DISARMING THE BARON

Courting a Curious Lady, Book 3

Lexi Post

ARE YOU SIGNED UP FOR DRAGONBLADE'S BLOG?

You'll get the latest news and information on exclusive giveaways, exclusive excerpts, coming releases, sales, free books, cover reveals and more.

Check out our complete list of authors, too!

No spam, no junk. That's a promise!

Sign Up Here

www.dragonbladepublishing.com

Dearest Reader;

Thank you for your support of a small press. At Dragonblade Publishing, we strive to bring you the highest quality Historical Romance from some of the best authors in the business. Without your support, there is no 'us', so we sincerely hope you adore these stories and find some new favorite authors along the way.

Happy Reading!

CEO, Dragonblade Publishing

Additional Dragonblade books by Author Lexi Post

Courting a Curious Lady Series
Uncovering the Lord (Book 1)
Confounding the Earl (Book 2)
Disarming the Baron (Book 3)

Marrying a Mabry Series
Stealing the Duke (Book 1)
Painting the Earl (Book 2)
Revealing the Viscount (Book 3)
Once Upon a Haunted Haven (Novella)

Acknowledgments

For my husband Bob Fabich, who has shown me what adventures are all about, whether we are walking the hills on the Isle of Arran, taking a helicopter to a glacier in Alaska, buying a new hat in Sorrento, or living on the Caribbean Island of St. Croix. I couldn't imagine enjoying these escapades with anyone else.

For my sister Paige, who gave me the kernel for this story and approved it after it was written, and for making sure I answered all her story questions in the epilogue.

Thank you to Marie Patrick, my reliable critique partner, who keeps me on track and helps me get unstuck when my characters do something I didn't expect.

A special thank you to my Lexi's Legends, and especially Rachael Bromley and Roslynn Ernst, for coming up with great names for some of the aristocracy. I also want to thank Joy Palmer for helping me decide on the ice cream flavor for this story. It just wouldn't be the same without ice cream.

They say writing is a lonely profession, but I'm never lonely with all these wonderful people keeping me company.

Author's Note

The Courting a Curious Lady series was inspired by two of my three favorite books of all time—Louisa May Alcott's novels, *Little Men* and *Jo's Boys*, published in 1871 and 1886 respectively. These were the next two books after *Little Women*, and I fell in love with Jo's school for boys. In Alcott's novels, there are a dozen boys as well as a few girls, all of whom go through the trials and tribulations of growing into adults. In *Stealing the Duke*, Lady Joanna sets up a school for ladies of the peerage modeled after Oxford and Cambridge. It's called the Belinda School for Curious Ladies.

Disarming the Baron is specifically inspired by Jack in Alcott's books. Jack is considered one of Jo's failures in *Little Men*, yet she sees hope for him in *Jo's Boys*. Jack is sly and sharp, and so is Lissette. He is also cheap, always looking for a way to make money. Lissette has grown up in war-torn France and so sees money as a way to survive. Like Jack, she not only survives but rises above her class thanks to her grandmother's machinations. Her grandmother puts Lissette at the Belinda School for Curious Ladies in the hopes that she will learn enough to capture the eye of a peer next Season. Unfortunately, like Jack, Lissette has her own mind and, while loyal to her grandmother, is determined to avoid marrying a peer at all costs. That she will be successful at what she puts her mind to is not the surprise for her. Rather, it is what that success will look like that catches her unawares.

CHAPTER ONE

The Belinda School for Curious Ladies
Silver Meadows, Northampton
Late October, 1817

MADEMOISELLE LISSETTE FONTAINE could see Lady Eleanor was confused even before her classmate spoke. "I don't understand how this formation could possibly keep the soldiers safe. Wouldn't Alexander the Great's enemies simply ride between them on their horses?"

"They couldn't because the soldiers stood shoulder to shoulder." At Ellie's frown, Lissa tried to think of an instance in astronomy, Ellie's favorite subject.

Unfortunately, she was rather ignorant about that subject, having only used the stars to guide her on her way home at night after foraging for food during Napoleon's wars.

"Lissette, surely you can explain. You know so much about these weapons." Ellie crossed her arms over her ample bosom, which was far larger than Lissa's, and raised her brows in expectation.

Lissa glanced around the sectioned area of what was once a very grand ballroom, but was now a library and the heart of the Belinda School for Curious Ladies' studies. Her gaze lit upon a shield hanging on the wall to remind students to focus on history.

Rising from her chair, she pointed. "I'll demonstrate." She walked to the wall and unhooked the shield. It was far smaller than what Alexander the Great used, as it was more modern, but it would do. The shield was well balanced, the straps feeling good on her arm, though it was heavy, as it should be. "Come, stand next to me."

Ellie rose and joined her.

"Stand right by my side. Now can you see how the enemy couldn't come between us?"

Ellie shook her head, sending her bright red curls swaying.

It would help if they had two shields. There were no other shields on the wall, but there was a painting. "Wait here." Lissa set down the shield and strode to the painting, lifting it off the wall. It was a bit larger than the shield, but it would do. She returned to Ellie again. "Now think of this as your shield. Hold it in front of you like this."

Ellie took the painting and held it before her. "It's heavy."

"Most weaponry is heavy so as to protect the bearer. Besides, Alexander's men were strong. Be careful not to catch the frame in your dress. You said that one was your favorite blue."

Once her classmate had adjusted the painting, Lissa stood shoulder to shoulder and overlapped the painting with the shield she held. "See? The enemy couldn't get between us. Plus, the soldiers would have spears in their other hands, so even before the enemy made it to the shields, they'd hit the spears."

Ellie's blue eyes rounded. "Oh, I understand now. But what about my other side?"

"You'd have a soldier there too, and if you were on the end, then"—Lissa moved to Ellie's other side but perpendicular to her—"you'd be protected by this soldier. It would be a large square of soldiers standing shoulder to shoulder that the enemy would have to face. That's the phalanx."

The painting came to the floor with a thud before tipping over as Ellie lost her grip. "Oh, dear."

"Oh dear, indeed." At the sound of the duchess's voice, they both looked up, startled. "I thought you two were reading Plutarch."

Lissa shooed Ellie away, not wanting her to do any more damage. "We were. I was demonstrating what a phalanx is." Lifting the artwork, she returned it to the wall, though it didn't hang straight. "We were reading about Alexander the Great."

The duchess eyed the shield, and Lissa quickly picked it up to return it to its place on the wall. Lady Joanna Northwick was not a harsh teacher by any means. In fact, she welcomed them all with open arms, expecting open minds in return.

For Lissa, the school was a haven…of sorts. It was a relief to not go to bed with a rumbling stomach or the fear of soldiers interrupting her sleep. But as her grandmother's plans moved forward, it put her in a difficult position. If anyone discovered her middle-class origins, they would be appalled.

Her ability to mimic her betters had brought her this far, but even so, she was quite sure the duchess sensed she wasn't gentry. Fortunately, her grandmother had saved the life of Lord Blackmore, the man they called the Captain, back in France. And since Lady Blackmore was the duchess's sister, Lissa found herself at the school.

Making sure the shield was secure, she returned to her seat at the table to join Ellie. "Did you wish us to change books?" She hoped not. She enjoyed reading about battles and weapons. She'd practically grown up with them.

"No. I need you to come to the parlor. You have a caller."

A caller? Could it be the young merchant she met in the Northampton village? But even as the thought came, it evaporated. It would not be him. He had mentioned he would be sailing out on his next ship. Oh, to travel the seas to exotic lands. The thought made her wish she could have gone with him, not that he would have asked her.

No, the only people who called on her were Lord and Lady Blackmore or her grandmother. Except for the Curious Ladies past and present, she knew no one else in England except

Anthony Taylour, Lord Blackmore's lieutenant, whom she hadn't seen since he'd left France three years ago.

Rising, she pulled on her gloves, secretly hoping it was one of the Blackmores. She pushed the book toward her classmate.

"I'll just read ahead a little." Ellie's shoulders slumped forward, most likely because she didn't truly understand war and there was quite a bit in the book.

As Lissa walked toward Her Grace, the woman smiled oddly. "I should perhaps be clearer on who was requested. This caller actually asked for Dague."

Lissa halted, startled, and looked over her shoulder at Ellie. Only the Curious Ladies called her that.

Ellie clapped her hands and smiled warmly. "It must be Dory or Elsbeth, then."

Of course. Lissa turned back to the duchess and followed. It had to be Dory, as she had been such a good friend before marrying Lord Harewood and leaving the school.

As they approached the parlor entry, the duchess halted. "I will announce you."

Lissa frowned. "Why?" It was unheard of for a duchess to announce anyone.

"Let us just say it is appropriate in this instance." With that, Her Grace entered the parlor.

Something was afoot, and it made Lissa nervous. She examined the entryway for clues and noticed a top hat, but as it was not yet very cold, there was no coat to give away the caller's identity. Still, it was a man's hat, and he'd asked for Dague.

A thrill went through her. Only one man that she knew had been told her nickname, and only because Dory told her husband that Dague was a weapons expert when he mentioned that Mr. Taylour needed one.

Her Grace stepped into the doorway. "As you requested, Mr. Taylour. Here is Dague." The duchess swept her arm toward the hall.

Lissa stepped through the doors, the skirts of her white day dress swishing when she stopped. It only took a moment to be sure the man with the strong jawline, blue eyes, and blond streaks in his hair was Anthony. Even as she smiled, memories assailed her of their scouring the countryside for food and valuables, she dressed in her usual trousers and shirt, he eschewing his uniform for her deceased father's farmer clothes. He refused to enter houses with locked doors, so she'd slip in through windows and open the doors to let him in, circumventing his gentlemanly ways.

His gaze roamed over her, no recognition in his eyes, though there was plenty of appreciation. How could he look at her so? Disappointment filled her. It was the stupid muslin dress with the sage ribbons that she wore. Never did she miss her masculine clothes more.

"Anthony!"

His eyes widened. He was clearly startled by her familiar address.

Striding forward, she took his face in her hands and kissed each cheek, silently urging him to remember her. She let go and stepped back, but not before inhaling his clove scent, which threatened to conjure up more memories.

"Lissa?"

Relief flowed through her, and she lifted her chin. "*Oui*. Do you not recognize me in a dress?" She held the dress out with her hands to emphasize the oddity for him.

"The truth be told, I don't recognize anything but your face. Last I saw you, you were dressed as a boy, and were not as, hmm, as grown. You have…changed."

She smiled warmly and took his hand in her gloved one, wishing the glove gone. "Come. Her Grace said you need my help."

She pulled him to the settee, but as she tugged on his hand to sit, he balked. He stepped away, and she let go.

"Your help?" He looked to the duchess, who still stood in the doorway grinning.

Lady Northwick strode in. "Yes, *her* help. You requested my weapons expert, Dague. This is she. You two obviously have much to catch up on. I will be over here in the dining room." The duchess waved toward the dining area that opened onto the parlor through a large archway.

There, Lady Northwick could keep her eyes on them without overhearing their conversation. Not that they needed a chaperone. They were old friends, bonded by the experience of war.

Anthony seemed to gather his tattered composure, and he gave a slight bow. "I thank Your Grace for your kindness."

"It is no special kindness. After all, I'm sure Lissette will tell me everything after you leave." The duchess winked before turning her back on them and strolling toward the connecting room.

Lissa shook her head, so he would know she had no intention of telling the duchess everything.

His shoulders relaxed, and he finally consented to sit next to her. He gazed at her in silence, making her uncomfortable.

She cocked her head. "What is it?"

"I'm trying to equate the urchin who rode double with me on my horse, crawled under a fallen barn wall to gather fresh eggs, and who reminded me daily that life was made to be enjoyed, with the beautiful woman before me."

Non, she would not accept such talk from her Anthony. "I am that same person, *mon ami. Oui,* a bit older and wiser, but no different inside. It is only the clothes that are different." She touched her chest above the neckline of her dress. "It is still me. I'm still Lissa. Please do not treat me as a lady. You know more about my life than anyone here in England." Which was true, except for her grandmother.

He shook his head, even as his gaze roamed over her once again. "That is difficult, but I will try. It is more than your clothing. This is a very different setting as well. We are not in the partially destroyed farmhouse where you lived because your family's mansion had been gutted by fire. You do not have to steal for your dinner, and your grandmother isn't out searching the dead for valuables she can trade."

"No, it is an easy life we live now. Though I will tell you I much prefer the freedom of male clothing. I would do much for a new pair of pantaloons." She smirked, as she had enjoyed being disguised even if it was to keep out of the hands of the soldiers. She looked far too young to be pressed into service like her father and older brother had.

He shook his head, clearly trying to remember how she looked back then. "It was a simpler time in France, when all that mattered was staying alive. I will honor our friendship and endeavor to treat you as the Lissa I first met, but you must understand, it's not easy. You are much older and no longer a boy."

She chuckled, beyond pleased to be conversing with him again. "My poor Anthony. I was never a boy, but a woman all along. But tell me, are you well? Her Grace told me you almost died." She swatted his arm with the back of her hand as she often had. It felt good to be on familiar terms with him again. "How dare you put yourself in such danger."

He leaned away and lifted both hands up. "Peace. I didn't know I was in danger. I was attending the wedding of Captain Blackmore."

"Well, you should have known. You always know when danger is lurking."

He grimaced and looked away as if embarrassed. "Obviously, not always. The man who shot me came out of the wood as I rode to the church." His gaze returned to hers. "But what of you? Are you enjoying your studies here?"

She looked over her shoulder to see the duchess reading the news sheets. "I suppose." She faced him again. "The lessons are interesting. It's the manners I do not like so much. That and the inactivity."

"But the other students treat you well?" His voice had lowered as if the duchess could hear them, but his concern was clear.

That he did still care about his old friend warmed her heart. "They do. Do not worry. All the ladies are very friendly. Lady Dorothea was my very good friend, and I miss her though she's barely been gone a fortnight, but Lady Eleanor decided that she must step in as my confidante." She wiggled her nose. "One does not naysay Lady Eleanor."

"Then I'm very pleased you are here and everyone has taken you in. I know it can be difficult learning the ways of the peerage."

She barely kept from wrinkling her nose again, a habit Ellie said would make her old before her time. Since she was already older than everyone thought, she had to overcome that urge. "It is, and that is why it is so good to see you. I have missed your company. I thought you avoided me purposely."

"No, of course not. Please do not think so ill of me. I have been busy helping Lord Blackmore, and then the duke, and now Lord Harewood." He leaned in and lowered his voice again. "It is quite interesting how little these high peers know about each other and those they do business with. It is as if they expect all will act honorably with them. They do not understand that everyone they encounter does not have the exact same background they do."

She smiled knowingly and kept her voice low as well. "I see it among the ladies, too. That is why it is so refreshing to talk to you." She lowered her brows. "And yet you have not come to visit me, but to see Dague. I am quite angry at you." Folding her arms, she let her pique be known as she met his gaze with her own.

A flush ran up his neck. "Yes, I must humbly beg your forgiveness for not making time to visit you and see that you were well. Can you forgive me?"

She didn't let her gaze waver, knowing how charming he could be, but he was here thanks to Dory, and he could be of great help to her. She continued thinking in silence, pleased that he grew uncomfortable, which proved how sincere he was for his neglect. "I suppose I must. But you must promise not to forget me again. You and Grand-maman are the only two people I can speak with freely. Do not make me wait so long to see you next time, or I will refuse you."

He laid his hand over his chest. "I promise."

Though she continued to study his face, she did not wish to hurt their friendship after so long a time apart. Finally, she nodded. "Very good. Now why do you need Dague?"

His brows lowered as he frowned. "Do you mean to say you are truly Dague?"

"Of course. Dague is French, is it not?"

He took a moment, probably to make the connection. "You mean you are known as 'Dagger'?"

She set her hand upon his arm. "Only to the ladies here. Dory said I needed a nickname."

"So she decided upon a weapon that is sharp and deadly?"

He was clearly insulted on her behalf. It was charming but hardly needed. She gave him a knowing smile. "But is that not me?" She lifted her hand from his arm and held it out in question. "Dory says I'm quick to understand. Ellie says my wit can kill an unwanted suitor in a trice. And Her Grace assures me my expertise in weaponry has opened her eyes to new knowledge." She glanced over the settee to look at the duchess again before turning back to him. "To be truthful, I've learned far more from the books at my disposal since landing on England's shore than from my use of the weapons available to me back home."

"Do not underestimate your past skills, Lissa. They were of great value and served you in good stead. It is simply that now your extended knowledge through reading is of more value and more in concert with your new life here. You are in England now, with no war to threaten you. Did you not wish to study something else?"

She frowned that he could so easily dismiss her past. "You sound like everyone else here. I thought you, of anyone beside Grand-maman, would appreciate the skills I acquired at home. I am sorely disappointed. I had hoped you could still care for me as I was, and not as I'm made to be." Why must her clothing determine her life? She wished she could go back in time, back to France, where she was simply the daughter of a lady's maid and farmer. She looked down at her gloved hands, barely holding back the urge to whip them off.

LISSA'S WORDS HIT a familiar chord in his heart. He'd spent his life being who he wished, doing what he wished, but much of his family simply dismissed him as unimportant. He couldn't do that to her.

He held out his hand, palm up. "I do care for you as you are. I fear it is this dress you wear that has played with my perception. I will endeavor to remember the person within its confines and not be swayed by the appearance of you now."

Though it was incredibly difficult, since she looked so beautiful, like a porcelain figurine of the most delicate mold. The only difference being that the cold porcelain figure would be pale white and cold to the touch. Lissa, as always, had sun-kissed skin, though much lighter than when they were in France, and she was warm with anyone she considered a friend.

It was not easy to equate the rough, young boy she had appeared to be, though he'd known her a young lady, with the beautiful and tantalizing woman sitting next to him now. When she'd first stepped into the parlor, he'd been stunned at the exquisite beauty of what he thought a new acquaintance, every part of him appreciating the view. Her black, silky hair, no longer short, was caught up behind her head, so it framed her delicate face, accentuating her high cheekbones, small, sharp nose, and dark-brown eyes. But now he couldn't see her eyes, as she stared at her hands as if she'd hadn't heard him. He resisted the urge to lift her chin, as he would have never done so in the past.

She finally lifted her head of her own accord, her dark eyes filled with sadness. "I appreciate your effort. I tire of being what I am supposed to be. I wish desperately to put on pantaloons and live my life in the country somewhere." She shook her head. "But I know that cannot be." Her gaze drifted away, as if she dreamed often of such a place.

He did not like seeing her spirits so low. Even in war-torn France, he'd never witnessed her in such melancholy. Her vibrancy was dampened here, and it was difficult to accept. "Then perhaps you could help me with my current investigation."

Her gaze snapped back to his and her eyes lit with the old fire he remembered. "Oh, *oui*. I would like that very much." She grabbed his forearm. "Do tell me how I can be of assistance."

Pleased that she'd overcome her despondency at his suggestion, he glanced at the duchess to see that she'd taken up a book and was happily reading. He leaned toward Lissa, the scent of apple filling his nostrils, reminding him of their close friendship. "I have seen an odd weapon and need to identify it, so I might ascertain what it could be used for."

She cocked her head and squeezed his arm. "This is in regard to your work for Lord Harewood, no? Is it important to the safety of Dory?"

He stiffened at how quick she was in her deduction. Not necessarily pleased by it, but also not surprised. He answered carefully. "I am not sure yet how this weapon weaves into the threads of my investigation. Knowing more about it may help."

"I see." She let go of his arm. "Do you have a drawing of the weapon?"

"I don't—I can tell you what it looked like, though my glimpse of it was not long, as it was transferred from one person to the other in a clandestine meeting."

"Then it was not meant to be seen for some reason." She paused as she thought. "Either it is to be used for nefarious purposes or it is not legal."

"Or it could have been obtained without the owner's

knowledge." He nodded, pleased at how quick she was to see the many facets of the situation.

"Tell me about it." Her eyes seemed to darken with the intensity of her gaze.

Happy to have assistance, he held up his hands about a foot apart. "It was a long dagger, about this length, but not like any I've encountered before. There were large notches on one side of the blade about a finger width apart. There was some kind of pattern to the notches, but the lighting was faint. I wasn't able to see it clearly. I'm postulating that the opposite side of the blade was sharp. The weapon had a cross guard and one side ring at the hilt. Does that sound like anything you know of?"

Lissa didn't answer immediately, but she did roll her lips in as she thought, something he'd seen her do dozens of times in France—but this time it was different. He wasn't sure if it was the dress or her age, but the movement had him waiting anxiously for her to release them, knowing her lips would appear redder. Finally, she let her lips return to their resting position, making her look like she'd just been thoroughly kissed. Unfortunately, it put the idea of kissing her into his head, an act that would probably horrify her.

"I do know of a couple of weapons that fit that description, but they are old, and not used anymore. If you could allow me to review my papers, I can sketch out the possibles, and perhaps you can identify which it is?"

He snapped his gaze from her lips to her eyes at her question. "That would be very helpful. You can send the sketches to Ravenridge. I visit with Lord and Lady Blackmore regularly."

She shook her head. "*Non.* We meet in the forest between the estates. I want to see you again. Either we meet, or I cannot aid you."

His gut tightened, but he wasn't sure if it was with excitement or a warning. He had no doubt the limited physical activity at Silver Meadows was Lissa's motivation. He could not in good conscience deny her. Besides, it did not appear he had another option, beyond requesting Her Grace to allow him to comb through hundreds of books on weapons, which would take far too much time. It had taken him months of following Lord Leighhall to finally discover the man had other activities beyond bedding married and unmarried women. If there were more to be discovered, he did not wish to wait. "I am quite pleased to meet with you again, but you must be chaperoned."

"*Mon Dieu*, not you too, Anthony. Do not speak to me about such idiocy. It is you and I. Friends. We need follow no such rules in the woods. We had no such chaperone when we looted the Grand Manse or filched the jewels from the Comte de Gondrin's broken-down coach. Do not insult me so."

As usual when she felt strongly, her French revealed itself. As much as he understood how hard her new life was for her, it was still best that she continue to live according to English Society decorum. "Very well, but you must bring a groom. I would not want anything to happen to you, or for you to fall and have no one about to aid you."

She opened her mouth to argue, and he held up his hand. "No. I will not be gainsaid on this. Those woods housed the very man that shot me, and though he is gone, it only proves that no area can be deemed safe for a young, unmarried woman."

Her bottom lip protruded a bit farther than her top as she met his steady gaze. "Very well. I shall bring a groom for appearances' sake." She shook her head. "There is so much more to life than appearances, but these English make them a priority. There are some things I will never understand."

He frowned, not a little disturbed by her conclusion. "Surely before the war, you followed the dictates of the French gentry."

She looked at him blankly as if she had no idea what he meant.

Understanding came to him. "Of course. I forgot that before the war you were most likely far too young to understand. Do not judge us English so harshly. We are not so far different from your French society."

"I will try." Though she didn't smile, she did appear to relax. "It will take me a couple of days to thoroughly research this weapon. I will meet you at eight in the morning in the woods on the path that connects the two estates two days hence. We will solve this mystery." Her shoulders straightened as if she were ready to vanquish any foe, which made him grin.

Though surprised by the early hour, he reminded himself that she was often out and about in France before the sun had even risen. "I very much appreciate your help." He stood, prepared to take his leave.

Lissa jumped to her feet. "Do you not wish to stay for tea?"

Her eagerness to have him near touched him. The only other person to wish him near in the last decade had been Lord Blackmore, but now he had a wife, with a child soon to come. "I would very much like to stay in your company, but if we are not to meet for two more days, I must resume my investigation."

Her shoulders, held so high just moments go, slumped.

He laid his hand upon her shoulder as he had so often done, not a little surprised by the warmth beneath the thin fabric. "I promise I will share with you any other information I have on weapons, should I discover more. I know you will be invaluable to my investigation."

A cough from the duchess reminded him where he was, and glancing over, he found her watching him. Quickly, he removed his hand.

Lissa gave him a short nod. "I will. I look forward to our next meeting."

He smiled at her, pleased that he would be seeing her again soon. Turning, he gave Her Grace a short bow. "I must take my leave, but I thank you."

The duchess rose and walked toward him. "I'm very glad that we were able to assist. Please tell my sister I will be calling on her tomorrow."

"I am happy to be of service." With another short bow, he turned and left.

By the time he'd descended the long steps from the doors of Silver Meadows to the ground, his horse was brought around. Mounting, he set off at a leisurely pace toward Ravenridge. He would give Lady Blackmore her sister's message, change into clothing more appropriate for following the Viscount Leighhall, and head back to the inn where he'd been staying.

Leighhall was visiting a young widow in the area, but could leave at any moment, and Anthony planned to be there when the viscount departed. Part of him wished the man would obtain another interesting weapon, just so Lissa's eyes would light with excitement again. But even as the thought was born, his instinct smashed it down like a nut beneath his heel. Though Lissa was indeed a very good friend, she was now a lady, and despite what she might wish, their relationship must change, for her sake.

CHAPTER TWO

LISSA BROUGHT HER horse to a halt just within the shade of the wood. She waited patiently for her groom to catch up, having raced over the fields to escape detection. It wasn't unusual for her to ride early in the morning. In fact, she often was accompanied by one of her classmates, but this morning was different.

As the groom slowed to enter the woods, she took the coin from the pocket of her newly purchased trousers and held it ready. As soon as the young man noticed her and moved his mount forward, she spoke. "I want you to stay here until I return."

"But I am to go with you, my lady."

She'd given up correcting the staff after a month of being at Silver Meadows. They insisted on addressing her as "lady," which was far from the truth. "Yes, I know. However, that is not my wish. You have done admirably to escort me thus far. Now I will continue down this path." She pointed to the well-worn dirt track. "If I need assistance, I will whistle loudly."

"Whistle?" The groom seemed quite taken aback by that.

She sighed. "Yes, whistle." She puckered her lips and whistled, not too loud, but not softly either.

The groom's eyes widened before he frowned again. "But—"

She held up her hand with the coin. "This is to keep you

company. If you are here when I return, I will give you another as long as you keep my chosen clothes and my activities to yourself."

His gazed riveted to her hand. Finally, he looked at her and nodded.

She walked her horse closer and handed him the coin. "Remember, no one is to know, not the other grooms, your family, or your lover. Understand?"

Again he nodded. "I shall wait here unless I hear a whistle, and will tell no one."

"Good." Turning her horse down the path, she kept it to a slower pace, not wishing to be obvious about how excited she was to see Anthony. It never behooved a woman to show she was excited to see a man she needed. And she did need Anthony, but not in the way most women needed a man. Only he could give her one last adventure. Only he knew her.

She hadn't expected to see him again after three years had passed since he left her and her grandmother in France. Her last year in London she had spent attempting to catch the eye of well positioned men of the middle class, but Grand-maman was having none of it, saying she'd suffered too much to get them to this point and only a peer would do.

The next thing Lissa knew, she was meeting the students of the Belinda School for Curious Ladies, and despite her wish to remain apart from such aristocratic women, she'd been welcomed wholeheartedly.

It was both a relief and a problem. Tucked away at Silver Meadows, she despaired of finding a suitable man for marriage before the next Season. Suitable to her was far different than to her grandmother, who was determined to see her live out her life with a boring peer. She needed more, either the excitement of helping a husband succeed or a complete lack of attention, so she could do as she pleased. Despite multiple visits to the village of Northampton and the local parish, no middle-class prospects had come to fruition.

But Anthony, who knew who she was, would understand why a peer was out of the question. He could help her find a wealthy man, and then she could satisfy her grandmother by giving her the life she wished. In return, she could aid Anthony in his quest and enjoy one last bout of freedom. Her plan would make them all happy.

Pleased with herself, she was envisioning the future of her dreams when she sensed something different about her surroundings. She slowed her mount, noticing a distinct lack of birdsong. Was he close, or was there someone else about in the wood?

Slipping her hand beneath the large man's shirt she wore, she grasped one of her daggers. Though she didn't like the constriction of having her now-bigger breasts bound, she'd been careful not to impede her arm movements. If she hadn't gained so much weight since living in England, she wouldn't have such a problem, but living during a war, when foraging for food was the norm, was far different from living in luxury with others cooking for her, and worse, waiting upon her. Even her only pair of pantaloons had been far too tight to wear in public.

The chuff of a horse confirmed her suspicions. Directing her own mount into the wood, she turned it about and watched the path, waiting. She had learned patience, among many other skills during the war, and it felt good to be back in her own element.

The soft sound of horse hooves coming down the path had her tensing. Finally, a horse of mediocre breed came into sight with an old man upon its back. He wore dark-brown trousers and a dirty shirt. He had bushy gray brows that hid his eyes, along with equally gray hair and a long beard. She relaxed, accepting that she would have to wait a bit longer. It could very well be that she was still early.

As the old man slowly moved past, something about him caught her attention. She shook her head and smirked before raising her dagger, then sent it flying across the man's path and into a large tree next to him. As she expected, he reacted far too quickly as he pulled on the reins, spinning his horse around, a flintlock appearing in his hand.

She laughed, walking her horse out onto the path. "You move far too fast for an old man, Anthony."

"Lissa! How did you know?" He shook his head as he returned the gun to its hiding place.

"Old men don't sit straight in the saddle." She grinned, pleased that she'd recognized him, despite his disguise. She waved toward his clothing. "Does your investigation require such subterfuge?"

He brought his horse up next to hers, so they were face to face. "It does, mainly to keep my real identity from being discovered. I find dressing as a villager makes it easy for me to be overlooked by the gentleman I'm following."

Though she couldn't see his mouth well with all the hair, his blue eyes shone with glee. Anthony had always enjoyed surprising others.

"I see you have also disguised yourself." He held his hand out toward her. "This is the Lissa I remember."

Relieved that her clothing had done what she'd hoped, reminded him of who she was and their friendship, she shrugged. "It is what I am most comfortable wearing." She dismounted, holding the reins of her horse. "How fares your investigation?"

His posture slumped, much like it should have when he rode the path. "Not as quickly as I hoped. The man I watch spends far too much time with women." He dismounted as well and brought his horse next to hers. "At first, I thought it was to hide his real activities, but now I fear women are his primary goal, while the weapon he came into possession of is merely a distraction. I sincerely hoped it would be the opposite." His gaze wandered as he appeared to review the many details in his mind.

That concerned her, not only because she knew how much he enjoyed discovering answers, but also because this time it had to do with her friend Dory. "Is the lord's interest in his ladies not enough for what you need to protect Lady Harewood?"

He returned his gaze to her and shook his head. "I'm afraid

much of it would be more damaging to said ladies than to the viscount, so it is of little worth to me."

That he spoke freely to her of the ladies had her feeling much more confident that their friendship was back to how it had always been. "Then perhaps what I discovered about the weapon may be of help."

He straightened, immediately focusing his attention on her. "Yes. Tell me what you have found."

Though she hated to stretch their friendship, survival, as always, remained her first priority. "I do believe one of the two drawings I made will be your weapon. However, I also need help, and I'm hoping you can be of assistance."

"Of course. You know I would be happy to aid you in whatever it is you need."

Beyond pleased with his offer, she gave him a smile. "*Merci*. I knew I could depend upon you. I need your help in finding a very wealthy tradesman or merchant to wed."

The bushy gray brows lifted. "I was under the impression that you would be coming out in the next Season."

"That is what is expected, which is why it's imperative that I find a husband before then. Grand-maman wishes me to wed a peer so she may have a comfortable old age. I cannot fathom being married to an aristocrat." She placed one hand on her hip and cocked her head. "Truly, can you see me married to a Lord Stiffboard, or worse, Lord Boring?"

Anthony nodded. "I do see your dilemma. But it might not be as bad as all that. There are many good chaps like Lord Blackmore who might be very enjoyable company."

She just stared at him, waiting for him to come to the same conclusion she had. Though she did need to provide for her grandmother, and she didn't look for love, since she'd already loved and lost, she couldn't imagine having to pretend to be an aristocrat for the rest of her life and do nothing but host visitors and make babies.

"What?" He lifted his shoulders. "It's possible."

She shook her head, a bit disappointed. "Look at me. This is what makes me happy. Do you see me happy, even with a man like the Captain?"

"But I thought you enjoyed the Belinda School for Curious Ladies and all that you are learning there?"

She hadn't understood how strong his beliefs in Society were until just now. She sighed. "I thought you, of anyone, would understand."

His shoulders tensed and he looked about, obviously uncomfortable. "In truth, I suppose I do, far more than you know. I also find the rules of Society tiresome more often than not and do not abide by them. But I am a man."

Seeing her opportunity, she grabbed his wrist. "Yes. But I cannot do as you. My only chance at a contented life is to find someone who is not anxious to be accepted, but happy in their own right, who doesn't need a lady wife." She squeezed, hoping he could understand.

Finally, his arm turned within her grip, and he wrapped his hand around her wrist.

Relief flew through her. It was *their* grip, a sign of solidarity with each that other they only used when in a crisis.

"I pledge to aid you, even if I'm not completely convinced it's the right course."

"*Merci, mon ami.*" She released his arm, and he did likewise. Now she could freely turn to other matters.

"Of course. But I won't be able to introduce you to anyone until I have found what Lord Harewood is searching for with Lord Leighhall. I must complete this task first."

Worry slipped up her back. She barely had three months. "How long will that be?"

"I could be done in a month or two, but it may take longer. It depends on what you have found for me." His beard appeared to lift, so she could only guess that he grinned.

Non, there would not be enough time. Frantically, she searched for a solution, unwilling to come so close to achieving her goal of marrying on her terms. She had despaired until Anthony had walked into her life. He was her only chance. "I cannot wait so long. Allow me to help with your investigation beyond the research. With both of us, we can solve it sooner." And she could enjoy one last escapade.

He shook his head, but she refused to give up. "In fact, as you go about following Lord Leighhall, I could help. There are many things a boy"—she gestured to her trousers and vest—"or a woman can learn that a man cannot."

He'd stopped shaking his head, but the gray, bushy brows were lowered.

"And like you, I can be disguised as a maid or a countess if needed." When he didn't say anything, she tugged on his memory. "Or I can be a frail old lady who is just looking for her lost chicken."

He shook his head again even as his brow puckered. "I still do not know how you convinced that merchant that your darling Rosalie had escaped her pen and joined him."

She lowered her voice and made it shake. "But I so love my dear Rosalie."

He laughed, his eyes crinkling beneath the bushy eyebrows. "Yes, so much that you had her for dinner."

She shrugged, going back to her normal voice. "True, and she gladly gave her life so that we could live another day." She sobered. "Allow me to assist you, Anthony. You know I can help."

"I do know you could, but you are a lady now."

She wrinkled her nose at him and held out her arms. "This is me. I can be many people, but I am *not* a lady at heart."

He rubbed the back of his neck, clearly considering her request, but having difficulty accepting. "Even if I say yes, I never know where I will be. It's not as if you can leave the school." He resumed shaking his head. "I—"

"Dory. I can ask Dory to help. She can invite me to Denton Hall. She has before. No one ever questioned it. If you need to travel, I can go with you, dressed like this, and no one will know. I know Dory will keep my secret."

He stopped shaking his head, but was obviously not convinced.

She held out her hand, palm up, imploring him to understand. "What is the worst that could occur? I could be discovered and considered no longer a lady, but I am that now. So no true harm is done, except that I would then be forced to be a mistress in order to keep Grand-maman as she wishes." She could tell he wavered, his gaze giving him away as he thought of all the possibilities and problems. "And if there is someone you think I should meet along the way, I'll happily dress accordingly and do my best to charm them. It could well happen that I become betrothed before your investigation is even complete."

She was quite certain his lips quirked up based on the movement of the beard.

"You have always known how to sway me." He paused. "However, you are far above being a mistress and do deserve to live a comfortable life after all you have endured and all you have done for the Captain." He held up his hand as she opened her mouth to object. "Allow me my piece. I do understand your request and your limited time, so yes, you may aid me in my investigation, but only in ways that I feel will keep your identity hidden and your reputation intact."

It wasn't what she wanted, but she was quite sure she could obtain no more…for the moment. "I understand. Now, do be plain about what you need to accomplish in order that we may search for my future husband posthaste."

"You must not share this with anyone. Do I have your promise?"

"You do."

He hesitated as if trying to determine how best to explain.

She let out a loud sigh. "Truly, Anthony. Out with it. This is me, Lissette."

From the movement of his frame, he silently chuckled.

"Thank you for the reminder. My goal in this investigation is to find something that Viscount Leighhall would prefer not become public knowledge."

It sounded as if Dory's husband wanted to blackmail the lord. "Why?"

"Viscount Leighhall became a bit obsessed with Lady Harewood before she married. He set out to ruin her reputation by putting her mother in a compromising position."

She waved him off. "Yes, I know all about that."

"You do?"

"As I said, Dory is a dear friend."

"Then I should tell you that Lord Harewood is worried that since he married your friend, Viscount Leighhall was not able to complete his plan against her. Since the viscount never forgets what he considers a slight, Lord Harewood would like information on the lord to ensure he does not make any further attempt to hurt Lady Harewood's character."

Even as Anthony explained the situation, she felt herself burning with anger. Poor Dory was helpless in the situation and never invited the problem. It was a feeling she, herself, had felt many times. "Then have you determined what would make the errant viscount toe the line?"

Anthony pulled his head back, clearly surprised by her question. "I will not know that until I can determine what his secrets are."

She cocked her head. "But if his secrets are only from a particular mistress, they would not be of great value. However, if he is concerned about his standing in Parliament, then learning a secret about that would be better. If we know what he values, then perhaps we can narrow our focus."

"That is very true." At his excitement, his horse shuffled, pushing into hers.

Quickly, she guided hers away before halting.

He moved closer once again. "That is something I need to think about. In the meantime, you did say that you have identified the strange weapon?"

Having completely forgotten about her research, she has-tened to pull the sheets of paper from her vest pocket. "I have two possibles." She separated the pages, holding out one in each hand for him to peruse.

"That's it." He pointed to the one in her right hand. "What is it?"

She looked at the paper. "That is a sword breaker." She gave him the paper and folded the other one, returning it to her pocket.

"A sword breaker? I've never heard of this. What do you know of it?"

She pointed to the paper. "I know that some collectors are having these made, so it could be a question of whether it is from the seventeenth century, where it wasn't used often, or if it was made in this century. It is a *main gauche*—left hand—weapon to be used when fighting with swords."

He studied the drawing. "I can see how these cuts between the arrow-shaped steel separators could capture a sword, but can it actually *break* a sword?"

She shrugged. "It is difficult to know. I imagine in the time period they were used, when swords were more likely to break, they could. However, capturing a sword is more advantageous than breaking one, as your opponent would be open to a thrust."

He lifted his gaze to meet hers. "That's true. I forget you have so much knowledge on weapons. So I have one last question for you about this. Why would someone obtain such a weapon?"

That was something she'd been thinking about as she gal-loped across the fields. "I believe it depends upon the age. If it is an authentic sword breaker, I imagine a person wishes it for a collection. I have seen two country estate houses since arriving here that have elaborate arms displays."

"And if it was forged today?"

"If it is a new version of this old weapon, then it may be wanted for battle of some kind. It's not for the purposes of a stealthy assignation, but rather a defensive weapon that also can serve in an offensive capacity if one were expecting to be attacked with a sword, which seems highly unlikely here."

His gaze moved back to her drawing once more. "Unless it is not to be used here in England—or if it is, a challenge is expected to be thrown down." He folded the paper along the creases she had made. "Thank you for this. You have given me much to contemplate."

"Myself as well, especially as it pertains to Dory."

He slipped the paper into a pocket in his own vest, which didn't quite button over whatever he'd used for padding his torso. "I do not think it directly relates to Lady Harewood. So there is no need to worry." Turning, he mounted up.

Quickly, she pulled herself up onto her own mount, so as not to be forgotten so quickly. "What is our next step?"

He stiffened, but he didn't shake his head this time. "I don't know, as I can only follow and watch for now. I will send you word when we can next meet." He lifted the reins in his hands, turning his mount around.

She gave him a hard look and spoke in a strong tone. "Do not forget me, *mon ami*."

At her French, he halted, turning his head to look at her. "I promise, I will not. You have already proven invaluable to me."

Convinced he was sincere, she gave a nod. "Until then."

She flicked the reins and headed back toward Silver Meadows with a new hope filling her. There had to be a wealthy merchant looking for a wife somewhere in Lord Leighhall's travels, and if not, she'd just have to find out what the lord hid as soon as she possibly could. In the meantime, she would look forward to escaping the confines of the Belinda School for Curious Ladies.

As she came upon her groom, he mounted up. "Glad I am to see you, my lady."

She bit her tongue and handed him another coin. "We'd best make haste if we are to get back to the stables without being seen." She didn't wait for him to acknowledge her statement, but sent her horse into a gallop across the field.

As soon as they arrived, she left her mount in the groom's skilled hands and headed for the servants' entrance. When she'd first arrived at Silver Meadows, she had chosen the room closest to the servant stairs. Her choice had proven well made more than once. No one noticed one more servant in such a large household.

Quickly, she strode through the herb garden and up the back stairs, her step lighter than it had been in months. As much as she preferred to keep her plans to herself, she was finding that having help was indeed beneficial. She had complete confidence that Anthony wouldn't tell anyone. Even in France, he'd kept her secrets from her grandmother, though there weren't many. He would keep this one, too.

Reaching the top of the stairs, she halted and looked around the corner. No one was about. She walked to her door and slipped inside, pleased that no one had seen her. Turning toward her armoire, she halted in surprise.

"Where have you been, and why are you dressed like that?"

CHAPTER THREE

M ERDE. WHAT WAS Ellie doing in her room, especially at this hour? It would be best to brazen it out. "I went for a ride, as usual." Striding over to the chair by the fireplace, Lissa pulled her right boot off.

Lady Eleanor Compton of Dulac was anything but meek, especially as she stood there scowling, her red hair as yet unbrushed, her blue dressing gown barely tied. "There's nothing usual about this." She waved her hand emphatically before settling it on her hip. "I came in here with an offer of help, only to find you gone. Then you arrive dressed like a man?"

Lissa couldn't help grinning and lowered her head so Ellie wouldn't see as she yanked off the other boot. Finally, she looked up and shrugged. "It's how I got about in France." She frowned. "Sometimes I miss home so much, I need to recapture it."

Usually such emotional tactics worked, but as Ellie crossed her arms over her ample breasts, it was clear she wasn't impressed. "You escaped from poverty and war to our shores. Don't try to tell me you long for that again."

Her classmate was far too honest to brook any dissembling. Rising, Lissa gave an exaggerated sigh. "True." She lifted the boots and brushed past Ellie to deposit them in the back of her armoire, their respective daggers remaining hidden from her classmate. Closing the door, she faced Ellie. "You said you came to help me?"

Ellie moved to the chair she'd just vacated and sat. "Not until you tell me why you went riding dressed as a man." Her eyes narrowed, suspicion clear in her gaze. "Tell me you took a groom."

Lissa leaned back against the armoire and crossed her arms. "I took a groom."

Her friend eyed her then nodded, finally convinced she told the truth. "At least you are being safe. Now tell me why you are dressed so."

On one hand, Lissa would like nothing better than to take one of her classmates into her confidence. On the other hand, the fewer people who knew about her adventures, the less likely she'd be caught. "I'd rather not."

Instead of being affronted, Ellie shook her head. "Tsk, tsk. I thought I could help, but it appears you won't tell me. Then I guess you'll just have to tell the duchess."

Lissa's breath caught in her throat, and though she didn't move a muscle, fear crawled up her spine. Not fear of the duchess per se, but fear that her one chance to enjoy life again would be snatched away.

The Duchess of Northwick managed the Belinda School for Curious Ladies, and as forward thinking as she was, she would not look kindly on riding about in men's clothes, meeting an unmarried man, friend or not, and searching for an unmarried tradesman with that friend while discovering the secrets of a degenerate viscount. Even as Lissa thought of all the problems the duchess would have with her new life plans, she knew her course.

She purposefully moved her gaze, studying Ellie. The woman was someone who could not easily be discounted either for her intelligence or her sheer force of will. Ellie also tended to mother them all, looking out for them like a protective hen despite the fact she was only twenty-four herself. She was much like the planets and stars she so loved, a force of gravity and impossible to ignore. Yet, unlike those cold celestial orbs, Ellie had a heart as large as the Continent.

There were worse classmates to be caught by. Lady Rose was far too proper, and Lady Sophie, though very quiet, was far too observant and would go straight to Lady Northwick. Lady Georgina couldn't keep a secret any better than Dory.

Finally, Lissa pushed away from the armoire and unbuttoned her trousers, the shirt beneath covering her to her knees.

"Shall I fetch the duchess, then?" Ellie was far too confident, but she had reason to be.

Still, Lissa ignored her and pulled the men's shirt over her head. After untying the material she'd used to bind her breasts, she took a deep breath, surprised at how constricting it had felt. She used to bind them all the time at home. Walking in her stockinged feet to the bed where she'd left her shift, she pulled it on to cover her nakedness before gathering the material and clothes up and adding them to the back of the armoire. Finally, she moved to her bed and sat upon it with her legs crossed, facing Ellie. "Very well, I will tell you." She had no doubt that Ellie had made note of where she kept everything, so she would know the woman didn't support her if anything came up missing.

"I'm listening."

She held up her hand. "First, you must take an oath not to tell anyone."

"I cannot take such an oath until I judge it is possible to do so based upon the information you relate."

Lissa bit down on a grin. Ellie, though the daughter of an earl, was as blunt and straightforward as herself. "Then I fear we are at an impasse."

"No, we aren't. You are. You can speak to me with no oath or speak to Her Grace."

She should have known that Ellie would not make any promises. "So you mean to ruin my entire future?"

At that, Ellie laid her hand on her chest. "I have no such intention. Come, Lissette, tell me what you are about. Perhaps I can help."

And there it was, her wonderfully big heart, obvious in her offer and her softening tone of voice. It was that characteristic that reminded Lissa of her own mother. "Very well. I rode out in disguise to meet a friend who has agreed to help me find a husband before the Season begins."

Ellie's eyes lit with delight before they narrowed. "Then this friend was a man, and perhaps an unmarried one at that? Was it Mr. Taylour?"

Startled that Ellie had deduced so much so quickly, Lissa hid her surprise. "Why do you suggest that?"

"Simple." Ellie crossed her arms and raised her chin. "The reason I came to your room was because your spirits have been much higher since you saw Mr. Taylour the other day, and I was going to suggest a dinner party."

Lissa's heart warmed at her friend's thoughtfulness. "I thank you for that. But Mr. Taylour and I are old friends. I have been in good spirits, as you say, because he is the one who will help me find a husband."

"But how can he do that. Is he a peer?"

She chuckled, relieved that Ellie seemed far less shocked than she'd expected. "No. He served in the military and before that was with the Bow Street Runners. He earns his living and so will be able to introduce me to other men of that class who have a bit more in their pocket than he." She lowered her voice as if to impart a great secret. "My grandmother expects a comfortable old age."

Ellie's forehead furrowed and she dropped her arms. "But why would you not wish to marry a peer?"

And here Lissa was again, trying to explain something she couldn't, all because her grandmother wanted a peer and would accept nothing less. But Grand-maman was in a townhouse in Bath at the expense of Lord Blackmore and so was not about to say what must be. "I am not comfortable with such status in your country. I do not wish to remember every manner and proper etiquette of a great lady. It is different for you. You have grown up so."

"Yes, I have, and still I fail at the worst times." Ellie's shoulders slumped, her own lack of success during the Season lying heavily on her.

"Do not fear. Some fine lord is bound to see your warm heart and kind demeanor."

"Thank you. It is my endless hope."

Ellie's lack of success did raise the question of whether the school was the right place for her, but since she enjoyed her studies, it was most likely a happy distraction. Unfortunately, there was little Lissa could do to help Ellie, and much the woman could do to help her. "Will you keep my secret?"

"I will, but only if you promise not to put yourself in danger. Being alone with a gentleman could ruin your reputation. Even among the middle classes, I doubt that is acceptable."

Having been affianced before, Lissa had thoroughly enjoyed showing Etienne how much she loved him both in and out of bed. War put things into perspective, and she would never regret loving him fully before he lost his life. But that was far too removed from Ellie's sheltered experience. "I promise not to ruin my reputation. I'm quite sure Mr. Taylour would never allow that to happen."

"Yes, of course, especially if he is a family friend." Ellie rose. "I would ask one boon of you."

"Of course. Being my confidante, you have relieved my mind very much."

Ellie's cheeks reddened with pleasure as she stepped up to the bed. "Will you share with me whom you meet and what you think of them? I may well have to find someone of equal quality if my next Season is also not successful. I just want someone who is kind and will be happy that I am in his family."

Lissa's heart ached for Ellie, and she promised herself she would be sure to remark upon anyone who could appreciate such a loving woman. "I will be pleased to share."

Ellie reached out and squeezed her hand. "Thank you. Now I should go, as it is almost time to break our fast, and I'm sure your maid will be in presently."

Lissa let go of Ellie and watched the woman walk to the door, her long, thick red braid swaying back and forth with her purposeful stride.

After the door closed, she returned to the armoire and pulled her three daggers from her male clothing then slipped them beneath the pillow. Her maid was aware she wore a dagger on her thigh, as was Her Grace, but no one was aware of how many she carried. Though she had no need of them at Silver Meadows, it was a habit she was loath to break.

Hopefully, she wouldn't need to use them while helping Anthony. Maybe the man she eventually found to marry would welcome a wife who came to him well prepared.

ANTHONY STOOD OUTSIDE the book shop in the village of Esterburn and watched the people going about their daily lives. How simple it was for the average person to get about, each with their own goals for the day. His goals were far more complicated. Today, he waited for Leighhall to emerge from the inn across the road.

Two days ago, he'd discovered whom the viscount was tupping—a Mrs. Anne Boscawen, who was on her way home to visit her family. She was also a laundress and seamstress for Queen Charlotte. That in itself would not have had him taking notice, except for the strange circumstances. It was rare that servants were allowed such time, and then to interrupt her trip for Leighhall had him wondering if they were old friends. Had she worked for the viscount in the past?

Mrs. Boscawen had no relation to Lady Amherst, whom the viscount had spent the last sennight with, nor was there a connection with the widowed baker in Bedford. It truly did seem that the man simply took his pleasure where he would. Still, Anthony kept detailed ciphered notes, so as to catch any pattern. So far, the only change had been the evening Leighhall had met with a man in the woods and accepted the sword breaker.

As the door to the inn opened, Leighhall stepped out alone.

Immediately alert, Anthony did not show it, remaining where he was, leaning against the front of the building in one of his favorite disguises. He looked like an aristocrat a few years older than he was, with black hair, trimmed black beard, and a long, light scar on his right cheek. When he was dressed all in black, people in the street did not engage him, which was exactly as he wished.

Leighhall remained just outside the door, no doubt waiting for his coach. The man was easy to spot. He prided himself on his appearance, so not only were his brown tail coat, tan pantaloons, and top hat of the highest quality, but his blond hair had been cut to show off his classic features in the best way. Women obviously found him attractive, which made the man's exploits that much easier.

After a moment of perusing the people on the street, Leighhall turned and began walking.

A bit surprised, Anthony remained where he was a little longer, keeping the viscount in sight. Then he began to walk in the same direction, only on his own side of the street. No one made eye contact with him, which suited him perfectly.

Leighhall looked up at a sign on a shop before halting as if to make sure he was in the right place. Then he walked in.

Quickly, Anthony crossed the street. As he strolled by, he noticed two things. First, the shop was a cobbler's. Second, looking in the window, Leighhall was nowhere to be seen.

Anthony continued his stroll, turning at the corner of the street, his destination the back of the shop. However, the alleyway behind the row of buildings was not a place a peer would wander, and in his disguise, he would definitely attract attention. So he continued on before turning and walking back up the side street until he reached the main road once again. He crossed and entered a confectioner's, taking a seat at a table next to the window. After ordering coffee ice cream, he waited.

He had long eaten his sweet and just finished his second cup of tea when Leighhall emerged with a large package. It was far too large to be shoes or even boots.

From his vantage point, Anthony studied it, noting how round it was and the protrusion from the center, though it was wrapped in brown paper. It was almost the shape of an open parasol, but the handle area was far too short. Leighhall started walking back toward the inn.

Rising, Anthony waited a moment before exiting the shop. He'd just started down the street again when Leighhall's carriage came to a stop before him, and the viscount entered it. The carriage had been loaded with Leighhall's many trunks, so it was no surprise that it continued out of the village.

Quickly, Anthony crossed the road and stepped into the cobbler's. No one was in the front of the shop, so he took time to scan the contents. Nothing had the shape of what Leighhall had left with, which meant it was a custom design or had nothing to do with boots.

A young man of maybe a score emerged from the rear of the building. "My lord, can I be of service?"

"I was hoping to find my friend, Lord Leighhall, here. He did say he would be stopping in."

The man didn't answer immediately. Instead, he studied him. "I fear he has already left. If he returns, can I tell him who looked for him?"

Either the cobbler didn't know Leighhall was on his way to Corby, or he hoped to gather information from Anthony to give the viscount. "No, it's of no matter. I'm sure to see him in a few days' time." Anthony gave an aristocratic nod before exiting the premises.

Now to retrieve his belongings and head for Denton Hall.

There was no reason to follow Leighhall to Corby, where he'd be visiting his mother. It was highly unlikely the viscount would be bedding his usual women there.

The next three days would be a good time for Anthony to return to Lord Harewood and report his recent discoveries. It would also give him a day to take Lissa into the village at Talley on the Green. No doubt she had already met everyone in Northampton, as she was nothing if not thorough.

He grinned, causing a young woman on the street to shy away from him. He kept forgetting about the scar. When he smiled, it made him look quite dangerous. Changing to a slight frown, he continued to the inn.

It took little time to have his small trunk loaded on his coach before he was off for Denton Hall, and Lord and Lady Harewood. He'd purposely purchased a coach with no coat of arms. Being recognizable did not further his occupation. He thought he could give up his need to investigate and bring men to justice after leaving the Bow Street Runners to join the calvary, but he'd been mistaken. It wasn't as if what he did with his life mattered to anyone. As he was the fourth son of a duke, three of them married, two with children, the family line had been secured by time he attended university. His life was his to do with as he pleased, and he was quite pleased to do what he enjoyed, which aided those who needed his services.

Now, Lissa was the one who needed his services. He smiled fondly as memories of their time together in France flooded his mind. He'd always known she was a woman, but she was rough and tumble like any young man, and they'd become fast friends, comrades in survival while Captain Marcus Stratton, the Viscount of Blackmore, recovered at her grandmother's home from multiple wounds on the battlefield. If he hadn't been so bent on solving the mystery of where Captain Blackmore had disappeared to, he would have never met Lissa.

Seeing her in a dress for the first time had been a shock. She was beautiful, not in an angelic way, but in a way that was far different from her old self. She looked fragile with her paler skin and long black hair. He was quite confident he could find her a wealthy gentleman to marry. Now that he thought upon it, he would make a few inquiries of the vicar at Talley on the Green. It wouldn't do to introduce Lissa to a man that was not wealthy enough to provide well for her and her grandmother.

He also looked forward to discussing the odd-shaped object Leighhall had taken with him. If it were another weapon, how did it connect to the women he bedded? And if it weren't a weapon, what could it be? And would it be of any help in discovering a weakness to exploit for the sake of Lady Harewood?

Some might be frustrated by the lack of information, but he found it exciting. There were so many possibilities, and he enjoyed discovering them all. That he could share this particular puzzle with a good friend just added to his pleasure. Yes, he would definitely take Lissa on a ride with the proper chaperone, so that she might also appreciate the complexities of the case. The best part of it all was that he could be himself.

Lifting the wig off his head, he scratched his scalp. Being himself for a few days was definitely something he looked forward to.

CHAPTER FOUR

L ISSA TOOK ANTHONY'S hand as he helped her down from his coach. She stepped aside to allow Ellie room to descend. It also gave her time to digest the newest bit of information she'd just learned about him. The coach was no hired hack, but his own and of very high quality, according to Ellie. Did working for the peerage provide such a substantial income, then?

There was so much she wished to talk about with Anthony. As soon as she'd been informed by the duchess that he wished to escort her and Ellie to the village of Talley on the Green, she'd been anxious to discover what else he'd uncovered in his investigation. That he had chosen this village, which was farther away from the school than the one in Northampton, also piqued her curiosity. Were there perhaps some men he hoped to introduce her to?

Mrs. Kingman, their chaperone, and a new instructor at the school, addressed them once Ellie had alighted. "What a lovely little village. It appears we will have plenty with which to occupy ourselves. Mr. Taylour, did you have any suggestions as to where to start? I admit, since I am rather new to Northampton, I have never visited Talley on the Green."

"Then might I suggest Miller and Sons first? It has a plethora of items, from scents to books." Anthony gestured to a sign on the right side of the street.

Mrs. Kingman raised a brow. "Truly, all in one shop?"

"Indeed." He gave her a nod.

"Then we shall start there. Come, Eleanor. I'm sure we can find something to purchase as a memory of our day here." With that, Mrs. Kingman and Ellie started forward.

Anthony held out his arm. "May I suggest we follow?"

Lissa hooked her arm around his as she'd been instructed, not particularly comfortable. "Yes. I'm curious why a shop would have such a variety of items. Is the owner in trade, then?"

"He is. However, the reason for his variety of items is that this is a small town, and if he simply stocked one particular product, he would not do well."

She found intelligence an excellent trait in a husband. "Then I should meet him, *oui*?"

Anthony shook his head. "That was not my intention, as he is already married." He glanced at her. "You can enjoy the experience of the day in addition to finding a husband."

Not happy that she had to turn her head to see him due to the lace on her bonnet, she wished Dory hadn't talked her into adding the material. Now, she was sure she would rip it out as soon as they returned to school. "I can enjoy my days once I am settled. I have little time to avoid marriage to a peer."

He returned his attention to the street in front of them. "Then I would suggest that after this shop we go to the Woodcock Inn, which serves hot cocoa in addition to being the place where many of the tradesmen in this area gather in the afternoon."

A feeling akin to that which she had just before breaking into a seemingly abandoned house back in France filled her. It was not knowing what or whom she might encounter inside that caused the anticipation. Pleased she would soon begin the journey to a happier life than the one planned for her, she took time to enjoy the sights and sounds of the village.

It was not unlike the one she grew up near, with its single-lane road lined with building next to building for a short distance and then nothing but fields or woods. Most likely the closest field was used for fairs or traveling shows. As they drew closer to Miller and Sons, she could hear pounding coming from a blacksmith's shop near the end of the street. Directly across from them as they arrived at their destination was a tavern.

She removed her arm from Anthony's as they all entered.

"Oh, this is quite impressive." Mrs. Kingman waved toward the back of the shop, which was a bit larger than expected from the outside, though there was absolutely no organization to it. "I'm sure we can all find a bit of something here."

As the woman strolled forward, Ellie looked over her shoulder and winked before directing their instructor toward a shelf of books.

On tables throughout the shop, there were teacups and plates next to tools divided by piles of cloth. Shelves along the walls held figurines, more books, silver, and even sweets.

"And is there something you might like to purchase?"

At Anthony's question, Lissa shrugged. "Doubtful, but I'm happy to look. It is not every day I am able to escape from school."

As she started in the opposite direction from her instructor, Anthony was quick to respond. "Escape? So you are not as content as you had me believe?"

"Oh, I am, for now. It is just I'm still getting accustomed to not having the freedom I had back home." She gave him a lopsided grin as she raised a pretty silver candleholder. "It's not as if I can ride out into the night and find something pretty like this to trade with."

He didn't smile like she expected him to. "I would be happy to purchase that for you. You no longer need to survive on your own. You have friends here, and you are free to thrive."

He said it so seriously that it made her uncomfortable. She was not who he thought her. The more he treated her as if she deserved something better, the more he put distance between them, though he obviously didn't realize that. She studied the candlestick holder, turning it this way and that. "No, I do not wish it." She set it back upon the table and moved forward, for once happy to have the bonnet lace to keep him from studying her.

Anthony never simply looked. He examined, studied, analyzed, but he rarely *looked*. She was quite sure even now he scrutinized her dress or her gait.

He stopped and lifted an apricot-colored ribbon from a tiny wooden rack set upon the table. "Perhaps this would interest you. It matches your dress exactly."

She looked down, having forgotten which dress the maid had laid out for her. She didn't care for day dresses, as they were so light that she could only hide two daggers when wearing one. Not that she ever expected to need them, but she felt safer for their presence. "I appreciate the offer, but I fear I have more ribbons and frippery than I'll ever use."

He returned the ribbon to its resting place. "Of course. I'm sure the Captain has outfitted you and your grandmother with all that you need. So maybe we need to find something you *don't* need."

She turned at that, confused. "Why would I purchase something I don't need?"

His gaze softened. "I forget when you are dressed in such lovely clothes that your life has been difficult."

She wrinkled her nose. "My life has been wonderful, not difficult. I have *lived* more in France than my friends have lived here in their well-kept homes."

"I meant no offense."

"I do not take any. I simply state facts." She smirked. "However, if you wish to buy me something I do not need, I will put forth effort to find something."

"Excellent." He held his hand out to the tables still to explore.

As she studied the variety of items, she searched for something with no purpose. The figurines could, in fact, be such, but they were not to her taste. So she changed her strategy and looked for something that a woman wouldn't need. There were many male items, but not useful ones like pantaloons, boots, or knives, but then again, the item was *not* to be useful. As she approached the last table, she could sense Anthony worried she wouldn't find anything.

Irritation filled her. He'd never worried if he could please her before. He looked at her differently, reacted to her differently because her clothing wasn't what it was in France. He no longer wore a uniform, but she still saw him as her friend. That he couldn't see her in a similar light was disappointing. Annoyed, she had reached for a cravat, just to fill his need to buy her something, when she spotted a cravat pin just beneath the frills and picked that up instead.

It was a cockerel, but not just any cockerel. It sparkled with small blue gems, a white one for the eye, and a red wing and comb. It embodied her two favorite symbols of her country, the French colors and the bird who symbolized the common people, new birth, a new day, a fresh beginning. Her throat closed and her chest tightened at what it could mean that she'd discovered it this very day.

"What did you find, Lissa?"

At Anthony's voice, she turned to show him, her pique forgotten as she held the pin in the palm of her gloved hand.

"Ah, your taste is unparalleled. Those rubies and sapphires in this rooster truly represent your place of birth."

Rubies and sapphires? She thought them glass. Disappointment filled her and she started to close her fingers over the pin, intending to return it.

"Wait." Anthony's warm hand covered hers. "Do you not wish to have it?"

She looked up at him, surprised he stopped her. "It is far too expensive."

His lips split into a wide grin. "Not at all. Please. Allow me to offer you this small pleasure."

Not a little confused, she didn't move. "But I cannot repay

you for something such as this."

Once again his gaze softened, an expression she wasn't sure she liked coming from him. "Lissa, it is like pin money to me."

Lord and Lady Blackmore, her sponsors, provided her with pin money. It was not much, and she squirreled it away in case she needed it, but with everything provided to her, she had yet to use it. "How can that be? Does working for the earl provide such a substantial income, then?"

He gave a soft chuckle, not the full one she was used to. "I have my own estate with tenants. The investigations I conduct are simply to help others." He leaned closer and lowered his voice. "And to have a bit of fun. The payment is to make them feel comfortable with the arrangement."

She blinked. Anthony was wealthy? Her mind spun at the possibilities.

"Now, allow me to gift you with this small token of your homeland." He released her hand and held his out, palm up.

Still not sure what to make of the man she thought she knew, she nodded and opened her hand so he could retrieve the cravat pin and find the proprietor.

She let her gaze follow him, trying to equate the wealthy gentleman with her old friend, the lieutenant from France. His actions, mannerisms, and even his conversations were completely different, but she hadn't truly understood until that very moment. Which was the real Anthony—or was there one?

"He is a fine gentleman, is he not?"

At Ellie's words, Lissa turned to find her classmate just behind her shoulder. "Yes, he is, but different from when he was my friend back in France."

Ellie waved her hand to dismiss the point, and the cravat on the table floated to the floor. "Oh dear." Bending over, she retrieved the white silk and tried to dust it off, but only succeeded in smudging the dirt from the floor across it. Quickly, she dropped it back on the table. "As I was about to say, different environments call for different manners, wouldn't you agree?"

Though Lissa wished to delve into Ellie's suggestion further, she did not wish to do so in public, as Ellie's voice was a bit loud and Mrs. Kingman as well as others in the store were glancing toward them. "I do agree. So did you find something here that you would like to purchase?"

Her friend grinned and lifted her arm, showing her drawn-tight reticule. "I found the perfect color of ribbon."

Though she couldn't see through the cloth of the reticule, Lissa had doubts the ribbon was the perfect color, as Ellie didn't have a good eye for matching her accessories to her dresses, but it all depended on what it was used for. "Then we must see what else this village has to offer."

"Yes. It is such a refreshing break from our studies."

Lissa agreed completely. She had only just started her "first year," as the ladies dubbed it, which meant general studies. She'd never read so much and was very thankful for the tutors Lord Blackmore had provided for her in France. Still, she much preferred learning by doing. Luckily, the duchess understood and allowed her to spend one day a week practicing with various weapons in addition to studying them, as long as she applied herself to the other subjects. She wasn't sure why she needed to learn philosophy, Latin, or Ellie's favorite, astronomy, to get along in life. She never had before, and so far, she saw no practical use for them, except to follow the stars home at night, which she would never need to do again.

Anthony approached, his stride that of a man confident in his place in the world. At least that hadn't changed. He held out a small brown paper package. "Would you like me to carry this for you?"

She cocked her head and lifted her chin as she'd seen a dowager duchess do upon counseling a young relative. "No. I believe I am capable of carrying it."

His brows lowered before one side of his mouth quirked up. "Of course."

Pleased he saw how silly his question had been, she lifted the brown paper from his hand and slipped it into a deep pocket she had added to her dress, then buttoned it. It might make her hips appear somewhat crooked, but she could keep her arm down against it if she found a gentleman she wished to be introduced to.

Mrs. Kingman joined them, a large package in her hand. "I believe I will need the footman to carry this to the carriage. Shall we go outside and explore further?"

They all agreed, and their instructor led the way. After the woman dropped her package into the hands of the footman, they continued down the street.

They hadn't gone far before Ellie stopped. "Oh, I must step in here. Would you mind?"

Lissa looked in the window to see what appeared to be both a seamstress and milliner's shop. "Please, go ahead. I can wait here with Mr. Taylour."

Mrs. Kingman frowned, clearly not happy with the arrangement.

Anthony held his hand out to the large window of the shop. "Might I suggest that Mademoiselle Lissette and I stand here, so I can be sure she is safe, and you can still be in view of both ladies?"

"An excellent idea, Mr. Taylour. Thank you." Mrs. Kingman gave Anthony a grateful smile and motioned to Ellie to follow her inside.

Happy to have Anthony to herself, Lissa looked up at him. "That was most ingenious. Now perhaps you can tell me what progress you have made on Lord Weaponeer." She kept her voice lowered, not wishing any passerby to hear.

Anthony chuckled then waited as a person did, in fact, walk by. "I do like that name, though I'm not sure it applies as of yet. But I have made some interesting observations, one of which I would appreciate your insight on."

Thrilled that his investigation moved forward, she nodded. "What can I help you with?"

He looked across the street, then behind him before glancing past her and finally answering. "He left a cobbler shop with a large, odd-shaped package, and while I do not know that it was a weapon, I also don't know that it was not, but I have tried to think of what it could be and have nothing to compare it to. It was definitely not a new pair of hessians."

This sounded promising. "Please. Tell me what it looked like."

"It was round like a parasol, but instead of having a long handle, it was half that length and pressed the outside paper in a cylindrical fashion. From the way he carried it, I would say it was not light, perhaps as heavy as a wall shield. Do you know of any weapons that fit that description?"

As she thought of what it could be, she noticed Ellie inside exclaiming over a hat, which would no doubt be purchased forthwith. "It could be a shield, but the protruding element doesn't fit. I will definitely need to research this."

Instead of being disappointed, he grinned. "I'm very pleased that you are willing to do so. I have many avenues I'm pursuing, which take most of my time."

That he had then taken time from his tasks to escort her to Talley on the Green meant that much more. "We are friends and we aid each other in our pursuits, do we not?"

"Indeed, we do. In fact, as soon as your instructor and class-mate exit, I suggest we go to the Woodcock Inn for refreshments. It will be an opportune time to further your personal goal. I know many of the tradesmen in town, and already spoke to the vicar to understand who might best suit your needs."

She greatly appreciated how seriously he took her goal, but she wrinkled her nose at him. "It's me, remember? You can state simply that you determined who was wealthy enough for my grandmother."

"I stand corrected. I am still adjusting to thinking of you as I always have instead of a lady of breeding, which is particularly difficult when you look so lovely in that dress and bonnet. I have no doubt that you will draw the attention of many a gentleman."

She sighed. Though she understood, she didn't like it. It must be why he was acting the gentleman. "Remember, I do not seek a gentleman, just a wealthy man."

He gave her a short bow. "I will keep that in mind, my lady."

At his address, she opened her mouth to curse at him when she noticed the laughter in his eyes. Now *that* was the Anthony she'd always known. But before she could reply in kind, Mrs. Kingman exited the shop with Ellie.

"Oh, Lissette, I found the most perfect gift for the duchess." Ellie touched her own bonnet. "It's a hat with little paper books on it! They will deliver it on the morrow. It will be a surprise, so please do not say anything at dinner."

"I will keep your secret. I promise."

Mrs. Kingman looked upon Ellie with affection. "It truly is perfect for Her Grace. Mr. Taylour, I do believe you said something about cocoa?"

"Indeed I did." Anthony gestured toward the end of the street. "If we continue in this direction, we will come upon the Woodcock Inn."

"Then let us go there directly. I find I'm quite parched." Mrs. Kingman took Ellie's arm, and they moved forward. Lissa took Anthony's offered arm, and they followed.

As they entered the dining room, she could see there were private rooms off it and hoped they would not be secluded. Fortunately, Anthony made the arrangements and they were soon seated at a table, cocoa and rout cakes ordered.

Mrs. Kingman looked about. "This establishment is the most crowded we've seen today."

"It always is at this time." Anthony nodded toward the room. "It is where much business is conducted. I believe your husband has come here on occasion, Mrs. Kingman."

Mrs. Kingman's eyes widened. "He has?"

Anthony nodded sagely as he sat straighter in his chair. "Yes, I have seen Mr. Kingman here. He has an excellent reputation among all." He nodded toward a table in the corner. "There are two people your husband regularly does business with, as one is the silversmith and the other is a purveyor of scents. Both are quite well established and comfortable. I imagine that has much to do with your husband's success."

"Oh." Mrs. Kingman, who was only recently married, seemed quite impressed. "Is there anyone else he does business with here?"

Lissa bit down on a smile so as not to alert the lady that there was more to Anthony's tale than simply her husband's contacts. It was obvious his explanation of the gentlemen was to let her know who was a possible husband.

He didn't disappoint either of them. "Now, Mr. Brown over there has done well also thanks to your husband, which makes his wife very happy."

She mentally crossed Mr. Brown from her mental list, which she didn't mind, as he was rather ruddy in complexion and sneezed quite a bit.

Anthony continued. "However, I don't believe your husband has had any dealings with Mr. Stochbury and Mr. Ozell. They are both lawyers retained by the aristocracy in the region. They each have an estate halfway between Northampton and Bedford."

Ellie jumped in. "Who's that by the window?" She waved her hand toward the area in question.

The three ladies at the table next to them stopped their conversation, obviously overhearing. Mrs. Kingman gave Ellie a quelling look, and the poor woman turned almost as red as her hair.

Lissa couldn't resist touching Ellie on the arm. "They look like they may be peers. Mr. Taylour, do you know them?"

Anthony studied them for a moment then leaned in. "Yes, I recognize the Earl of Trente, but the two he is with are unknown to me." He kept his voice low, probably in hopes that Ellie would answer in kind. "Lady Eleanor, do you wish me to make their acquaintance for you?"

Ellie looked at the men then turned toward Anthony. "No,

but I thank you for the offer. I must wait for my mother to approve any possible suitors."

At that moment, their cocoa was brought along with their rout cakes, and they all indulged.

Lissa watched the men Anthony had mentioned. From outside appearances, she wouldn't mind meeting the silversmith, but the purveyor of scents was not to her liking. Both the lawyers seemed well formed and most likely were quite intelligent, and also, no doubt, busy. That would be an excellent trait in a husband—a man too busy for a wife would allow her more freedom.

As Ellie engaged Mrs. Kingman in the positive attributes of the town, Anthony leaned in, but kept his voice low. "There is also a tradesman of Mr. Kingman's status by the door. He is actually the man's competitor. He's talking to the owner of three establishments, a tavern, a tea house, and a mercantile in a neighboring village."

Taking a sip of her cocoa, she looked over the brim of her cup to see that both men were deep in conversation. Such men would be very busy, and she added them to her list. Putting her cup down, she replied, "Thank you. How do you know so much about the people in this town? It's not in close proximity to Ravenridge at all."

"I make it a point to know the area where I reside and those nearby. This is not so far as all that on horseback."

She cocked her head. "Especially if one were to ride through the forest?"

"Shh. I would not want my secret to become known." Though he made the statement with all seriousness, his gaze held laughter.

"Then I must determine what boon I receive for keeping it from public knowledge."

His eyes rounded before he sat back, shaking his head. "I find your wit much unchanged."

His compliment, whether meant to be one or not, had her

feeling rather accomplished, which was silly. It wasn't as if she hoped to impress him. He already knew her. She studied him as he answered Mrs. Kingman. He may know her, but as it turned out, she didn't know him. If he had such a vast fortune that the cravat pin he bought her was no more than pin money, then perhaps she needn't look further for a husband.

She turned her head to view each man Anthony had mentioned. None were as handsome as he, but all were well built and had wealth. She'd never considered outward appearances important. If she had, she would have never fallen in love with Etienne. The scar he had on his cheek from a fall as a youth had significantly diminished his looks. Yet his heart had been steadfast and his loyalty and honesty unquestionable.

What she must determine was if she wished a new start with a man of means or be comfortable with a friend. Her immediate thought was that a friend would demand far less of her, but did he know her *too* well? And she didn't know how Anthony felt about marriage. She would have to delve into that subject next time they were alone, which she hoped would be soon.

Not willing to limit herself, to keep all possibilities open, she observed the silversmith, lawyers, tradesman, and merchant for a while longer. If there was one lesson she'd learned at home, it was to always have multiple escape routes.

CHAPTER FIVE

ANTHONY STRODE INTO the stables at Ravenridge only to halt at the sight of his friend, the Viscount of Blackmore, talking to the stableman, Mr. Clancy. The opposition of the two gentleman reminded him of his various disguises. Marcus had fine hair as dark as midnight, and Mr. Clancy's was rough and gray. And while Marcus stood as straight as he had while commanding troops in the war, Mr. Clancy's curved back proved the toils of his trade had left their mark.

"Ah, here he is now." Marcus waved him over. "I know you're busy on another investigation, but I was hoping you had a moment to give us your opinion."

Anthony did not wish to be late to meet Lissa, but since his captain housed him, he didn't feel it appropriate to deny the request. He strode forward. "I'd be happy to impart what little knowledge I have. What do you need from me?"

Mr. Clancy chuckled, his grin as wide as the stable door. "The lad here don't think he can trust his own judgment. But I told him it shines everything else down, I did."

Having mingled among the lower classes quite often, Anthony understood the old man's reference to something quite impressive, and his curiosity was piqued. Striding up to them, he turned to where Mr. Clancy pointed.

On the ground next to the stall was a wooden rocking horse.

It was far from the typical, as it had been painted to look like a real horse. Not only that, but the tail and mane appeared to be horsehair and the eyes were onyx stones. What made it truly an artistic creation was the leather saddle with tiny stirrups. Obviously, this was to be for the lord's coming child.

Anthony pretended to give it a careful examination and crouched. Lifting the small reins, he set the horse in motion. Eventually, he stood and looked at his former captain. He scanned Lord Blackmore from head to toe, then looked at the horse again. Finally, he spoke to his friend. "It is well made and more lifelike than any I have seen, but…" He let his voice trail off.

Marcus frowned, clearly concerned. "But what? What's wrong?"

"I don't think it will hold your weight." He barely kept his laughter at bay as his friend's brows lowered even further.

"My weight? Why would—" Realization dawned, and Marcus shook his head. "It's for the baby."

"Well, in that case, I believe the baby has a first-rate ride. What will you call it?"

"Call it?"

Mr. Clancy chuckled. "My lord, Anthony wants to know what its name is."

Understanding that his friend was new to fatherhood, while he had two brothers who had already reached that status, Anthony explained, "As you and Lady Blackmore hold horses in such high esteem and provide each with a fitting name, I would suggest that you may want to have a name for your child's first horse so they understand this is expected."

Marcus clapped him on the shoulder. "Excellent idea. I will think upon it."

"Then I will leave you to your thoughts and look forward to hearing what you decide upon. You cannot as easily tell us that you will wait to reveal the name until it is born, like you have with your child, since this fellow or filly is *already* born."

Marcus grimaced at the reminder of what he and his wife had

told everyone, but didn't say anything.

Anthony walked his Irish Hunter out of the stables and mounted. He was about to set out when the lord came outside. "Wait. You didn't tell me what you think."

"But I did."

"No, I mean, I wished to know if you think Mariel will like it. Lady Sommerset painted it to look as real as possible, and I had the saddle made specifically for it."

He held back a chuckle. Did the man not realize his wife loved him so much that if he presented her with a simple rattle with a horse engraved upon it, she would be overjoyed? "Lady Blackmore will be absolutely delighted with it."

"Do you think so?"

"I do."

Marcus finally appeared to relax. "Thank you. I appreciate your honesty."

As his former captain, now friend, turned for the stable, Anthony smiled, kicking his mount so he could let out his laughter without anyone hearing. He shook his head even as he set a quick pace. He'd never met anyone so in love with their wife. His own brothers seemed happy, but not besotted like Marcus. He counted himself lucky he need never worry about marrying or children. Being the fourth of four boys did come with advantages.

He slowed his horse as they entered the wood, finding himself anxious to see Lissa again. He'd like to believe it was his interest in what Leighhall carried, but he recognized that he had missed having her about. Though escorting her about the village had been a unique experience. She was quite beautiful, something he'd not recognized in France, though he'd known that she was attractive. There was something about seeing her as she must have looked before the loss of her family and home, long before the war came to her lands, that had him appreciating exactly how adaptable she'd been.

He had little doubt that if she set her cap for any of the men he'd drawn her attention to in Talley upon the Green, they would quickly appreciate having her as a wife. But he didn't want to limit her choices. She'd endured much and deserved to consider as many as she wished. He'd have to arrange an outing to Woodford Chase. He'd spent time there as well, and with help from an acquaintance, he could provide her with at least half a dozen others. Maybe he should—

The thought left as a feeling of being watched filled him. He had no disguise, so his senses were much more attuned to his surroundings. He slowed his mount, hoping it was Lissa, but preparing as if it were another with bad intentions.

The snort of a horse had him turning around, only to have his top hat lifted from his head. Instinct took over and he reached out, grabbing the arm that sought to steal from him.

"Good it is to see that you are still quick, *mon ami.*"

He looked up and took back his hat before letting Lissa go as she dangled from a tree branch upside down in her usual shirt and trousers, not a little concerned at her precarious position. "Am I to expect an attack upon my person every time I meet with you?"

She held her arms out. "Who is to say?"

"Let me get your horse, so you can get down from there."

"No need." She lifted her torso and grasped the branch, then dropped her legs, only to swing her feet onto another, shorter branch, before climbing down to the ground.

Dismounting himself, he waited as she fetched her horse from behind the bushes along the other side of the path.

As she strode back toward him, he only saw the old Lissa, her gait that of a young man, not the graceful walk he'd witnessed on their outing eight days ago. She stopped twenty feet away, the reins in one hand, her other on her hip. "I thought you forgot about me."

"Hardly. If you remember, I'm tracking. As much as I wished to meet with you, I had to stay with Leighhall."

"Why meet now?" She cocked her head, obviously not pleased with him.

He'd thought taking her to Talley on the Green would satisfy her for at least a fortnight. "Because Leighhall is currently at a house party where he is dancing attendance on a number of ladies, much like the one Lady Harewood attended." He paused as a thought occurred. "I can only hope he does not come away wishing to do damage to one of their reputations as well."

She finally moved closer even as she shrugged. "Then if you find anything on him, you can sell it to that lady's parents. I'm sure they'd be grateful."

Her suggestion surprised him, as he'd willingly offer such intelligence freely. It reminded him once again that she'd done what she had to in order to survive. Part of him wished she'd never had to experience war, but the selfish part of him was thankful she had, or he would have never had such a good friend. "Did you find anything in your research on weapons that might be what Leighhall carried out of the cobbler's?"

"I did." She crossed her arms. "But if I tell you, will you forget about me again?"

"Lissa, I would take you with me, but that is hardly proper."

She glanced past him at nothing in particular. "I so wish I didn't need to pretend to be a lady. I'd rather jaunt about with you and experience life." She flung her hand out toward the path to Silver Meadows. "They read about life, think about life, talk about life, but they do not experience it. At least while in London, they went about a bit. It is not for me."

Something had seriously changed in their time apart. She had not complained so much before. "What has happened?"

She snapped her gaze back to his. "I did not say anything happened."

He raised his brows, not letting her look away. "I know you, remember?"

At first it seemed she wouldn't give in, but then she threw her hands up. "Grand-maman wrote me. She has a list. A list! She said she's going to arrange for the Blackmores to bring me to London early so I can be outfitted." She stalked across the pathway. "*Oui*, she wishes to dress me up for auction. Sell me to the highest peer.

This is what she wants." She stalked back across the path. "She is boxing me in. *Mon Dieu*, I do not want this. But what I want— What are you smiling for?"

He couldn't help grinning. "You have no need to worry about going to London early. Lady Blackmore will not be able to travel. In fact, I doubt she plans to attend much of the Season."

Lissa stilled. "She won't?"

"No, she won't. She is in a delicate way. I doubt that she will travel before April. So, you see, you have a reprieve."

She frowned before her eyes widened. "She's with child? I was not aware." Even as Lissa's spirits seem to lift, her shoulders slumped. "Grand-maman will just have Lord Blackmore ask Lady Northwick, who I know will accept."

He hadn't thought of that, but what she said could very well happen. He tried to think of what might help her. "You only need to heed your grandmother until you are twenty-one."

"Is this true?" Her eyes lit with excitement. "You do not jest?"

"Not at all. If you can avoid a proposal from a peer for a couple of Seasons, you can then do as you wish." But could she? As a lady, she was stunning, and many a man did not look past a lady's appearance and manners.

A sly smile lifted her lips. "But I won't—wonder if the duchess could convince my grandmother to wait another year."

If he hadn't been watching her so closely, he would have missed it, the slight movement of her nose when she hesitated. He'd only seen it once before when he'd caught her lying. Their friendship was built upon respect for each other's abilities and honesty. Not a little hurt that she sought to dissemble with him, he folded his arms. "That was not what you were going to say."

She opened her mouth then closed it.

"Why do you seek to lie to me now? What is of such import than you cannot tell me?"

Her gaze lowered. "It is habit. I apologize."

It was habit to lie? She had lied daily in France, but now there was no reason for it. "I cannot accept your apology unless you tell me what you were about to say." As she rolled her lips in to think about how to answer, he lost his patience. "Tell me now."

Her gaze snapped to his. "Very well, I'm not nineteen."

When she didn't continue, he scowled at her. "How old are you?"

She didn't look away, but her shoulders stiffened. "I'm twenty-four."

He dropped his arms. "Twenty-four?" He wasn't surprised. He was shocked.

"*Oui*. Far too old to be marriageable material, which is why Grand-maman told all I was younger. She has her plans for me."

And Madame Fontaine called *him* the trickster? Several requests the old woman had made of Lord Blackmore over the years started to coalesce. As the one who fulfilled those requests, Anthony had sometimes wondered, but it made more sense now. The old woman had wished for tutoring for them both so they could come to England and converse appropriately. The other tutors for Lissa were to teach her to be a lady by English standards, evidently so she could be married off.

He had to admire the old woman's patience. Did she know her charge was not as interested in complying as she'd hoped? Now that he'd inadvertently given Lissa the information she needed to break away from her grandmother, would she? That question lay heavy in his chest, and he had to have the answer before aiding her further. "Now that you know you can ignore your grandmother's wishes, what will you do?"

Lissa moved closer to her mount and idly stroked it as if it helped her calm her racing thoughts.

He did not interrupt her musing. It was a life-changing decision, and she needed to evaluate her options. In fact, he wouldn't be surprised if this were the first time she had the opportunity to determine her own future. Until this very moment, it had been survival, and then aiding her grandmother, and now doing as her grandmother wished.

Finally, Lissa stepped away from her mount as if she didn't

want to depend upon it for making her decision. "What you have told me provides me with a certain freedom I didn't know I had, yet I am still bound to my grandmother. I could not have survived without her any more than she could have survived without me."

He could tell she had more to articulate, so he waited, anxious to understand the very core of who she was. Was it the woman who thought nothing of selling information to save another woman's reputation instead of offering it freely? Or would she honor her relative, her only surviving family member?

She straightened her shoulders, mimicking the actions of a young man more than a woman. "I will continue on the course I have set, to find a wealthy tradesman so that my grandmother can end her days in luxury. She deserves that. If I cannot do that before I must enter the Season, I shall seek a compromise with her, letting her know that I am aware I no longer need to do as she wishes."

His muscles relaxed, though he hadn't realized he'd tensed. Her answer sent a wave of relief through him that she was the honorable woman he'd always thought her to be. Upon the heels of that thought came another, and he blurted it. "Do you think your grandmother knows this law?"

Lissa nodded with no hesitation. "I am sure she does. I'm also sure it is why she made me the age she did, so if I weren't successful in my first Season, there would be another before she'd no longer rule over me. She did not expect me to learn of this." She gave him a soft smile, one he'd not seen on her before. "Thank you for this gift."

He swallowed hard as he gazed at her, the pull on his heart very strong. "I am pleased I could be helpful. And I promise I will continue to be, so that you need not reveal to your grandmother what you know."

She gave him a regal nod, as if she were in a ball gown accepting a dance, when she stood there in shirt, trousers, and boots, her hair tied back in a queue. She practically embodied contradiction. It was, perhaps, what had always intrigued him about her, her ability to adapt.

"Now that I have assuaged your fears regarding the upcoming Season, could you tell me if you found any information to aid me in my investigation?"

Her eyes widened as if she'd forgotten why they had met. "I did." She shoved her hand into the pocket of the trousers and pulled out a folded piece of paper. "If what your quarry carried was this, it does begin a pattern."

He opened the paper and stared at the sketch of two figures. One looked like an old shield with a hole in the middle and a small grate above the hole. The other, presumably the back, had straps and what looked like the butt of a gun of some sort. "What is this?"

"It's a gun shield." She grinned triumphantly. "Henry VIII of your country had a number made based upon an Italian design." She moved to stand next to him and pointed at the front of the shield. "That hole is where the shot comes out, and this grate allows the shooter to see to aim."

The light scent of apple filled his nostrils, sending him back to France again. "What kind of gun is this?"

"It's a breech-loading matchlock pistol." She pulled her hand back but remained next to him. "The shield itself is wood, with pieces of metal over the front."

Forcing himself to concentrate on the images, he examined the smaller details. "So this would be a weapon from the early Renaissance. Do we use anything like this today? I've never seen it in the military."

She shook her head then held up her arm, as if holding a shield, and pretended to shoot over her forearm. "While the idea appears sound, the actual use of it was awkward, and after your king's initial interest, it was lost to history."

"So it's another unusual antique weapon."

She stepped back and held her arms out. "Exactly. It's the start of a pattern. Not only a pattern, but it may just answer the question about what this Leighhall is using these for."

He immediately understood what she meant. "It's not in order to use them, unless he plans some ancient battle or a stage play." He paused because he wouldn't discount those two possibilities completely. Peers could have *very* odd interests. "However, the most likely reason he has these is for a specific collection. Now we just need to discover if it's for a museum or for himself."

"I would wager it's for himself. A man who beds so many women is highly selfish." She winked. "Unless, of course, he's an excellent lover. In that case, he could be considered generous."

Not a little shocked by her comment about Leighhall's bedroom skills, he stared at her.

She waved off her deduction. "It's more likely that he would sell such weapons to a museum, not donate them. Unless of course he wished to have a room named after himself."

Unable to remain silent, he finally stopped her analysis. "I suggest that you not delve into the man's amorous affairs. That is not a fit subject for a young woman to dwell upon."

"*Mon Dieu*, Anthony, do not attempt to stifle my speech when we're alone." She threw her hands up. "I'm not in some stifling parlor conversing with Lord Monotonous about the color of a vase. Are we or are we not partners in this investigation?"

Her tone had taken on a hard edge, one he was familiar with. Though he understood why she was upset, he couldn't fault himself. As much as he tried to think of her as the urchin with which he'd scrounged for food while staying in France as Blackmore healed, he couldn't. She was more than simply that person now. He would not apologize, but he did need to assuage her anger, as she was a valuable asset to his investigation. "I will endeavor not to. However, I will not have it held against me that on occasion, I may treat you more as a lady than as young man."

She held his gaze, but he did not waver. Finally, she sighed. "Very well. I will let such remarks pass and focus on our goal instead. I would like to hear your thoughts on Leighhall's gathering of odd and ancient weapons."

Pleased that they had an understanding, he reviewed every-thing he knew so far. Finally, he shook his head. "I'm not sure as yet what these weapons tell us. But if the man is simply adding them to his own collection, then I fear there is nothing to that which would help Lady Harewood."

Lissa's brow furrowed in obvious concern. "Then we must unearth more about the man. What do you propose?"

He'd been biding his time until he knew more, but now seemed the right time to infiltrate Leighhall's household. "I plan to disguise myself as a servant and apply for a position. I have heard that the man hosts his own house party on the last weekend of every month after the Season ends. I'm quite curious as to who his hostess is. It may be his mother, but my instinct tells me it will be whomever he's bedding at the time."

Lissa's brown eyes seemed to lighten with her excitement. "That's an excellent idea. But what will your disguise be? You know servants gossip, so it will have to be a disguise that is not easily removed. Also, you will want to get into the house, so a common laborer, which would be fairly simple for you, won't help."

It was a true pleasure to strategize with someone who had similar experience. "I'd thought to pose as a footman or butcher."

She raised her brows, a small smile playing about her lips. "A butcher? And what do you know about butchering? I mean besides cutting off the head of my dear Rosalie."

He chuckled at the memory of Lissa showing him what to do to dress a chicken for cooking. "As a matter of fact, I have had more training since then in the butchering of cattle, so I should be able to handle a lamb, goat, or whatever else might be required. First, I will go to the village of Melton, where his estate is located, and get a feel for what it is like working for him and what he expects so that I am not turned away. If I can find out what the man wants—or rather what his butler wants—in a footman, I can speak to that upon applying."

"That's an excellent idea. When do you propose to go?"

"Two days hence. It is but a half-day's ride on an inferior mount, which will leave me half a day to discover what I need."

She set her hand on his arm. "That is a sound plan. I will be ready and will meet you here at this time in the morning."

Surprised, he stepped away, taking his arm from her hold. "What? You cannot come. What would the duchess say? You must remember, I owe her my very life."

Lissa waved off his concerns. "Her Grace will never know. I will simply have a migraine, something I claim at least once a month to take a break from the monotony."

"But…" He stopped himself from continuing, as all his objections were centered upon her being a lady. He switched tactics. "How will you disguise yourself?" He gestured toward her clothing. "This will not work anymore now that your hair is long."

She grinned, clearly pleased with herself. "Do not worry, *mon ami*. Like you, I have other forms of dress, and for such an outing, I do believe a village lass who has experience as a maid will do quite well." She dropped her grin and cocked her head. "After all, women are more likely to gossip than men when it comes to an employer, *non?*"

She had a strong point. He had no doubt she could garner far more information as a maid than he could as a footman or butcher. He searched for another reason she shouldn't go, but again, they all came back to her status as an unmarried lady. "Are you sure the duchess won't discover you've left?"

"I'm absolutely sure. I've done so before with no one the wiser."

It was on his mind to ask her about the other times, but he decided he'd rather remain ignorant. That she was resourceful, he was well aware, and he'd just have to trust her abilities. His unease was no doubt caused by the fact that this was England in peaceful times, not France during a war. There were different rules that governed society. Then again, her social aspirations were not particularly high, so everything considered, the risk was low. He just didn't wish to incur the duchess's wrath.

He finally nodded and held out his arm. "Two days hence I will see you here, and we shall endeavor to learn more about the Viscount Leighhall's preferences in staff."

She grasped his wrist. "Agreed." He grasped hers in return, then, releasing him, she turned, mounted her horse, and raised her arm. "To our success." She didn't wait for a response, but spun her horse about and headed back from whence she came.

He stood there long after she'd gone, after the sound of her horse's hooves no longer echoed in the wood, even after the birdsong returned. He had an unsettling feeling, not about his mission, but about Lissa. That worried him, only because he cared for her wellbeing. England was not her home, but any home she had back in France was gone. If she didn't care so much for her grandmother, he would refuse her help, as much as he needed it. He just hoped that the honorable woman he'd known in France held sway over the young woman who craved the exhilaration of challenges.

Finally, he mounted up and headed down the path toward Ravenridge. Despite his misgivings, he couldn't ignore the anticipation in the pit of his stomach at the thought of riding to Melton with Lissa and discovering all they could to be hired by Leighhall. It felt good to have her by his side once again, if only for a short while. He hadn't realized exactly how much he had missed her or how much she could add to his success.

As his horse stepped out into the morning sunshine, he set her to a gallop, his spirits rising as he planned for the coming trip.

CHAPTER SIX

L ISSA CARRIED HER basket with the newly purchased loaf of bread as she wove in between the crowd of people. It was market day, and the farmers and bakers filled the town square of Melton. Though the maid's dress itched a bit beneath her arms, it fit fairly well and concealed her daggers nicely, especially with the half sleeves that weren't too tight. She still glowed with pleasure at Anthony's approval over her brown-and-white maid's gown, beige bonnet, and red cloak.

Noticing a bench outside a confectioner's shop, she headed that way, hoping to find a servant about as ladies enjoyed a sweet. Just as she reached the shop, another woman plunked down on the seat of the bench. She stopped in her tracks.

"Oh, did you wish to sit? I can make room." The young woman, who appeared at least six or seven years younger than her, wore an ivory work dress, white apron, and white bonnet that didn't quite hide all of her dark hair. She moved to the side of the bench, pulling her own cloak to the side and leaving just enough room.

Lissa smiled warmly. This was exactly the type of person she needed to talk to. "Thank you." She sat and set her basket on the ground next to her. "I'm Margret, but people call me Meg. I have been walking all over the market looking for soap. The weather is much warmer than I expected for November."

"I be pleased to make your acquaintance. I'm Annie. Mum says we always get this heat just before a cold snap."

"Your mum is a smart woman."

Annie smiled with affection. "She is, and well I know it. She's the housekeeper for Lord Emyn.

"Do you know if she needs any additional maids?"

Annie sighed as she shook her head, her expressive hazel gaze showing true regret. "Mum said with the Emyns traveling, what she has too much of is staff."

Lissa let her shoulders slump forward. "Then I guess I will apply at Woburn Manor. Do you know if Lord Leighhall is in need of another maid?"

Annie's eyes rounded, and she grasped her package closer to her chest. "You do not want to work there."

Surprised by the reaction, Lissa forced herself to remain calm, tamping down the excitement of learning something of great import. "Why wouldn't I want to work there? Are the wages so poor? I thought he was well established."

Annie shook her head, but didn't lessen the hold on her package. "It's not that. He offers very good wages. He has to because no one stays very long." She looked up as two men walked by.

Lissa did as well and noticed Anthony talking to a man near the blacksmith's across the square.

When Annie didn't continue, she nudged her with her elbow. "Why don't people stay long?"

As if she'd forgotten what they were discussing, Annie blinked, then her brows rose. "Oh, I don't truly know why, but there's been talk over the years." She nodded. "Yes, much talk. Mum says I shouldn't listen to gossip, but there have been so many stories, I'm sure part of them are true." She gave a little shiver.

Now this sounded promising. Lissa leaned in. "I've always believed gossip to be at least half true."

"You do? So do I."

She waited for the woman to continue, but she seemed to

have forgotten the track of their conversation. Not wishing to start from the beginning once again, Lissa led Annie toward what she needed to know. "What do they say about working for Lord Leighhall?"

"They say—and I only tell you what others say, not what I know—but they say that the maids and such must beware of the lord's roving hands."

Lissa widened her eyes as if in shock, though she didn't doubt it was true. The man obviously had no respect for the gentler sex.

"I know you doubt me, but I heared that three women were so ashamed that they left his employ and never returned to their villages. No respecting woman here would work there, so they all come from other places. And what's worse is that strangers like yerself will come here to work for him and they are never seen again!" The last was whispered loudly.

Lissa clutched her hands in her lap. "Surely you do not mean they were murdered?"

Annie shrugged. "No one knows. But they do say there is a locked room at Woburn Manor that the lord doesn't allow anyone into, not even to clean it. Some say he does terrible things to his staff in there."

"No, it cannot be." Lissa endeavored to look duly shocked, though she doubted that people were killed in the man's home. If they came to work for him then left his employ, they most likely returned to their own village or found another position. There would be no reason for anyone in Melton to see them again. But the locked room was intriguing, if such were true.

Annie nodded sagely as if she were the keeper of all truths about Lord Leighhall. "I swear to you, it is what has been said."

"I cannot thank you enough for telling me. I must find my brother and tell him we cannot go there for work."

Annie breathed a sigh of relief. "I'm so pleased I sat here and spoke to you. There are only these two estates in this area, but you may want to try those near Pickwell."

Lissa rose and looped her basket over her arm. "Thank you

for your kind help. I must find my brother directly."

"Of course. I wish you well."

Quickly, she took her leave and headed for the blacksmith's, only to find Anthony was no longer there. Not seeing him in the vicinity, she continued toward their meeting place, an old well, just past the butcher's at the start of the village.

That Leighhall could not keep his staff said much about him. She doubted the man gave references, and without references a maid or footman was in dire straits. Of course, they could say they were attending a sick parent for a time and use older references. That was what she would do.

So what did the Leighhall do—accost every maid, beat every footman, test out his ancient, odd weapons on them? Though she doubted that could be it, she'd heard of such goings-on in France, especially during the war. And what about the room? He may not allow servants into it, so perhaps he had nobility in? Maybe he was a spy for a foreign country and met with his contacts inside. Or maybe he hoarded gold and jewels in the room and didn't trust his staff not to rob him. For all she knew, it could be a room of mirrors where he danced naked to admire himself.

She smirked at the thought. Dory had said the man was attractive and used that to his advantage to hide his evil intentions.

Whatever Leighhall's reason for keeping a locked room from his servants, if that were indeed the case, it meant that Lissa and Anthony would have to find a way into that room. Anyone who locked something away was either keeping a valuable secret or was as a mad as King George. She didn't fully understand how England could have a mad king and a prince serving as regent, but they did. Since neither influenced her life in any way, she rarely gave it more than a passing thought.

As she rounded the corner of the butcher's shop, the village well came into sight. The forest bushes and trees seemed to encroach upon it, closer than when it was first dug, but the posts that held the hoist to lower the bucket appeared fairly new, as if added in the last year. If there were a cup available, she wouldn't mind a sip of cold water while she waited.

Walking down the narrow, worn path of dirt through the dry grass, she concluded that the well was still used by the people in the area who needed it. At that thought, she sensed someone else near and turned to see who it might be. As she suspected, someone else trod down the path, and from his smile, he'd often done so. The young man with dark, curly hair couldn't be more than sixteen or seventeen, but what had her slowing was his clothing. He was also of the servant class and might have valuable information about Leighhall.

She stopped a few steps from the well. His lanky stride quickly closed the distance. It wasn't until he was but an arm's length away that she recognized the look in his gaze. He had no intention of stopping to chat. Just as she moved her free hand toward the sleeve on her other arm, he reached out and grabbed her basket. She yanked hard on it, and since he didn't let go, he lost his balance.

Slipping the blade from her sleeve, at the same time using his momentum to swing him around, she heard the thud as his head hit the well post. Like a cuirassier intent on an enemy, she slammed her elbow into his stomach before knocking his chin back and holding the knife to his throat. "Do not move, *comprende?*"

The young man's eyes remained unfocused. He was clearly still reeling from his head hitting the post.

She pressed her blade against his throat. "You would dare steal from me?"

His Adam's apple moved above her blade. "I just wanted to feed me mum. We haven't—"

"*Arrêt!*" Anthony's voice rang out behind her.

At the demand to stop in French, she pulled her blade back a bit, but didn't remove her dagger altogether. "Why should I stop?"

The soft swish of Anthony's footfalls as he strode through the tall, dry grass toward them told her he was close, but she didn't let her attention waver from the youth who would steal from her.

Anthony stopped just behind her culprit. "Let him go."

"Let him go? Why? He thought to take my bread." They should bring the young man before the magistrate or whatever law ruled the village. Or would it be Leighhall?

"Sister, do not forget where we were but three years past. What would you wish if you were caught in Talant?"

At the reminder of the night she'd almost been hauled off to prison for stealing a horse, she stilled. It wasn't that she'd forgotten who she was, but more that she had returned to those days when fighting over a precious piece of pig meant the difference between going to bed hungry or with a half-full belly.

She looked into the youth's eyes, which seemed able to focus now, and he appeared absolutely terrified. *Mon Dieu.* He was just a lad, as they said in England. Releasing her hold, she stepped back.

The young man didn't move.

Slowly, so as not to scare him, she retrieved the bread from the ground where it had fallen, the dry grass keeping it away from the dirt and bugs. "Here." She held it out to him. "I apologize. Sometimes I forget that I am not like you anymore."

He eyed her suspiciously, no doubt expecting her to stab him when he reached for it, so she returned the dagger to the sheath beneath her sleeve. "Here. Take it. It's for you. I can buy another."

"She will not hurt you." Anthony stepped up beside her. "She knows what it is to go hungry."

Still, the young man didn't move.

Anthony took the bread from her and held it out. "You may take this. Then tomorrow, go to the blacksmith. Tell him William recommended you. He is looking for someone willing to learn. Are you willing to learn?"

The youth nodded.

"Then take this for tonight, and tomorrow you can start buying your food instead of stealing it."

The young man looked at her and back at Anthony, then finally grabbed the bread and spun around, running into the wood.

"Do you think he'll go to the blacksmith?" She hoped the young man did, because he wasn't very good at stealing.

"I don't know. But better the blacksmith than Leighhall."

She turned toward him at that. "You also learned that no one from this village will work there?"

"Yes." Anthony moved to the well and lowered the bucket. "The man goes through servants rather quickly. From what I learned, he's not in residence but one weekend a month, when he hosts a different kind of house party."

Intrigued, she leaned her hip against the well and faced him as he dropped the bucket and slowly pulled it up. "What kind of house party?"

"Let us just say it is only partially a Society occasion."

She cocked her head and stared at him. "Anthony, do not be so coy. Be plain with it."

He pulled the bucket to the well wall and set it there, holding it as he answered. "Very well. It's for men and their mistresses only."

"That fits the man's personality. From what I learned, his lack of respect for women includes his servants. He thinks because he employs them to cook and clean for him, it entitles him to touch them whenever he chooses. I imagine they quit after one of those weekends."

Anthony's brow lifted at that before he scooped the tin cup attached to the bucket into the water and offered it to her.

"Thank you." She took a sip. As the cool liquid flowed down her throat, she let her eyes close. There was no feeling like a cold drink of water on a beautiful sunny day. After taking a few more sips, she handed the cup back to Anthony.

He took it and threw the rest back in one gulp before filling it in the bucket two more times. The third time, he dumped it over his bare head.

She chuckled as he pushed aside his damp hair. "I've never much appreciated bonnets and caps until this very moment."

He grinned, then doused himself with two more cups of water.

As the water flowed down his neck, it soaked the golden hairs of his chest seen clearly by the open V of his coarse shirt. The small hairs darkened when wet, and the oddest inclination came over her. She suddenly wanted to lick them dry.

Shaking her head, she dismissed the feeling. "I learned something as well."

He set the bucket to the side and leaned against the post the youth had so recently vacated. "Anything about weapons?"

"No—at least, I don't believe so. There is gossip that Leighhall has a secret room in his home that remains locked, and not even the staff are allowed in there to clean it."

"Now that *is* interesting. Is there any suspicion as to what is in there?"

"Of course there is." She grimaced. "Everything from a room to torture servants to outright murder."

"And do you think that's what it's used for…if it exists, based upon your source?"

"I do not." The problem was, she had no clue as to what it may house. "The only way to know is to get inside Woburn Manor and investigate."

He pushed away from the post and walked to where her basket lay on its side, scooping it up. "That had been my intention, but being a servant isn't going to allow me the access I need."

"Then the only other way is to get invited to his special house party." She smirked. "Surely you can disguise yourself as a peer." Even as the idea took root, her heartbeat increased. The possibilities of what they could discover were endless.

He frowned as if he had no idea what she meant before understanding dawned. "You mean for me to go to this weekend party of debauchery?"

"No, not at all. I mean for *us* to go to this weekend of debauchery. I shall pose as your mistress. Unless, of course, you already have one and wish to take her." She didn't like that idea at all. Imagining Anthony partnering with another woman bothered her greatly.

He dropped the basket. "No!"

She cocked her head, not a little confused. "No, you don't want to go, or no, you don't have a mistress?"

"No, I mean…" He picked up the basket and handed it to her. "I mean, yes I plan to attend if I can garner an invitation, and no, you cannot attend with me as my mistress."

"Why can't I?"

"First of all, you're a lady now."

She scowled at him, her irritation quick to take hold at his consistent need to think of her in terms she couldn't even begin to aspire to. What lady held a man at knifepoint when he attempted to steal from her?

As if he understood the error in his logic, he quickly continued. "Second, you could not make a convincing mistress. Third, we don't know how dangerous the man is yet." He held up his hand as she opened her mouth to respond. "No, hear me. True, he may not be dangerous at all, but that is not a chance I can take with a peer. It is too easy for him to bring up charges if he thinks something is amiss. I will not have you thrown into Newgate."

Beyond frustrated with him, she straightened, intending to stalk off, when another idea hit. Instead, she set her basket on the ground and pulled her bonnet from her head. With a few jerks, she removed the pins that held up her long, dark hair and let it fall about her in waves. Then she untied her cape and dropped it before tugging at the handkerchief that covered her chest and bosom, letting it fall, revealing the bit of cleavage between her breasts as they were held up by her stays.

His eyes darkened from their sky blue to a deep azure.

She gave him a sultry smile before sauntering up to him and brushing back the hair from his forehead. "But *mon ami*, I know much about how a woman can pleasure a man." She pressed herself against him, finding his chest harder than she expected. Rising on her toes, she whispered in his ear, "Do you prefer me against a wall or on my hands and knees?"

His heart thundered against her own chest before he took two steps back. "Lissa."

If he'd thought to yell at her, his harsh whisper was anything but. She smiled seductively, not a little surprised by how quickly her own heart had begun to race. "Yes. I am here and I am yours. What would you have of me? Would you like a taste?" She pushed her breasts higher, her nipples threatening to show themselves.

Anthony's gaze riveted to her chest, his Adam's apple moving hard as he swallowed twice.

His singular interest had her blood heating. For the first time, she looked at him as a would-be lover and was pleased by the possibilities. With no one to stop her, she sauntered forward until she stood before him once again. "Perhaps I can convince you." She pulled his head down and pressed her lips to his.

That was all the invitation he needed. His arms wrapped around her and his mouth took over their first kiss, but it was no gentle meeting of the lips, as with young lovers. It was a demand from a man who needed her, or perhaps any woman. The thrill of his tongue thrusting into her mouth had her wrapping her arms around his neck in full supplication.

His hands roamed over her, one finding her backside as the other ran up her side to cup her breast. His fingers moved over her bare skin to dip into her dress, searching and finding her hard peak. The suddenness of her desire caught her by surprise, intensifying every feeling. She pressed her hips against the evidence of his need and moaned.

Suddenly, his hands were gone and she stumbled back, confused, blood pounding in her veins.

"I cannot in good conscience..." He didn't continue, just stood there staring at her as if he didn't know who she was.

Tamping down her frustrated desire, she retrieved her handkerchief from the ground and wrapped it around her neck, tucking it in beneath her stays. Crouching down again, she found three of her pins, picked up her bonnet, and then, as if he weren't still standing there watching her, coolly wrapped her hair up, fastened it, and tied her bonnet. Lastly, she swept the red cloak about her and fastened it.

She walked over to her empty basket and looped her arm through it before facing him. "We've learned quite a bit today. Shall we return home now?"

"No." His voice sounded normal, though his countenance was anything but pleased. "We will talk about this." He waved his hand between them. "Where did you learn to entice a man so? Does your grandmother know? Did you know this back in France?"

Relieved that he would not hold her actions against her, she moved toward him, but when he took a step back, she halted. "If you wish to know if I was a virgin when you came to find the *Capitaine*, the answer is no. Before you arrived, I met Etienne." A part of her heart still hurt when she thought of the man she'd loved. "He and I were to be married, but we did not wait for a ceremony to fully show our love for each other. It was wartime and every moment was precious, no day assured." She paused, waiting for the sting of pain to subside. "He, like my father and brother before him, was forced into the war and killed. He is the one who taught me about love and fulfillment." The memories were bittersweet—more sweet as the years passed.

"I didn't know. You never told me."

She shrugged. "There was no need to. It was in the past."

He took a step forward and stopped. "But it's a part of you, what made you who you are."

There was no censure in his voice, but she was well aware of the mores of the English. "*Oui*, so you can see more now that I cannot marry a peer. You know how they think." Even as she said the words, she shivered. If only she didn't have to marry at all.

But there was her grandmother to think of.

Anthony appeared lost in his own thoughts, though why her revelation would concern him so much was a puzzle. Unless he was considering her suggestion. "That is why I can easily pass as your mistress if you can find a way to obtain an invitation. I don't suppose you can steal one?"

That dispelled his pensiveness. His lips quirked. "No, I can't steal one. An invitation to someone's home is delivered only to the people invited."

"Then you must get invited." She strolled past him. "Now, we'd best get that horse you used and get back to Northampton, or we'll be traveling at night, and you know how thieves like to lurk about at night." She winked, since they had once been those very thieves.

In short order, they had retrieved their horse and mounted. She was once again behind him and didn't mind holding on to him. She'd never noticed exactly how pleasant cloves could smell. Then again, it might simply be his particular clove scent. "Have you ever thought about getting married?"

He chuckled, his body moving slightly with his humor. "Now why would you ask that?"

"You know that I once planned to marry, so I was curious."

"The answer is no. I have four brothers—three are married and two have children. There is no reason for me to wed."

She found his answer odd. "What about for love? Have you ever been in love?"

He shook his head as he guided the horse to the left at a split in the road. "That tender emotion has never visited me. It is just as well. I could not imagine having to stay at home with a wife and family when there is so much going on around us."

His answer wasn't a surprise—still, it did not bode well for her suggesting they marry. Then again, she wouldn't mind if he continued with his investigations.

Or would she? Being absolutely honest with herself, she was sure she'd want to help. Maybe after this one was completed, she could bring up the possibility.

His first answer, though, had her puzzled. "Did none of your brothers marry for love?"

He shrugged. "I don't know. I'm not privy to their thoughts and feelings. I rarely see them as we each have our own—"

At his sudden pause, she prodded. "Own what? Life?"

He twisted around to look at her. "I think I know how I can get an invitation."

Excitement at that prospect had her heart racing. "How?"

"My brother."

"Your brother?"

He turned back to face the road. "Yes. He can most definitely make it happen, but I'm sure he'll require payment of some kind."

Payment? Why would a brother pay another? Her brother and she never required payment from each other. "Your English ways will never make sense to me." She shook her head, completely baffled.

"It's not necessarily an English way, but more of a Taylour way of operating. My family is nothing if not creative."

"Your family does not sound like any I've known before."

He laughed. "That describes my family perfectly—not like any other."

As they turned onto the lane before reaching the path to Silver Meadows, the sky turned a pale pink, signaling the setting of the sun. She was used to returning to the house in the early morning or in the dark of night. But with her maid's clothing, she could simply walk in the side door and no one would be the wiser. She should have thought of the disguise long ago.

"Would you like to meet my brother?"

At the surprise invitation, she immediately questioned the motivation, but then again, this was Anthony. She could trust him. "Yes, I believe I would."

"And I believe I would prefer to enter the lion's den with you by my side, and maybe perhaps the duchess as well. After all, you'll need a chaperone."

"I will?"

"Yes. Be sure to wear your best day dress. Think of it as another disguise, preferably to intimidate."

Ah, now *that* she understood. "I'll be looking forward to it."

He stopped the horse so she could dismount.

She stepped to the horse's head to look up at Anthony. With his coarse clothing and disheveled hair, he appeared rather handsome. She'd always thought him well made, but in the pink light, he practically glowed with vitality. That was what had made them friends from the start. "When should I expect you?"

"Two days hence. I'll need to send an invitation to the duchess. She may choose to send a different chaperone, so if there is anything you can do to convince her to take this day journey with you, that would greatly aid our cause."

Seeing an opportunity to press her advantage, she gave him a decisive nod. "I will as long as I can join you once you're invited."

He was obviously still not convinced, but he didn't shake his head. "That is a weighty request. Allow me these two days to look at it from all sides."

She didn't see that there were many sides, but she would accept that he couldn't make the decision so quickly. He liked to examine the ramifications of risky enterprises, but he almost always engaged in them anyway. "That is acceptable. I shall do what I can to entice the duchess to join us." She grinned. "If your brother were to have a well-stocked library, it would be so much easier."

"As it happens, he does, and I'm quite sure he rarely uses it."

That was perfect. Lady Northwick was of the mind that any library not used for reading should be stripped from its owner. "Now I'm quite certain I can entice her."

"Then I will see you in a couple of days. I shall wait here and watch that you make it inside un-accosted."

She opened her mouth to object to such a waste of time, but he held his hand up.

"No, do not argue with me. While you are with me, I must be sure you're safe."

She chuckled as she remembered a particular night when it was she who had kept him safe. "As I did with you, *mom ami?*"

She couldn't be sure in the fading light, but his face appeared to color. "Yes, we must keep each other safe."

Having made her point, she nodded then turned and walked briskly across the field to the gardens. Anyone inside would think she'd been in the woods gathering mushrooms with her basket. Either that or she'd been trysting with her lover.

The memory of Anthony's mouth on hers flared to life, causing her to walk faster. She wouldn't deny she enjoyed every moment of being in his arms. Nor would she deny that she would like very much to be so again.

Heat filled her as she slipped in the side door and hurried up the servants' stairs, myriad ideas crashing against each other as she reviewed the possibilities of attending Leighhall's weekend of debauchery—not the least of which was seducing one Anthony Taylour.

CHAPTER SEVEN

Anthony, dressed in his best maroon tailcoat, brown paisley waistcoat, and tan pantaloons, waited for a lull in the conversation between the women opposite him—Her Grace the Lady Northwick and Lissa.

Lissa had not only convinced the duchess to be their chaperone. She looked absolutely aristocratic in her white day dress, decorated with pale blue embroidery around the scooped neckline. Her hair, pulled back, gave her a proper appearance beneath her bonnet, but the tendrils of black hair that fell about her face made her appear almost angelic. He was not surprised that she was as good at masking who she was as he.

What had surprised him was the kiss they'd shared and the words she'd whispered. Somehow, knowing she wasn't a virgin, and quite possibly a seductress, had put thoughts in his head he'd never contemplated, nor did he wish to. Yet he'd spent the next two nights dreaming about touching the bare curves he'd felt as she pressed herself against him. At the memory of those dreams, he shifted his position.

As if his movement caused him to become the focus of attention, the duchess turned from Lissa and looked at him. "Mr. Taylour, how should we address your brother? You haven't even told us his name. All I know of him is that he has a library that he ignores."

He cleared his throat. Now that it was time to reveal all to two women who had saved his life on different occasions, he found the words stuck in his throat. He swallowed hard. "You may address him as Lord Ferncroft."

While Lady Northwick nodded as if it solved some puzzle she'd been working upon, Lissa's eyes widened in obvious shock. "Your brother is a peer?"

"He is." He dismissed his feeling of guilt. Though they had always been honest with each other, they had no agreement to tell each other everything. After all, where would he start?

"Come, Mr. Taylour, tell us his position and about his home. Are you two good friends?" The duchess's gaze was absolute, as if she'd will him to speak.

"I would not say we are friends, but we are family. You must understand, he is the oldest and I the youngest. We were not in each other's company very often."

Lissa had recovered, and her gaze turned shrewd. "And what title does he hold? I understand families can have many titles."

It was as if she'd already guessed, which shouldn't surprise him. She was both observant and quick to make sense of the clues. "Lord Ferncroft is a marquess." Even as he made the announcement, he could almost see Lissa's thoughts. Would she figure it out now or later?

"And he doesn't use his library?" The duchess hmphed as if that were a significant crime to lay at his brother's feet.

Though he didn't feel a strong obligation to defend Darius, he didn't want the duchess to start off the visit on the offensive. "He does use the room, and I'm sure the governess finds books for his children to read. He is recently widowed, so I'm afraid his library is not his primary concern."

Her Grace looked to Lissa. "The poor man. I suppose we must put aside our differences to allow for a pleasant visit, then."

Lissa nodded, but didn't say a word, no doubt irritated with him. He'd have to make it up to her, except he was well aware of what she wished, but after the way his body reacted to hers, he could not allow her to go with him to Leighhall's. He would simply point out there was no way for her to leave Silver Meadows for an entire weekend.

"I always knew there was more to you than you allowed us all to see. Does my brother-in-law know?" Lady Northwick raised her brows in expectation of his answer.

"The Captain? I mean Viscount Blackmore? No, he doesn't. I have had no reason to discuss my family with anyone. As they are all scattered about the country and rarely see each other, I don't often think to discuss them." He gave the duchess one of his charming smiles. "To be fair, they don't particularly approve of my various employments, but as I do my part to help others, I do not believe their blessing necessary."

The duchess gave him the side-eye, clearly understanding his reference to his work for her husband.

He was thankful she lapsed into silence at that. Unfortunately, Lissa found her voice.

"Well, do not leave us in suspense, Mr. Taylour. Tell us about your family. Do your parents host a gathering at Christmastide? Do your brothers all have titles? Do you expect to carry on the Taylour line?"

"Lissette, we don't ask such personal questions here." Lady Northwick frowned at Lissa, who quickly looked away.

He could remain quiet, but since Lissa was such a part of his investigation, she deserved the truth. "I do not mind, Your Grace. I'm sure Mademoiselle Lissette is curious about the complexities of life among the *ton*."

Not only did Lissa whip her gaze back to his in surprise, but the duchess gave him her full attention, obviously curious herself.

"Then if you don't mind, Mr. Taylour, I'm sure we would both enjoy the conversation to wile away the time as we journey northward." Her Grace offered him an encouraging smile.

He cleared his throat. "I'm not certain it will take that long. As you know, I'm Anthony Taylour and I am one of four sons of the Duke of Roxburgh. However, my parents tend to enjoy life far up north, so I see them only occasionally." His heart filled with warmth at the thought of his mother. "My parents were injured in an explosion at a factory they visited, and my mother prefers being around only people who know her well."

"Oh, no. I'm very sorry to hear of such an event." The duchess held his gaze, making it impossible to look at Lissa to see how she reacted to the revelation. "Whatever were they doing in a factory?"

"My mother's heart knows no bounds. She insisted on helping those of the working class and brought my father to witness the conditions there, which she felt were unsafe for the children." He grimaced. "She proved her point. Unfortunately, my father was with her as well, and he lost part of his leg. My oldest brother now serves as the figurehead of the family."

He turned his head to face Lissa, her dark eyes unreadable. "My brother, the marquess, has a daughter and a son, and my brother the earl has two sons, so there is no need for me to keep the family name alive."

She didn't react to his statement, but her gaze didn't waver.

"And your other brother?" The duchess obviously wanted to learn every detail. "One is the marques we are about to visit and the other an earl. What of the other?"

Reluctantly, he moved his attention back to Her Grace. "My next brother is the Viscount of Livermore further north, and I am the Baron of Bellamore, my lands even closer to the Scottish border."

"You're a baron?" Lissa's question was not surprising, though the tone of disbelief did make him cringe.

"I am." He wanted to explain, but the duchess clapped her gloved hands.

"I knew it. I cannot wait to tell James."

Though the duchess was practically laughing with enjoyment, Lissa remained pensive. He waited patiently. It was only a matter of time before she would request more information.

"Well, my Lord Bellamore, it is a pleasure to know you." Her

Grace beamed with pleasure.

He held no misconceptions that all Her Grace's family would soon learn of his heritage. While he had expected it to be so, it was necessary in order to move forward with his plan for infiltrating Leighhall's house party. He needed both women with him for his brother to give his ideas credence, and he did want a bit of advice, if Darius was in a pleasant mood. He never knew with this particular brother.

"Why then do you tell everyone you're Mr. Taylour?" Lissa's tone was far calmer than he expected.

He wished he could explain to her alone, but the duchess was listening avidly. "Because it is the way I wish to be addressed. I am, after all, Mr. Taylour. This is the name I most identify with. Can you imagine what they would have said to me when I wished to join the Bow Street Runners or even the military? They would have made assumptions about my abilities, wealth, and connections. But by being Mr. Taylour, I am perceived simply as a man that someone needs to become familiar with before passing judgment."

"I see." Lissa didn't make any movement to tell him she truly understood and would forgive him for hiding his parentage from her. He wanted more than anything to have her ask more questions, rail at him, or simply refuse to be his friend.

His heart skipped a beat at that thought. He hadn't realized how much he valued their friendship until that very moment. Maybe he hadn't considered all the possibilities of his plan. Losing Lissa was not worth impressing his brother. But was he to keep his identity a secret from her forever?

The duchess laid a hand on Lissa's knee. "I'm sure you are quite surprised after being friends with Lord Blackmore and Mr. Taylour here." She turned toward him. "I believe I understand why you have not used your title. And I promise, my husband and I will keep your secret. It is something only you should disclose, and I'm honored that you took us into your confidence."

"Your Grace, I had no such expectations, but I am thankful

for your understanding."

He looked at Lissa to see if she would offer any assurances as well, but her gaze was directed to the passing scenery.

She was angry. No doubt she felt betrayed, but he hadn't betrayed her. Mr. Taylour was who he was, not Baron Bellamore. His mother had taught him as a young man that a person's station in life had nothing to do with their worth. It was a radical idea, but considering his mother's beginnings, the sentiment had become the foundation of his life.

Silence filled the coach. With the knot in his stomach, he was not inclined to break it. As the miles passed, he focused on what he would say to his brother in order to obtain the invitation. Since Leighhall lived much closer to Darius than to himself, it would not be such an odd request, just somewhat unusual. Darius could paint him as his reckless younger brother, which was exactly what he thought of him anyway.

"Mr. Taylour." The duchess's sudden address caught him unawares.

"Yes, Your Grace?"

"Perhaps now is a good time to tell us why you are visiting your brother. I had, of course, assumed that you wanted him to meet Lissette, but I have reasoned that this is not the case at all and perhaps she is simply the excuse to have me accompany you."

He forgot to breathe for a moment. That the duchess was so observant had not occurred to him. He looked to Lissa, whose eyes widened before she quickly looked to him and smirked. No doubt she thought he deserved to be discovered.

He'd learned early in his investigative career that staying as close to the truth was best. "Your Grace, I can see why you opened a school for curious ladies as you, yourself, are the epitome of one. Your powers of deduction are frankly, remarkable."

The woman lifted her chin in acknowledgment.

"You are correct. It is not simply that I wish Mademoiselle

Lissette to meet my brother, which I do." He looked at Lissa to make sure she understood. When she gave him a regal nod of her own, he felt the knot in his stomach loosen somewhat. "I am also here to request a boon of my brother, and having a lady such as Your Grace in my company may perhaps persuade my brother that I have left Mr. Taylour behind and fully embraced Baron Bellamore, and therefore, I would be worthy of my request."

"So you wish me to, in effect, sponsor you to your own brother?"

He chuckled, hearing it put in such a way. "In essence, yes."

She looked to Lissa then back at him. "And may I know what the request entails? If I'm to play my part in what I can only imagine is your investigation for Lord Harewood, more details would be helpful."

He looked again to Lissa, who now grinned for the first time since entering the carriage. He wasn't sure if it was because she admired her teacher or enjoyed the position he'd put himself in. "I wish to obtain an invitation to a certain lord's house party so that I might follow my subject closer."

"I see. And the only way your brother would help you obtain this invitation is if he thinks you have settled into your role on your estate?"

Relieved she understood his odd family dynamics, he nodded. "That is correct."

The duchess looked to Lissa. "You know Mr. Taylour almost as well as Lord Blackmore. Do you think we should aid him in his quest?"

Lissa appeared to ponder the question carefully, then she looked at him intently, letting him know he would have to grant her wish to attend said house party were she to comply.

Finding himself in a position with few options, he could do nothing less than agree. He gave her a single nod. "Mademoiselle, will you help?"

Lissa didn't answer him, instead turning to the duchess. "Yes, I think we should aid him. After all, I believe his brother would expect no dissembling on our part as women."

As if she'd opened a door, the duchess immediately took up the subject. "I agree wholeheartedly. Many a man since the dawn of time has underestimated women. Of course, in instances like this, it is to our advantage that their limited views…"

Even as the duchess continued to speak energetically on the topic, Anthony was well aware that Lissa had received exactly what she wanted in payment for his not telling her he was a peer. Since she had an aversion to peers, she wouldn't attempt to seduce him at Leighhall's as she had in the village, so all in all, his plan appeared on track.

Now all he needed was his brother's help.

As the carriage pulled up to Hawthorne Park, the usual concern rode up his back. Though he'd written that he would be visiting with guests, he worried about his brother's mood. His "black days," as Darius called them, made him impossible to be around.

Stepping into the spacious entry of Hawthorne Park, he handed the butler his hat. "Is my brother available?"

The older man, who'd been with Darius since they were all young, knew exactly what he was asking. "He is, Lord Bellamore. He will entertain you all in the parlor. Tea will be served presently."

Relieved that Darius would be amiable, Anthony followed the ladies into the pale-blue room. Stepping directly to the right of the doorway out of habit, he perused the space before continuing in.

"Oh, how lovely." The duchess took a seat on a pale-blue settee, patting the space next to her for Lissa. "Your brother has excellent taste."

Ballocks! He'd forgotten to tell them about Dinah. Quickly, he strode up to both ladies. "This was my brother's late wife's décor. I would suggest not mentioning it, as he only lost her last year."

Lissa frowned, but kept her voice as low as his. "Is he not one of your brothers who has children?"

"Yes." Not wishing to have Darius come upon them while discussing him, Anthony moved toward the chair nearby to sit upon its arm before catching himself. Instead, he walked behind it to stand, resting his hand on the back. He didn't want Darius to have any issues with his manners, at least not today.

Within minutes, Darius entered the room. "Baron. It is a pleasant surprise to have you. When I received your letter, I quite rejoiced."

Despite his words, he looked anything but happy. Then again, it was difficult to tell when Darius was happy. He did look well, except for wearing his black hair rather long, and his gray gaze was quite keen.

Anthony walked around the chair and held his hand out to the duchess. "Your Grace, may I present my brother, Lord Darius Taylour, Marquess of Ferncroft. Brother, may I present Her Grace, the Duchess of Northwick."

His brother's right eyebrow rose before he gave the duchess an impeccable bow. "Your Grace, it is a pleasure to have you at Hawthorne Park."

Anthony quickly held his hand out to Lissa. "Lord Ferncroft, may I present to you Mademoiselle Lissette, a very good friend."

"Mademoiselle, you truly make this whole room so much more beautiful."

Lissa looked to Anthony. "My lord, you did not tell us what a charming brother you have."

He gritted his teeth, wishing he could speak plainly about Darius, but that wouldn't further his cause. Still, it irritated him that Darius chose to compliment Lissa. "I fear I have neglected to mention many aspects of my family." He gave her a wicked grin. "But I promise to remedy that on the way back to Silver Meadows."

Darius turned toward him. "I greatly doubt that the Taylours can be so interesting as that. I would hate for you to bore these fine ladies with our history."

"I suppose you're right. Then perhaps we could take a walk in your gardens, as I'm sure the ladies would enjoy the pleasant day among so many lovely patterns." Anthony held up his hand to stave off his brother's objection, as he needed to speak to him privately. "Yes, I know most of the plants are past their prime."

Darius eyed him curiously. "They are, and hardly worth seeing."

"Then perhaps, my lord, we could view your library?"

At the duchess's request, they both turned.

"My library?"

At Darius's question, Anthony quickly explained. "Yes. Her Grace has a particular love for libraries and books. As yours is rather large, I'm sure she'd enjoy seeing your collection of tomes."

His brother's brow furrowed, but he didn't argue. Instead, he turned to the duchess. "I would be happy to escort you there. If you like, I can have tea served among the many books."

Lady Northwick rose. "That would be lovely."

As Darius led the duchess out, Anthony followed suit with Lissa.

They had yet to clear the doorway before she leaned in and whispered, "Be sure to let me know the set weekend for Leighhall's. I will arrange to be 'visiting' Dory."

He slowed their progress so as not to be overheard. "Are you sure that is wise? Can she keep such a scandalous secret?"

Lissa gave him a sly smile. "Oh, I would never tell her the truth, but something else. Perhaps that I wish to surprise my grandmother. That way, if anyone attempts to find me, they will be looking in the wrong place."

He shook his head but didn't reply. While she was dressed so beautifully and looked as delicate as an orchid, it was easy to forget the sharp mind and strong will of the woman beside him. While that didn't bode well for him at Leighhall's, it did mean she would be an asset at the event.

As they entered through the double doors of his brother's library, the duchess awaited. "Come, Lissette. Let us explore this treasury of knowledge. We may even find a book we have not seen before."

As Lissa's gloved hand left his arm, he noticed how gracefully she walked as she joined the duchess and they began their perusal on the eastern side of the room.

Not wishing to lose the time with his brother, he walked toward Darius, not completely comfortable with how his brother continued to watch Lissa. "I have a request to ask of you."

His brother nodded, but didn't move his gaze. "I assumed as much."

Still, Darius didn't stop what could only be called ogling Lissa. "Marquess?"

"You said the mademoiselle is a friend. Is that true, or do you wish to court her?"

Surprised by the question and not a little irritated by his brother's interest, Anthony moved between Darius and the sight of Lissa. "She is simply a friend. However, I will tell you she has no wish to marry a peer. Are you contemplating marrying again?"

His brother finally turned away and strode toward his desk, clearly irritated. He stopped behind his chair. "I have no choice. I have but one son. It is too much risk to take with such a vast estate. I will need another, preferably one that is legitimate." The last was said with an accusatory tone.

Anthony moved closer so as not to be overheard. "If you insinuate *I* have illegitimate offspring, I can assure you I have not a one." He wasn't sure why his brother's assumption bothered him so much when he'd cast aspersions on his character before, but it did.

"Yes, well, you hardly have much to worry about up there." Darius waved his hand upward as if Northern England was of little consequence.

Taking advantage of the opening, Anthony quickly made his request. "Exactly, and that is why I am south, so as to find a fitting lady who would not mind living in such a remote place. I have come to you today to ask you to garner an invitation for me to Lord Leighhall's house party next weekend. I was assured by fellow peers that it is not to be missed."

Darius pulled his head back and cocked it slightly. "Can it be my little brother is seriously contemplating the prospect of finally taking on the responsibilities of his station?"

"Yes, I am." Anthony held his brother's suspicious gaze. If he wavered even the slightest, Darius would know he lied.

"Leighhall, you say?"

At the question, he relaxed. "Yes. I believe he has an aunt who plays host. The man's appearance attracts many a young woman, so I'm hoping to draw one away from him with my charm."

His brother closed his eyes for a moment as if attempting to find his patience. "Your estimation of yourself far exceeds anyone else's. However, if you are indeed serious in applying yourself to settling into your role as Baron Bellamore, then I will not stand in your way."

"Thank you. I had hoped you would be of help." Already, Anthony was contemplating how to act with Leighhall. Appealing to the man's ego would be the easiest way to find favor with him.

"I will require a boon in return."

His brother's comment dampened his excitement. "Of course. How may I be of service?"

Darius studied him for the longest time. So long that Anthony caught whispers of the ladies' conversation about a writer named Rousseau and a book titled *The Social Contract*. Finally, his brother opened his mouth then closed it and shook his head. "It can wait. When you return from this house party, I want a summary of your progress toward winning a lady. Then I will give you my requirements."

So Darius wasn't absolutely sure about him. The man knew Anthony far better than he wished. "I will be happy to return here shortly after and report to you on which woman or women I am bent upon courting."

Darius let out a heavy sigh before moving away from his

chair. "Your pride knows no bounds. Mind my words, baron. One day that hubris will be your downfall."

Anthony withheld a chuckle, not in the least bothered that Darius continued to call him by his title alone. His brother had started that years ago after a particularly long lecture on the duties of a peer. To be fair, he would have agreed with Darius if he truly expected to win over more than one lady, but as he had no intention of courting anyone, ever, he needn't worry about such a dire prediction.

Now he just had to wait for the invitation. Leighhall, like most peers, would view any request from one of higher status as an honor and a new connection to tout. The man's ego led him to exact revenge on the smallest slight, so a request from a marquess would be welcomed.

The doors to the library opened and a footmen arrived with a tea service. The duchess noticed immediately, and guided Lissa toward them. Now Anthony just needed to get through tea and remember to sit *in* the chair, not on the arm of the chair, and all would be well. All his plans were progressing perfectly.

CHAPTER EIGHT

Lissa waited in the wood, pleased that the weather had cooled considerably. Anthony's distraction of Ellie's coach had made it easy to slip out while the footmen were helping him get his coach back on the road. Now all she needed do was wait for Ellie's coach to continue on and join Anthony.

She felt so much younger, like she had back in France when she and Anthony had planned to rob the next coach to come down the road. Sometimes they would go the whole night with nary a traveler. Other times, the coach would hold those with little wealth and Anthony would refuse to take anything. She would grow irritated with him, but he always brightened her mood.

At least this time, there was truly no life-and-death danger. How much danger could there be at a peer's party, even if it was with mistresses? With such women about, she'd feel more comfortable, even if she'd never been a mistress. She had no doubt they would talk and she'd uncover much more to help Dory.

It was this anticipation she'd miss most once married. Or maybe it was the completion of the puzzle that was Leighhall that she would miss the most. Either way, marriage loomed just beyond the horizon, and she did not look forward to it. At least she could try to find someone in trade who traveled often, leaving her to her own whims.

She'd discarded the idea of marrying Anthony a sennight ago when she discovered he was a baron. A baron! She'd been so furious with him, especially as she couldn't give him the force of her full wrath with the duchess present. But that abated when she realized she could use his confession to make him take her on this foray to Leighhall's so she could help solve his mystery…if there was one. She truly hoped the lord held a dire secret, otherwise, there would be no way to dissuade him from his intent to ruin Dory's reputation.

Being able to help her friend and disguise herself to find the clues made Lissa feel more alive than she had since stepping onto England's shores. It was this experience that meant even more than Anthony's societal status. This adventure would be the very last of her life.

Unless…

Even as Ellie's coach moved on and Anthony stood about his, a new idea formed. Her grandmother wished a life of luxury, while for herself she wished only freedom. To her grandmother, the only course of action to a comfortable life was marriage to a peer. But what if she could amass a fortune another way, a way she had significant skill at?

She was about to enter a home that was sure to have much wealth under the guise of a mistress. What if there was a secret room and that room did hold precious jewels and gold? Even if no such room existed, she would be among strangers who were peers and would certainly travel with expensive items to show off among each other. As Anthony had said, high peers expected all to act honorably with them. Granted, she hadn't stolen anything in over a year, but such skill did not simply vanish. It was a worthy solution, and one she needed to contemplate more fully.

"Lissa?"

At Anthony's call, she moved out from behind the tall bushes where she'd stood. No sooner had she left their cover than Anthony whipped his head around, spotting her immediately.

The man definitely had a keen sense of space.

"If we leave now, we should be one of the first to arrive." He held his hand out to her, and she clasped it with her bare one, having eschewed the usual gloves for her more wanton role. She wasn't sure if it was the role or the man, but a tingle of excitement raced up her arm.

He cleared his throat as he walked her to his coach, which now sported a coat of arms.

She pointed to the symbol of a lamb upon a mountain. "Is that yours?"

He glanced toward the convenience. "Not at all. I may be attending this house party under my real title, but I see no reason to be identifying myself in any other way. I chose a rather meek coat of arms, as my plan is to pretend to be in awe of Lord Leighhall. The man obviously lives for adoration."

She allowed him to help her into the coach, then waited for him to settle in opposite her as the door closed behind him. "And *I* plan to learn as much as I can from the other mistresses and servants. I imagine some of the women will be ladies who were led astray in the past by a peer, or who had no choice due to their lack of wealth. Do you believe some may be from the middle class as well?"

"I do not know what backgrounds the women will have, but I do know the men will all be peers. I cannot say what to expect, as I have never been to a house party such as this." He winked. "We will learn all about it together."

Her heartbeat raced at the weekend to come. "While I'm interested in what such a house party is like, I have nothing to compare it to. Hopefully, I never will. However, I'm very excited to see what we can discover. I'm also looking forward to the challenge of acting the part of a mistress. I do hope the clothes I ordered are appropriate. I've never met one, so I had to rely on the seamstress's expertise."

Anthony chuckled. "So many of your packages arrived while I trailed after Leighhall last week that the Captain was certain I have a strong admirer. Though he was too much a gentlemen to ask, he did hint at it. I, of course, didn't explain anything. Were they all clothes?"

"They were. From what I understand, a mistress wears much more than I expected. They dress much like ladies do. I did have the seamstress modify one of my own dresses, so I could arrive in appropriate attire. I do hope everything fits."

He cocked his head as if mulling over something. "If anything doesn't, you may have time to make adjustments. I know many a lady who embellishes a gown or two."

She wrinkled her nose at the prospect. "Truly? You think the mistresses embroider and do mending? If so, then this portends a poor adventure. I do not wish to spend my time the same way I would while visiting the Blackmores."

"Then let us hope it is vastly different." He crossed one ankle over his knee and relaxed back into the thick cushion. "Now, we must determine our plan. First, who are we?"

She'd already thought about who she would be, since they had often done this when engaging in activities that were not quite legal. "I will go by Lizzie, Lizzie Laurent. My grand-maman calls me Lizzie, so I will be sure to react. I am a French courtesan, new to this country." She waggled her eyebrows. "You met me while serving in the war and took comfort in my arms. When you left France, you couldn't bear to leave me behind." She fluttered her lashes and clasped her hands together.

He stared at her wide-eyed before his lips twitched. "Lizzie? No, that is too close to your real name. Best to have something entirely different in case we leave on poor terms. There is the chance we could be caught somewhere we shouldn't be."

"You do make a good point." She went through the names she'd used before, but they were far too mundane. Then she grinned as the solution came to her. "I shall be Daguette."

"Little dagger?" His brow furrowed, but then he nodded. "Yes, that will do. No one but your classmates know you by Dague. Yes, that will be perfect. But we are simply lovers, not *in love.*"

She waved off his comment, having far too much fun. "Nonsense. What do you think mistresses are for, but to love physically and emotionally? That way you aristocrats can marry some stiff Society miss who will accept you into her bed for the sole purpose of having heirs, no emotion involved."

"And my brother wonders why I don't wish to marry." He shook his head. "Very well—I couldn't bear to leave you in France, but I hide you from my family."

"Agreed. I am the secret mistress. I like that. And what about you?"

He sat straighter. "I'm the younger son who wishes adventure, but I'm being pressured to marry, as I'm sure my brother mentioned in his letter to Leighhall. I have heard rumors of Leighhall's prowess in bed and wish to learn how he is able to stave off his own family while enjoying his life."

She could see Anthony sought to keep things as close to the truth as possible. "Does Leighhall have family?"

"He does. From what I understand, there is a married sister, a mother, and an aunt."

"We know our story, so what are our primary and secondary goals?" She hoped his were in concert with hers, or most of hers.

He pondered her question, his gaze moving to the window where the tree-lined road had just given way to rolling fields. "Our primary goal must be to discover anything that may help Lord Harewood keep Leighhall away from Lady Harewood's reputation. But to achieve that, we need to focus on those mysterious weapons, his secret room, if there is one, and the connection between the women he tups."

She bit down on her smile. "Tups?" Having lived in Town all of last Season, she'd been exposed to the more common vernacular, but to hear it come from Anthony while he was dressed so smartly made it impossible not to tease him.

He sat back, stretching his long legs out in front of him. He seemed particularly interested in his boots. "It's another term for 'to bed.'"

She laughed, unable to hold it back. "Yes, I know, but it would behoove you not to use such language while at Leighhall's, as it shows you are not the proper young baron you are pretending to be."

His head lifted and he smiled at her. "But I am not there yet. I am here, with you, Lissa. I did not think I needed to watch my tongue."

"True. I just thought to point it out." Pleased with their old camaraderie, she also stretched her legs out next to his and crossed them at the ankle, though he couldn't see her feet beneath her blue traveling dress. "I have not seen you in almost a fortnight. Have you discovered anything else about our profligate viscount?"

Anthony sighed as he crossed his arms. "More of the same. He spent a few nights each with Lady Bowmont, the actress Sarah Low, and a Mrs. Perry. I can find no connection between them. Lady Bowmont is a married countess who is known for her exquisite taste in décor. Sarah Low is unmarried and appeared in *The Cobler of Preston* on Drury Lane, though she is rumored to be the secret mistress of Lord Fitzlen. Mrs. Perry, also married, is known for her charity work with orphans."

Lissa contemplated the women along with those he'd mentioned before. "So they are all of different classes and both married and unmarried. Is this true of all his assignations?"

"It is. I'm beginning to believe that he simply has nympholepsy."

"That would be rather embarrassing. Is that not a feminine disease?"

He grimaced. "No, that is nymphomania, and those women with it are usually locked away. Nympholepsy is more of a frenzied passion for something, and in Leighhall's case, it would be women."

She didn't actually see the difference, but it could be simply that the English interpreted words differently. "And would such a label be enough to bring the vigorous viscount under control?"

"Not likely. It would be deemed an envious prowess that he could satisfy so many women. But the odd, ancient weapons may be a clue."

Though he had a point, that reasoning for the weapons could go the same way as the lord's penchant for bedding women. "Or it could be that he simply enjoys collecting them."

Anthony remained quiet for a long moment. Finally, he shook his head. "I would agree if it weren't for the secretive way he obtains them."

She pondered that. "If it's a secret, would that be enough?" Though she hoped it wasn't, or Anthony might turn the coach around.

"No. We need to discover why he collects them in secret. It is the obtainment of them which could tell us that they may be stolen."

She jumped in, immediately understanding what he was thinking. "Or is it his ownership of them? If he has them on display at his estate, it means how he obtains them is his biggest worry. But if they are nowhere to be seen, then he either is displaying them somewhere else or simply having them in his possession is a danger to him as well."

"Exactly." He pulled his legs in and sat forward. "But I know he doesn't have them displayed in his townhouse in Town, and with no other estates than the one we are traveling to, they would need to be there."

Mimicking him, she pulled her own legs in and sat forward as well, getting a whiff of his pleasant clove scent. She held her hand out in question. "And how do you know they are not displayed in his townhouse?" She could guess, but loved hearing how Anthony went about his investigations.

He took her hand in his and pulled it toward him. "Why, my charming Mademoiselle Daguette, I entered his humble abode as a footman when he was not in residence. I charmed a lovely maid into showing me the home, as I was considering applying. There wasn't a weapon to be seen anywhere, and I assure you, I was quite thorough." He lowered his head and kissed the back of her bare hand.

She shivered at the shock of desire his light touch sent through her.

It must have surprised him as well, as he dropped her hand immediately and sat back against the seat cushions.

Swallowing down the titillating feeling, she remained where she was. "Then we may have one answer once we get to Woburn Manor."

Anthony didn't respond. Instead, he turned his head and kept his gaze on the scenery.

Was he afraid of the desire he felt for her? She'd never known him to be afraid of anything, yet he seemed uncomfortable with this new attraction. She didn't mind it in the least. Though Etienne had been her only lover, the book she found in the library at Silver Meadows with the inside title of *The Illustrated Pleasures of Seduction* had taught her there was even more to experience. Who better to enjoy such pleasure with than an old friend?

It must be that Anthony still insisted on looking at her as a lady, even though he knew her to be "ruined," in English terms. Maybe if she took him into her confidence and told him she was thinking about not marrying after all, he would not be so averse to their mutual desire. It was something to contemplate.

As the coach slowed upon entering a village, he finally turned back to her. "We'll be stopping at the inn here for refreshments. We are halfway there, and I thought you may wish to walk about a bit."

She smiled at his gentlemanly ways. "That sounds lovely, Baron Bellamore."

He blinked for a moment at her address, but finally nodded. "Yes, we should definitely practice our roles."

The coach came to a halt in the yard of the Bell and Pheasant Inn. The place was a bustle of people coming and going, horses being changed out for those traveling far, and a few dogs hoping for a chance morsel to fall from the clothing of a patron.

Anthony helped her down and walked her inside. In short order they were led to a private room. She walked into the small area that sported a table and a cushioned seat much like the one she'd just left in the coach. Unclasping her cloak, she looked over her shoulder to find Anthony whispering to the waiter before turning toward her.

"Would you help me with my pelisse? It is far too warm in here to keep it on." Already the fur-lined garment that had kept her warm in the coach felt stifling inside the inn.

"Indeed it is." He stepped behind her and lifted the woolen fabric from her shoulders.

She turned to thank him, but his back was to her as he set the cloak on a hook.

He then doffed his hat and added it to their outwear. When he turned back, he stilled, his gaze raking over her as if he touched her.

She could feel her body heat with anticipation. "Do I look the role of a mistress?"

His gaze flew up to meet hers and he swallowed hard, his Adam's apple moving not once but twice. He opened his mouth, closed it, then appeared to find his words. "You look ready to be ravished. Are you quite certain this attire is what is expected?"

The appreciation in his gaze had her belly tightening. "*Oui,* the seamstress I used said she makes clothing for the mistresses of three lords, and one of them is a duke."

When she'd donned the carriage dress that morning and looked in her mirror, she almost didn't recognize herself. The bright-blue color, one she never wore, made her skin look lighter and contrasted greatly with her black hair. But it wasn't that as much as the high collar in the back which disappeared as the neckline plunged in a wide V that actually showed much of her modest bosom, since she wore stays but no shift. The seamstress had told her to leave off the shift if she wished to capture her benefactor's heart, and had lined the stays with satin for comfort.

However, instead of covering half her breasts, the stays fell beneath them, pushing them upward. Her nipples were barely held in by the muslin material and the ribbon that decorated the very edge of the neckline.

"I see." He remained exactly where he was, but his gaze returned to her chest.

The thrill his focus sent through her had her anticipating the weekend for a completely different reason. "Do you think you'll be able to keep your eyes upon me when faced with a room full of women similarly dressed?"

He didn't immediately respond, but as if drawn against his will, he took a step closer. As the room was small, there were barely two steps between them. Eventually, he raised his gaze to study her face. "You are far more beautiful than even I knew. I will be hard pressed to remember our purpose. No other woman could possibly compare."

His words, as unexpected as they were, made her heart race. "Your words are kind and do me great honor."

As if her choice of words recalled him to their purpose, he backed up and held his arm out toward the table. "Shall we sit?"

Though she would prefer they did something else, they were in a public place and they couldn't lose sight of their goals. However, she added another goal to her list, that of enjoying her very handsome friend to the fullest. She gave a ladylike nod, though she felt more wanton then lady, and slid behind the table.

Anthony did not immediately join her. "I almost forgot to tell you what else I discovered last week." He didn't look at her, but instead faced the wall to her left, which was a bit odd.

"You mean our quarry did more than tup?"

He grimaced as his gaze moved toward her. "Yes. He obtained another weapon."

Not a little put out that he hadn't conferred with her on it, she gave him what she hoped was a proper mistress pout. "And only now you tell me?" She crossed her arms, effectively hiding her bosom.

At her movement, he walked to the side of the table where he would sit. "I did not seek you out earlier because I recognized this particular weapon. It's a chakram, an ancient weapon of India in existence at the time of Alexander the Great."

"Yes, I know of it. It is a disc-like shape that is very sharp, and when thrown can be deadly."

"Yes." He slid in beside her. "It's not valuable for its brass and has no use today."

That Leighhall had obtained another obscure weapon did not surprise her. Many people were predictable, participating in the same activities, buying the same items, enjoying the company of the same type of people. "How did he obtain this one?"

"He dug it up."

Now that was different. "Peers don't dig in the soil."

He grinned, back to himself once again. "Our viscount does when he knows there will be a chakram wrapped in leather next to an old Roman road marker."

Her mind spun with the possibilities. "Was the ground disturbed as if recently dug?"

"It was impossible to tell. There was much mud in the area, as it had rained in the evenings the three days prior to his traveling there."

"And was it on a person's property or along a road?"

"It was along a road between the Countess Bowmont's estate and Mrs. Perry's cottage."

Obviously, the spot had been prearranged, but by whom? "Do you think one of the women sent him to that spot?"

He'd opened his mouth to answer when the waiter came in. The man set down the tea service then exited, allowing another to place a tray of sweets on the table. After they left, she uncrossed her arms and poured a cup for Anthony. "Do you still drink it black?"

When he didn't immediately answer, she looked up to find his gaze on her chest once again. She twitched her nose. "Anthony?"

He blinked before looking at her. "Yes."

"Yes, you take it black?"

He looked to the cup she held aloft but inches from the table. "Yes, black."

She set the cup before him then reached past it to lift what looked to be a berry tart of some kind. As she did, she felt her nipple slip past her dress. "Oh." She pulled her hand back, setting the dress aright again with her movement. "I forgot my manners. Would you pass me a berry tart?"

He took a plate and filled it with not only the tart but a scone and a piece of pound cake, which she quite liked. Then he set the plate before her. "These are your favorites, are they not?"

That he remembered what she enjoyed touched her. "Indeed they are. *Merci*." Not to be outdone by his thoughtfulness, she pointed to the Shrewsbury cakes. "Be sure to fill your plate. I will not have room in my belly for any."

"If you insist." Though he said it seriously, she noticed the quirking of his lips.

He really did have very nice lips, and when he'd kissed her, they were firm and commanding. She did like that in a lover.

As they ate, she contemplated Anthony, who continued to keep his gaze anywhere but on her. She'd always known he was handsome, especially now with a trim beard about his jawline that was far darker than his gold-tipped hair. It was her new awareness of his body that intrigued her. She'd always known him to be fit, based upon their many escapades back in France, but for the first time, she wondered how he would look *sans* clothing. The patch of chest she'd seen while they were dressed as servants was barely a glimpse, and she found her curiosity growing.

Would he be an attentive lover? Her instinct answered in the positive. Would he be an energetic lover? He certainly was capable. Would he be a creative lover? Now that was a question that could only be answered by experiencing him. Still, her imagination conjured up a scene involving a balustrade and steps like the grand staircase at Silver Meadows. Even as the scene took hold, her body heated.

"Daguette? Lissa?"

She snapped her head around to look at him. *"Oui?"*

"I asked if you would like me to order more sweets."

She gave him a seductive smile. "No, I have all I need right here."

His brow furrowed, but he didn't ask her to explain. "Then I suggest we continue our journey. I would like us to be among the first to arrive, so I might make an impression on the viscount and perhaps have a chance to explore the house."

At the reminder of their mission, she forced herself to refocus. "Then let us leave posthaste." Rising, she stepped from behind the table.

He rose at her movement, and she wondered if gentlemen did that with their mistresses. It was something she would watch for. He immediately lifted her pelisse and helped her don it, though he left the buttoning to her. She would have been perfectly happy if he had wished to do that for her.

"Wait here while I make sure all is ready."

Before she could answer, he slipped out. It was just as well, as she wanted to form a plan. She only had three days with which to accomplish all her goals, in addition to learning how mistresses acted. That was a lot to do in so short a time, but even if she couldn't manage to slip enough valuables from the Leighhall home into her hidden pockets, she was quite sure she could manage a few that would constitute a substantial start on her freedom. But she wouldn't forget Anthony's investigation. She hoped that she could find the secret room. If it contained gold, she could satisfy two of her goals at once.

The door opened and Anthony held out his arm. "The coach awaits."

She gave him a regal nod, practicing in case she was expected to act the lady despite her role as mistress, and placed her bare hand on his arm. When they arrived at the coach and he helped her in, she found a package on her seat. "What is this?"

He settled back against the opposite cushions. "Just a few sweets for the rest of the journey. After all, I am to be not only smitten but your benefactor as well."

She gave him a sly smile. "I didn't know being a mistress would entitle me to such lovely treatment."

"But there is far more than that." He reached into his waistcoat pocket and pulled out a necklace with a large oval sapphire and handed it to her.

"This is quite costly. I do hope I don't lose it."

He waved her comment away. "Don't worry on my account. It is yours to keep for your help with this. I could not embark on this next step in my investigation without you, and I am grateful."

She didn't know what to say to that, her throat closing over the wealth of the gift.

"And you'll want to wear this as well." He held out a large ruby ring with a small diamond on either side. "This makes it clear that you're mine."

His words made her shiver, as she wished to belong to no one, but she understood his reasoning. "You believe it will keep me safe from the other peers?"

"I do." He pointed to the ring in his hand. "Read the inscription."

She laid the necklace on her lap and lifted the ring from his palm. It was warm from his touch as she angled to read the inside. *"Le mien.* My own." She frowned and looked at him. "I don't understand."

He grinned as he cocked his head to the side. "I thought it fitting, since we don't wish anyone else to think you are available. Since you suggested I'm besotted, I'll ask Leighhall if he has advice on how much time I must spend on a future wife because I cannot bear to be away from you."

Relief washed through her and she promptly slipped the ring on her finger. "So you had a similar idea as to your role as I did."

"Of course. It makes the most sense." Still grinning, he motioned to the necklace. "I even took the liberty of having a small miniature of me done. I will give that to you once we settle in."

He'd thought of almost everything. "But what do you have of me?"

"I need nothing, as I have all of you." His grin transformed into pure possession and lust.

Not expecting such a look from him, she felt her pulse race. To give in to such a craving was very tempting, but a part of her couldn't imagine being at the whim of a man. The idea made her new goal to avoid marriage settle in as a survival plan. "That may be, but perhaps a lock of my hair would be appropriate. I will be sure to make one available to you soon after we arrive."

He didn't move for a moment, as if he couldn't, but finally his face relaxed and he shrugged, leaning back into the cushions once again. "That will be fine. I suppose if I am lovesick, then I should have something from you."

She took a moment to steady her breathing now that he no longer gazed at her. Gathering up the necklace, she slipped it into her hidden pocket. At least now she had some valuables that she could sell when the time came. Yet even at the thought, she stiffened.

It was one thing to sell a piece that was stolen and quite another to sell a gift. Berating herself for such sentimental ideals, which had no place in surviving, she surreptitiously studied Anthony. Then again, if she did manage to bed him, she could consider the jewels what they were pretending to be—payment for services, services she wasn't only more comfortable with, but actually anticipating.

CHAPTER NINE

"ONE ROOM?" ANTHONY stared at the butler in disbelief. It was hard enough resisting Lissa in her revealing dress at the inn. It would be impossible if he must share a room with her.

The butler, who looked to be better suited to a pugilist's ring than an estate, frowned. "Yes, my lord. Lord Leighhall only accommodates guests in two rooms when there are three people."

Three people? It took him a moment to understand what that meant, then he quickly recovered. "I understand. You'll have to excuse me, as this is my first visit to Woburn Manor."

The man waved over a maid who had to be at least two score. "This way, my lord."

Anthony held his arm out to Lissa. "Shall we?"

She smiled brightly. *"Oui."*

They ascended the grand staircase, which split, and were guided to the right. He studied the walls, paintings, even the floor beneath their feet. Everything was in good repair, though not lavish.

The maid stopped at a door halfway down a long corridor. "This be your room, my lord. A valet will be sent up with your luggage and will unpack. The viscount is in the billiard room, so when you are ready, you will find him there."

He thought to ask where the billiard room was, but held his

tongue. If he didn't know, he had an excuse to wander. "Thank you. And will a maid also be arriving?"

The woman's cheeks colored. "No, my lord. It is the viscount's custom to only provide a valet."

Ah, because women were not important, no doubt. "Very well, thank you."

Rather than discuss their lodging in the hall, he opened the door and stepped to the side, allowing Lissa to enter.

She strode into the room much like she did in trousers. "It's well appointed, but not in the best taste."

He closed the door then reviewed the room. He agreed with her assessment. The maroon wallpaper with gold quarter moons and burgundy curtains made it dark. The gold-accented chairs and table in one corner were a dark walnut wood. There was no dressing table, but a full-length mirror in one corner. A single settee, set before the unlit fireplace, had a deep-red cushion and gold accents as well.

Lissa opened the curtains, filling the room with light, which just made it look more like a brothel. "Well, this is interesting." She lifted what looked like a manacle chained to the headpost of the bed.

Ballocks. She didn't need to see that. Maybe she didn't know what it was for. "I'm sure we will find many interesting items here."

She didn't answer, instead moving to the armoire to open it. Seeing it clearly empty, she closed it and moved on. He should also detail the room, but he felt a need to be close should she find anything untoward.

At the thought, he grimaced. The whole situation was untoward. When he'd agreed to let her play the role of his mistress, he hadn't thought they'd be sharing a bedroom. Maybe there was a dressing room he could sleep in.

As she perused a narrow bookcase, which did indeed contain some books, he moved to the other side of the bed, relieved when he found another door. Opening it, he let his eyes adjust to the muted light before moving in and opening the curtain of the narrow window.

With light now streaming in, he turned and stilled. Though the room contained a bathtub, it contained other items for having sex, some of which even he was not familiar with. However, there were enough feathers, whips, ropes, chains, dildos, and clips for him to understand the sexual nature of the room. There was even a sling of sorts anchored to the ceiling that had him imagining many different positions a woman could get into for the pleasure of a man.

Hearing footsteps approaching, he spun and closed the heavy drapes before striding to the door.

"What's in there?" Lissa lifted her hand in question.

He closed the door behind him. They never lied to each other, but there was no rule that they couldn't withhold information. "More of the same." He gestured toward the bed. "And the tub."

She seemed satisfied with his answer. "This room has a very interesting library. I will say, though, I'm quite pleased there isn't an embroidery loop to be seen." She strolled to the bed. "Would you prefer this side or the side by the fireplace?"

As the realization they would need to share a bed filled his head, he swallowed hard. "I'd prefer this side."

She twirled around and walked to the other side. "Good, as I imagine myself sitting about on the settee in my shift eating sweets." She flounced upon the cushions and lay back. "No, this doesn't work with my travel dress and pelisse." She stood and unbuttoned the front, her back to him. "Would you?"

Having no choice, he strode across the room and lifted it from her back, careful not to look over her shoulder at her chest. Unfortunately, she spun around and took the garment from him. "Since there are no maids, I guess you'll have to help me on occasion to dress and undress."

At her words, his stomach tensed. How did his investigation become an assignation?

She opened the armoire then looked over her shoulder. "I

wonder why there are no maids. Do you think Leighhall can't find women to work here, or is he hoping we will all walk about nude?" She turned back to the armoire and hung her pelisse.

Now other parts of his anatomy were reacting to her words. Turning on his heel, he headed for the door. He'd just put his hand upon the knob when she must have seen him.

"Where are you going?"

He forced himself to turn and look at her. She looked like the most beautiful French courtesan a man could want, and he *did* want her. As if admitting that to himself were the worst of crimes, he stiffened. "I plan to explore before finding the billiard room."

"What about the valet?"

He forced a shrug. "I'm sure he'll take care of everything." Then, without another word, he yanked open the door and closed it behind him. Standing outside the room, he took two deep breaths before heading down the hall away from the stairs. He needed to concentrate on the reason he was in such a predicament to begin with.

There was not much activity in his wing of the house yet, as he confirmed by opening every door. In the hall, he made note of each room, vase, and bust as he strode back to the grand staircase. At the top, he searched the shadows for anyone about. Seeing no movement, he proceeded to the opposite wing. As with the one he'd just left, there didn't seem to be anyone occupying it at the moment. What he found curious was that every other room was quite typical of what was found on an estate, while the alternating rooms were decorated like they were in a brothel. Was this how Leighhall kept his sex habit a secret from his relatives, by assigning them rooms that were typical?

He came to the last door on the end and turned the knob, but it didn't open. Locked. Was this Leighhall's? Stepping back, he paced off the distance between the door and the end of the hall then the length between the door and the next. It had to be.

Crossing the hall to the opposing door, he opened it and

found it occupied. A woman with blonde hair lay asleep on a bed beneath the quilt. Two trunks were set on each side of the armoire, but he didn't stay longer to investigate. Quietly, he backed out, careful to be sure the knob wouldn't make a sound. He continued down the hall, listening at each door before opening it. He was just one away from the stairs when voices rose as people ascended.

Walking back the way he'd come, he stood before a door as if not sure it was his and waited for those arriving to make the top of the split in the staircase. When the maid moved down the opposite hall, he plastered himself against the wall until the three people entered a room a couple of doors down from where Lissa was. As soon as they were all out of sight, he strode for the stairs and quickly descended. If he were correct, there was only one other guest with Leighhall, and it was the perfect time to make himself known.

However, he made use of his freedom to find the parlor, library, dining room, and ballroom, before approaching the double doors where he'd heard men talking. A maid scurried by as he opened one of the doors. He stepped to the side, immediately taking in the entire room and the two men intent on the ball rolling across the billiard table. As the ball fell into the rope pocket, the shooter, Leighhall, straightened. "I'll be happy to play you again."

The other man, taller, thinner, and darker than their host, shook his head. "If I continue to play you, I won't be able to afford Violet."

"Ah, come now, Buswick. You know I'll be quite pleased to take on the patronage of Violet if you can no longer afford her *and* your wife."

Buswick grimaced then turned to fill his empty glass.

Anthony strode forward, smiling as if he'd just met his hero. "Lord Leighhall, I cannot tell you how honored I am that you invited me this weekend." He reached for the man's hand and pumped it vigorously. "Truly an honor. I'm Baron Bellamore, and I have to say I'm very impressed by your ingenuity. It is truly an honor."

Leighhall's blond brows rose over his light-blue eyes. "An honor? Yes, of course. How do you know so much about me? I don't remember us meeting."

Anthony tugged his tailcoat down as if he hoped to make a good impression. "No, we did not, but I have admired you from afar—your skill with Ceaser in the Epsom Derby and, if I may be so bold, your many feminine conquests."

As expected, Leighhall was clearly pleased with such acknowledgment. "It all comes with time. You are barely out of Cambridge, aren't you?"

"I recently returned from the Continent. I served our country proudly then stayed to enjoy the pleasures." Anthony leaned in. "One of which I brought with me here."

"You brought a French strumpet? How intriguing."

Buswick strolled forward. "Welcome, Baron Bellamore. Whisky?" The earl held out a half-filled glass.

Anthony accepted. "Lord Buswick, I did not know you would be here."

Buswick's brow furrowed. "Have we met?"

Anthony waved his hand, well aware they hadn't met, but also knowing he could convince the man they had. "Most assuredly, at the Stocktons' end-of-Season ball. I was with Lord Sommerset. We were discussing the sculpture exhibit at the British Museum."

"Ah, of course. That Stockton event is such a crush, it's hard to remember everyone. I do apologize."

He raised his glass toward Buswick. "Not at all. I'm sure we will get along famously here."

Buswick smiled, clearly pleased, but Leighhall seemed a bit put out, so Anthony quickly turned his attention back to the man. "What gave you the idea to have such an ingenious house party? I must say, I've been anticipating it since you sent the invitation. I do hold you in such high esteem."

As if immediately appeased, Leighhall clapped him on the shoulder. "I had grown bored with the typical house parties where every feminine person is judging you as husband material as if they have a say in their own futures. So I created the type of event I would enjoy most."

The viscount's opinion of women didn't coincide with his success with them. "And is your mistress in residence?" Anthony could imagine the man keeping her close.

Leighhall snorted. "Hardly. I see no reason to spend coin on a woman when I can have my choice for free. For my parties, I simply invite a couple whores to attend and then choose between them as the whim takes me. My appetite cannot be satisfied by just one, so sometimes I take both at the same time."

Anthony widened his eyes, not because the man had a *ménage à trois*, but at his attitude. "I do believe I can learn much from you."

"Of that, I'm quite sure, young Bellamore."

It didn't surprise Anthony that Leighhall referred to him as young, as the man appeared close to two score. He was about to ask another question when the doors to the room opened and a gentleman stepped in.

He decided to step aside and observe for a while. As Lord Rothbury spoke to Leighhall, Lord Buswick joined him by the fireplace. "I understand this is your first time here."

Anthony settled his attention on Buswick. The man was so thin that it appeared a strong gust of wind could knock him over. His long sideburns didn't detract from the illusion. "It is."

Buswick took a sip of his drink before continuing. "He doesn't often invite newcomers. We all prefer this weekend to be kept secret, so much so that we are only invited a few times a year. How did you know of its existence?"

"I admit to eavesdropping." Anthony held up his hand. "Not purposely, but I have admired the viscount for a while now, with his ability to enjoy his life as he wishes despite the pressures of his title. I believe I can learn much from him."

"If that's your concern, simply marry as I did and keep your mistress. Many of us do so." The man's tone made it sound as if Anthony were a simpleton.

"Of course, I'm aware of that." He let his pique be known, not wishing to appear too much of a sycophant. "However, I love Daguette and could not bear to be with another woman."

The man stilled as he reached for his glass again. "You are faithful to your mistress?"

"I am." Anthony nodded emphatically, playing the young, besotted lord.

Buswick stared at him oddly. "I do believe you will find this weekend eye opening in many ways."

That was Anthony's hope, but in a far different way than the earl was implying. "What should I expect?"

Just then another man entered, whom he recognized as Lord Pemberton. Though he didn't socialize with the peerage, he'd learned quite a bit about them through the Mabrys and his many times dressing as a footman or coachman. He hadn't expected Pemberton, since he was a bit older than even Leighhall and had a middle-aged man's girth.

"Tonight will be a dinner." Buswick gained his attention once again. "After which we will drink and then join the women for whatever games Leighhall has devised."

That sounded typical. "And the morrow, do we ride or hunt?"

Buswick grinned, clearly hiding something. "Yes, I do believe you could call it that."

Not particularly liking the man's expression, Anthony quickly responded, "Then it will be much like a typical house party but with our mistresses, correct?"

"Not typical in the least. Everything Leighhall plans is sexual. Did you not see your dressing room?"

At the reminder of the room, Anthony swallowed hard. "I did."

"Then you have an idea of how the time will progress." Buswick patted him on the shoulder. "I do hope you are well rested,

Bellamore." With that, he moved off to greet another guest who had just entered.

Anthony reviewed the men in the room, the very elite of the *ton*, and tried to imagine what sexual play would ensue. They all appeared quite typical in demeanor, but obviously this house party would encourage atypical behavior. As intrigued as he was, his investigation took precedence, and he memorized the men in the room. Including himself and Leighhall, there were seven. Were they all involved in Leighhall's search for ancient weapons, or were they all unaware? If they did rotate throughout the year, could there be one who attended every month and the others didn't know?

So far, besides them being peers, he noticed no obvious connection between the men. There were Whigs and Tories, those beyond two score and those like himself in their thirties. Each man was far different in physical build than the next. The only two who were relatively close were he and Leighhall. They both had blue eyes, though Anthony's were a deeper blue, and both had blond hair, though his was darker. They were also both broad in stature and attractive to ladies. That could help him in his supposed admiration, though he felt anything but. What truly stymied him was how Leighhall could attract so many women to bed with such an attitude. The man was proving to be a harder puzzle to solve than Anthony had expected, and he only had three days in which to figure it out.

"Gentlemen." Leighhall spoke loud enough to interrupt all conversation. "Welcome to Woburn Manor and my house party. It is my pleasure to be your host and allow you the enjoyments you cannot indulge in at other parties."

Soft chuckles filled the room.

"For those who have been here before, you know there are no rules unless I set them, and then they must be followed. Feel free to enjoy the pleasures of my home and those of your women."

Lord Rothbury raised his glass to that.

"Dinner will be in a few hours. You may remain here for billiards and bets, or you may return to your mistresses to make the most of the afternoon. The gardens and public rooms are at your disposal for this. Just don't enter any other bedroom because, well, bedrooms are boring."

Again, masculine chuckles followed.

"For those who have accepted my invitation for the first time"—Leighhall looked directly at Anthony—"I am happy to answer any questions, and my advice is free."

"Yes, Leighhall has more advice than all of us combined." Lord Pemberton laughed at his own wit.

"Well said, Pemberton. Let the pleasures begin." Leighhall raised his drink before throwing it all back in one swallow.

Anthony took a sip, as many of the other men did.

Two men strode toward the doors immediately, and he followed.

One man turned to the other. "I believe I need to show my demirep the parlor, as it has a writing desk at the perfect height."

"I'm taking Maria into the ballroom. She has a fondness for balls and hard columns."

The two men laughed as they strode up the stairs.

Anthony ascended a bit slower, curious that Leighhall would allow everyone to ramble about his house if he did indeed have a secret room. Which raised the question, did he actually have such a room, and if so, was he simply so arrogant he thought it couldn't be discovered?

Reaching the room he had to share with Lissa, he halted outside the door. Sleeping in the dressing room was out of the question. He had no doubt she'd already discovered what was in there, so that would be far too odd. Though she expected him to sleep in the bed with her, that was also out of the question. He'd just have to sleep on the settee. At least there was one. A number of the rooms he'd investigated earlier had a wingback chair instead.

With that decision made, he opened the door but barely took

a step inside before stopping.

"Oh, *mon amour*. I didn't expect you back so soon." Lissa handed the book in her lap to the woman sitting on the settee with her. Then she sauntered forward in her traveling dress that exposed so much of her.

She took his hand. "I did miss you, but look." She held her other hand out to the woman similarly dressed, only in a deep maroon, her bosom quite large, with a necklace squeezed between her breasts. "This is Delilah. She's here with Lord Rothbury."

"For the moment." Delilah rose and joined them, her gaze roving over his face as if she touched him. "I can see why Daguette is so happy to be here." The woman turned to Lissa. "Page six, Daguette." With that, she brushed by them. "I'd best see if Edward has need of me."

Her tone made it sound as if pleasing her benefactor were a chore, not a pleasure, and he found himself looking over his shoulder as she exited.

Lissa's hand turning his head back to face her startled him.

"Do not be lusting after women while we're here. Remember, we're here for another reason altogether."

Surprised by her reprimand, he studied her for a moment, almost sure he saw jealousy in her dark eyes, but that couldn't be. They were friends, despite his inappropriate kiss, and they had other matters than being bedmates to attend to. "I have not forgotten. Is she not happy to be with Lord Rothbury?"

Lissa let go of his head and returned to the settee, where she picked up the book and replaced it on a shelf. "Delilah was duped into believing an earl loved her. She gave him her body only to discover he'd already arranged a marriage contract with another." She faced him. "This life was not her first choice, but she does what she must to live."

His own anger surfaced to meet Lissa's. "Did her family not protest?"

"They couldn't. She is the one that gave in." Lissa sat back down on the settee. "This is why I do not wish to be part of this peerage. It is cruel."

He strode to the settee and sat next to her, giving her one of his charming smiles. "Surely not all of us?"

She wrinkled her nose and slapped his arm. "No, not all of you, Lord Baron."

Inordinately pleased that she did not count him among the typical aristocracy, he forced himself to keep his gaze on her face. "What did Delilah mean by page six?"

Lissa shrugged. "Just a page in the book we were reading." She waved her hand toward the bookcase. "It appears all these books are of young women being swept away by passion, though I had only looked at a handful before Delilah knocked."

He rose and walked around the settee to view the titles. *Lady Fancy's Fall*, *Pamela's Plight*, and *Bea's Journey to the Brothel* did sound rather salacious and repetitive. "Not much variety, I see." He scanned a few more titles before one book caught his attention—*Seven Ways to Pleasure Your Lord*. He sincerely hoped Lissa hadn't seen that one yet. He strolled away from the bookcase as if they were all rather boring, and noticed their trunks by the armoire. "I see the valet unpacked."

"Hardly."

At Lissa's irritated tone, he faced her, again making every effort to only look at her face. "But the trunks are here." He waved his hand toward them.

She rose and walked to hers. "Yes, they are, but only one is unpacked." She lifted the lid of her trunk to show it was still full of clothes. "We women are to unpack ourselves, since we are not ladies."

Though he could see how some men would view their mistresses in such a light, it still rankled. "Would you like me to help you unpack?"

Laughter filled the room. "*Mon ami*, I do not think that a good idea." She reached into the trunk and pulled out a thin shift that could hardly be called such, as it was made of crepe and absolutely sheer.

He swallowed hard, forcing his mind from imagining Lissa in it. "I understand."

She grinned before folding the garment and setting it back into the trunk. "I am not displeased by the notion of unpacking, as I'm sure you can understand. I was displeased with the attitude of the valet. I imagine he mimics his lord."

At the mention of Leighhall, Anthony found his mind in a better position to concentrate. "Yes, the man's attitude toward women is basically contempt, yet he is in so many beds. I'm curious how he does that."

Lissa closed her trunk and faced him again. "No doubt he hides it well from the ladies. I'm more interested in what he hides within his secret room, if it exists. When can we begin the search?"

"We can do so now. We have three hours until we need be in the dining room. Leighhall gives his guests full access to the house, except to unused bedrooms. Some of the men have already gone to fetch their mistresses and bring them to a particular room. Our viscount doesn't act like a man with something to hide."

Lissa rolled her lips in as she thought, which had him waiting for her to release them.

Quickly, he moved to the fireplace to stop looking at her. "I suggest we begin with finding this secret room, if it exists, and searching for these old weapons. If they are well displayed, then he has no need to hide them."

"Yes. And if we don't see them, he must hide them." Lissa strolled toward the bed and sat upon the maroon quilt, which made her stand out all the more in her blue dress. "If he has this secret room, it must be an inside room. If it had windows, it would be far too easy to find."

He had to admit, she made a good point. "True, if Leighhall is that smart."

She cocked her head. "I would not underestimate a man who

acquires weapons secretly."

He gave her a nod, wishing she would leave the bed. She was far too enticing in her gown. "If this supposed room is in between others, I would suggest the entrance to be in a place that would be highly unlikely."

"Like from the kitchen?"

"No, the servants talk too much. I don't think the entrance would be from the library or billiard room."

Lissa grabbed the foot post as she sat straighter. "So maybe the parlor or the dining room areas, usually the domain of a wife?"

Even as she said the words, her chest rose with excitement, which he couldn't ignore. "Yes." He forced his gaze upward. "Those are two excellent places to start." Except the parlor was being used. "Let us investigate the dining room."

She hopped off the bed. "If someone asks why we are there before dinner, we can simply say we were looking for it."

"As I said, Leighhall invited us to explore, so no need for an excuse." And if he needed one, he'd just pull her in for a kiss and no one would think twice…except maybe him.

CHAPTER TEN

LISSA RAN HER fingers along the gold wallpaper, hoping to find a crack or feel an airflow that didn't belong, but so far nothing appeared out of the ordinary. That, however, didn't dampen her spirits. Though they'd been investigating the room for nigh on two hours, she loved the mystery and the anticipation of discovery. Feeling like she did was how it had been in France. She craved a life such as that now as well. She just couldn't give it up.

Even after hearing Delilah's story, she nevertheless wished to move forward toward an independent future while still supporting her grandmother. If she had to, she could follow Delilah's route for a short while, but as she had additional skills, she doubted that would be necessary.

"Have you found anything?" Anthony's voice carried across the large room.

She answered as they had planned so no one would suspect. "You have hidden it too well."

"I can't find yours either." He sighed. "I will not admit defeat yet."

He sounded so sincere, she laughed. "Nor will I." She continued running her hands along the wall until she reached a large china cupboard. The glass doors and mirrored back made it appear there was twice the amount of crockery inside. She gave it a cursory glance, as the china was unremarkable, and continued to the other side to lay her hand against the wall. That was when she noticed the cupboard was anchored to the wall. How odd. The piece was far too large to be moved without at least two men. There was no reason to anchor it.

Curious, she walked back to the other side to find it also anchored. Not a little confused, as it would be much easier to steal the china from inside than to take the cabinet, she crouched down to see if perhaps the legs were uneven, making it necessary to affix the furniture to the wall.

"What do you see?" Anthony's voice had her looking over her shoulder.

"Nothing remarkable." She was about to get up, but since she was already on the floor, she knelt down and looked beneath the furniture. Her breath caught at the sliver of an opening in the wall. She ran her gaze along the width of the cabinet and found another sliver. Reaching beneath it, she pressed her fingertips to the opening. Cool air met her skin, and she shivered. Could this be it?

Pulling her hand out, she sat back on her heels and studied the cabinet.

"What have you found?" Anthony stood above her, his voice low.

"I'm not sure." She looked up at him. "Beneath this furniture, there are two breaks in the wall wide enough to be a doorway, but the china cupboard is affixed to the wall."

He cleared his throat before offering his hand. "Here, let me help you up so we can investigate further."

She took his hand and rose before studying the cabinet. "I think we should open it."

"I agree." He took hold of the knobs on the glass doors and opened the cupboard. "It looks like a typical china cupboard."

She licked her fingers then ran them along the back in the area where the breaks in the wall were. She definitely felt air. "The back of this must open somehow."

"Let me check."

Not excited about stepping away, but well aware he had more experience with hidden doors, she backed up and let him move into the opening.

As he ran his hand along the back, she kept looking over her shoulder to make sure no one was about. But when she heard a click, she snapped her head around to see his hand beneath the shelf with a china tureen.

"I've got it." His words were whispered, but the excitement in his voice was obvious. Slowly, he pulled, and the back of the cabinet shifted to the right, revealing the wall.

She looked over her shoulder again before whispering in his ear, "No one is near."

She actually saw the shiver that raced up his back before he stepped forward and pushed against the wall. It didn't budge. He ran his hand along one side and found a latch covered in wallpaper, but a keyhole could be seen if looked for. He pulled a slender lever, but it didn't move.

She had pins in her hair she could use to unlock it. Her heart sped at the opportunity to explore further, but the sound of voices froze her. "Someone comes."

She stepped back, prepared to cause a distraction while Anthony closed the hidden door.

Just as the voices sounded in the doorway, she found herself pushed against the wall next to the cupboard as Anthony's tongue dove into her mouth. Hot fire shot through her, and she immediately wrapped her arms around his neck, grabbing at his hair.

When his mouth left hers and he licked his way down her chest, she noticed the voices were silent. Opening her eyes, she found two men watching them. She should tell Anthony, but his tongue found its way beneath her neckline to her nipple, and the feelings coursing through her were too strong to ignore. Instead, she let her eyes close again and her head fall back against the wall, thrilled by the desire flooding her veins.

"I say, are you starting dinner early there?"

Anthony's head left her chest so fast, she would have fallen to the side if he still weren't pressed against her, his erection proving he'd lost the purpose of his kiss.

He looked over his shoulder. "Oh, Lord Buswick. Our host did say we could use any room, correct?"

"Indeed. And this room will be all about delectable treats, after all." The man stared at her, but could see little, since Anthony blocked his view.

She gave the two men a ladylike nod. "I look forward to meeting you at dinner, gentlemen."

The other lord's brows rose in surprise. "I do believe we've been dismissed, Buswick."

"Yes, so it seems. Let us try the library, then, shall we?"

As the two men turned and headed back out, she remained silent, not sure she could hold herself upright if Anthony stepped back.

He turned back to her, confusion in his blue gaze. "I apologize. Leighhall had said we could use any room with our mistresses, so it was the first action that came to me to hide our real purpose."

She wanted to kiss away his apology, but revealing how much she enjoyed his touch now would scare him away. "No apology needed. It was a brilliant idea." She fluttered her lashes at him. "*Mon amour.*"

He blinked before understanding dawned. "Yes. Though I do hope we need not resort to such activity again."

Feeling a bit more stable, she let her hands slide from around his neck. "I think we should investigate this room another time."

"Of course." Anthony stepped back, but stared at her chest.

Looking down, she found he'd pushed her neckline beneath her breasts in his hunger. She quite liked that, but still righted her clothing and pretended a coolness she was far from feeling. "Now that you found what you sought, my lord, shall we go up and change for dinner?"

Having turned away as she covered herself, Anthony held his arm out for her without looking back. "I believe that would be appropriate."

She took his arm and hid her grin. If he lost himself with her in a simple kiss, she couldn't wait to have him help her undress and dress.

As they entered the front foyer, they found a man carrying a woman over his shoulder as he climbed the stairs. The skirts of her dress were thrown over her head. She grinned at them just before she slapped the man's arse.

"Alice, you keep doing that and you won't be able to sit tonight." His words were followed by a loud whack and Alice laughing.

Lissa looked to Anthony, who chuckled before coughing. He tried to move toward the first step, but she halted him. "What was that?" It wasn't anything she'd seen, done, or read about.

"Um, it's hard to explain."

"Oh really, Anthony. It's me." She practically growled at him. She was no stranger to sex, but what she'd just witnessed appeared to be punishment. Yet the woman had asked for it and liked it. It made no sense.

He took a deep breath then finally looked at her. "Some people enjoy the sting, as it excites them before copulation."

She raised her brows, absolutely sure it was something she would not be interested in at all. "Do not attempt that with me."

His eyes widened. "Of course not."

Confident he was aware of her limitations, she made to move forward, but he didn't. Instead, he whispered in her ear, "Remember, this is not real."

She completely disagreed. The new attraction they had to each other was very real. "Shall we?" She gestured toward the stairs.

Finally, he moved, and they ascended in silence. When they entered the room, they discovered the valet there waiting to help Anthony dress. He'd already lit a number of lanterns in the now-darkened room. She couldn't believe her good fortune, as she had no doubt Anthony would hide in the dressing room if left to his own devices.

Moving to the armoire, she turned her back and opened the doors to choose her dress for dinner, having pulled out a few before the valet had arrived to unpack for Anthony. Choosing a deeper-blue dress with a daring square neckline, she laid it on the bed. It was far more suited to her coloring.

When she turned, she found Anthony facing her, bare chested and far more muscular than she'd expected from a man of the peerage. Then again, he didn't live that life. His chest was well defined and had a sprinkling of blond hair across the mounds. His abdomen rippled as he lifted his arms for a clean ruffled shirt. But before the shirt came down, she noticed a neat scar that jolted her memory. He'd been shot. If the duchess hadn't saved his life, they would not have been able to renew their friendship. That thought made her pause as her chest tightened. Anthony made the world a better place to be. Even if many didn't know it, she did.

As the shirt came down, it hid him from view, so she turned back to the armoire and closed the door before crouching down and opening her trunk. Pulling two additional daggers from its depths, she slipped them into the deep pocket of her dress. At the slight noise they made, she remembered the necklace Anthony had given her. Pulling it out, she decided it matched her dress perfectly. Rising, she turned to the bed to see Anthony standing in just his shirt. Unfortunately, it came down to the middle of his thighs, but what was revealed was impressive. His thighs were well muscled and his calves looked harder than the Arc de Triomphe in Paris. But they were not perfect, as two other scars, not nearly as neat, marred one thigh and the opposite calf.

"Do you see something you like?" Anthony's voice had her snapping her gaze to his.

She didn't need to play the role of mistress to answer him honestly. "I do. I look forward to this evening, when I can better explore all that I have seen." She licked her lips to indicate she would like to do more than touch.

Anthony's chest rose suddenly. "My love, you tease me unmercifully. We must attend the dinner and games."

Games? This was the first she'd heard of games. "What kind of games?"

He shrugged as he bent to pull on his trousers. "I do not know, but I'm sure we will enjoy them."

She hoped the night didn't go too late. She planned to rise as early as she usually did to get into the secret door before anyone was up, including the servants.

After laying the necklace next to her dress, she pulled out the two small daggers from her pocket. As they were in the enemy's home with many a randy man about, she preferred to be prepared. With one dagger strapped to her thigh and another to her forearm beneath her long sleeves, she felt comfortable with Anthony. But in case they were separated, she would add one to her boot and another within her pocket.

With nothing else to do as the valet finished dressing Anthony, she strode to the bookcase and found the book *Lady Fancy's Folley*, which she'd been looking at with Delilah earlier, curious about what was on page six of the story about a lady of quality who fell in love with a man of a lower class. According to Delilah, the lady's father would kill the man and sell her to a cruel duke. Of course, she ran away and made her living as a prostitute.

She opened the book and turned to page six. *Her heart recognized him as her match. She'd found her love. The one man who could make her happy forever. With that realization, Fancy opened her dressing gown and whispered his name.*

Now why would Delilah mention that page? Perhaps there was something else. Lissa looked further down the page, but the door closing as the valet exited interrupted her, and she turned to find Anthony looking particularly enticing in his black tailcoat and white waistcoat, though the colors were a bit severe for his personality. If she didn't know him, she would be quite impressed. Setting the book back onto the shelf, she moved forward.

"I do believe I will need to keep Alice from absconding with you."

His eyes rounded as he grimaced. "Yes, please do."

She strolled closer and walked around him. "Yes, you fit the part perfectly." She stopped in front of him and turned her back. "Now if you could unbutton me, I can dress for dinner."

Initially, he didn't react, but finally she felt his fingers on her dress. At first it was as if he were afraid to touch her, but by the fourth button, she felt his fingers brush her back. The touch sent heat flowing through her limbs, and she found herself wishing they didn't have to attend dinner, but she kept her purpose in mind.

"You are unbuttoned." His voice was raspy. "Do you not wear a shift with these gowns?"

She faced him, holding her gown in place. "No. I believe that would defeat the purpose. These stays are lined so as to be mostly comfortable." Though the padding at the top beneath her breasts to make them appear bigger was an odd feeling.

Turning toward the bed, she lifted the gown over her head. It was no easy task, but she managed, not willing to press Anthony's limits so close to dinner. Once free of the dress, she stood in nothing but her stockings, daggers, shoes, and stays, which pressed her small breasts upward from beneath. As she laid the light blue dress on the bed, she glanced over at Anthony to find he'd turned his back toward her.

She shook her head at how much of a gentleman he acted now, when in France, he treated her like a fellow soldier. Lifting the skirts of the dark-blue dress, she tunneled into it before straightening. Fortunately, the arms were quite loose, making the dress fairly easy to pull into place. Holding it up, she walked back to where Anthony stood contemplating the door. "I'll need your help with these buttons."

He turned, sweeping his gaze over her. "I am happy to assist."

She turned, but spoke over her shoulder. "I must admit, you are the handsomest lady's maid I've ever had."

"Thank you. I will take your kind words to heart." His chuckle belied his words as his fingers tightened her dress about her with each button. "There. I believe my work is done."

Instead of turning toward him, she strolled to the mirror in the corner to see the final result. At first, it was difficult to believe it was her. She looked almost five years younger with the square neckline that barely concealed her areolae. The darkness of the dress made her skin seem lighter, and the wisps of her hair about her face softened it considerably.

Lifting her hands to her hair, she pulled out all the pins, then rolled it into a loose knot and resecured it. The result made it look as if she'd just tumbled out of bed. "Perfect." She turned to face Anthony. "Don't you think?"

His gaze fastened on her face for a moment before sweeping over her like a lover's kiss.

Her body reacted with tingles along her arms and down her legs.

When his gaze returned to her face, he appeared stunned.

"Is it not perfect?"

Blinking, he finally nodded. "It is. You are."

"Good." She lifted her skirts and swept past him, in a hurry to break the odd spell his gaze cast upon her body. Reaching into the bottom of the armoire, she pulled out her soft kid leather boots. Definitely not indoor shoes, but for dinner, they would be fine. Sitting on the bed, she untied the laces of a boot before kicking off her shoe.

Anthony's shadow in the lantern light fell over her. "Allow me."

When she looked up at him, the lantern's glow highlighted the gold strands of his hair, making him appear like a sun god. "Do you know how to lace up boots?" She held out the boot in question.

"As a matter of fact, I do." Taking the boot from her, he knelt.

She lifted her skirts up to her knee, and he slipped the boot on, then expertly tied it. As he did the same with the other, her curiosity wouldn't let her remain silent. "How do you know how to do that?"

He rose, a comfortable smile on his face. "My nephew, Darius's son. I've laced his boots for him on occasion."

"You've spent such time with him?" That surprised her, as the brothers' relationship seemed strained at best.

"I have…when my brother is not about."

When he didn't elaborate, she didn't ask anything further. Instead, she took a dagger from the bed and slipped it into her right boot. Then, rising, she picked up the other dagger and dropped it into the sheath sewn in her left pocket, since she could wield them with either hand. When she'd finished, she stepped into the center of the room. "I believe I'm ready for dinner." She turned around in a slow circle.

Anthony shook his head then walked to the bed and lifted the necklace she'd forgotten. "Not yet. We must show everyone that I spend my fortune on you."

She wrinkled her nose. "Of course, a sign of ownership." It bothered her more in this setting than in the drawing rooms of London's elite, where wives had status.

He stepped behind her and laid the cool metal on her chest to secure it at the back. "Remember, Lissa, this is only a role."

She swallowed down her irritation. "Yes, of course."

When he stepped back, he offered his arm. "Let us join the others and see what we can learn."

She gave him a seductive smile. "About our host or the activities to ensue?"

"Both will be of benefit to us, don't you think?"

She set her hand upon his arm. "I do."

As soon as they entered the corridor, they encountered another couple going to dinner. Both seemed in a jovial mood, which made it much easier to get into the spirit of the party. All four of them entered the parlor together, Anthony pulling her to the right once inside. She glided along with him, used to his strange habit. He'd once told her it was to scout the territory, something he'd done since serving as an investigator for the Bow Street Runners.

The other couple moved into the room, immediately seeing others they knew. Anthony leaned in. "The blond man by the tall window is Viscount Leighhall."

Lissa studied the man. He was broad but more slender than Anthony, and almost as tall, with sharper features. His brows were thin and rose in a point. His straight nose ended in a bit of a bulb. Beneath it were clefts above and below his lips, easy to see, as he was clean shaven. His very short hair revealed rather large ears, which accentuated the oval shape of his face. Overall, he made a striking figure. "He is attractive, and if his manners are equally inviting, I can see why he has no problem finding a bedmate."

Anthony looked at her. "It is good to have an opinion of a woman, as I see him as no more handsome than Buswick there by the fireplace or Rothbury next to the writing desk."

"I understand, as I would not know if Delilah were prettier in the eyes of a man than Alice." She looked from the obviously sophisticated blonde woman to the red-haired one from earlier who sat on a wingback chair, one leg thrown over the arm. Of course, that could be because her arse still hurt.

"I assure you, mademoiselle, there is none here who could take my attention from you."

At Anthony's overly exaggerated comment, she chuckled and placed her hand on his shoulder even as she looked to her right to find a couple had moved near. "Anthony, you need not turn my head with flattery. My heart belongs to you."

"Oh, Lord Buswick. Please, allow me to introduce you to Daguette. My dearest Daguette, this is Lord Buswick."

Lissa surmised things were less formal in this setting. "Lord Buswick, it is lovely to meet you."

The lord gave a nod. "And Lord Bellamore, may I introduce Violet?"

Violet had hair of deep auburn and blue eyes so dark they did indeed appear violet. The woman gave a soft smile to Anthony before facing Lisette. "I have not seen you here before."

"I have not been here before. I do hope you can tell me what to expect."

The woman gave her a wide smile. "I will do so with pleasure."

"Daguette, I'd like to introduce you to our host before we settle in making new friends."

She wrinkled her nose at Violet as if she must appease Anthony, and then faced him. "I would be honored to meet him."

With a quick nod to Buswick, Anthony led her across the room. As they approached, she studied the woman on Leighhall's arm, hoping she would be able to shed light on the man. She was tall and thin and blonde, similar to him, but with a large bosom and hips, and a wide face.

As they drew closer, the man turned his gaze to her and swept it over her thoroughly, as if cataloguing all her attributes for a later time, before moving his attention to Anthony. "Ah, and here is young Bellamore. You must introduce me to this beauty at your side."

She pasted on a smile, not at all impressed.

"My lord, it is my distinct pleasure to introduce you to my dear Daguette. Daguette, this is Viscount Leighhall, our kind host."

She set her free hand on her chest. "My lord, it is an honor." She looked up at Anthony then back at Leighhall. "*Mi amour* has told me of his high esteem for you on more than one occasion."

The man lifted his chin in clear hubris. "I imagine I could teach him many things, but tell me, you hail from France, do you not?"

"Indeed I do." Again she looked upon Anthony as if he were her only reason for breathing. "My Anthony was there fighting when we met. I will always treasure that day." When she turned back, she could see Leighhall was clearly not thrilled with her constant reference to Anthony, so she changed tack. "When he told me of your brilliant idea for a house party, I said we must meet you. And then to hear from Delilah that you have been hosting such a lovely gathering for years, I must say I was intrigued by a man of such creativity and foresight."

"Mademoiselle, I simply saw a need and a way to fulfill it." Again the man puffed with pride. "It is not so easy to find the perfect person with which to share these weekends, but I am quite fortunate to have the lovely Selene as my guest." He gestured toward Anthony. "Lord Bellamore, this is Selene, a woman of incomparable attributes."

"It is a pleasure to meet you, Selene. I hope that you and Daguette will enjoy this weekend."

The woman gave them a secret smile. "I'm most sure we will."

"Leighhall!" The shout from the doorway had them all turning. "Is dinner not ready yet?" Lord Pemberton, as Anthony had identified him, strode in like a boar at a picnic, searching the room for his mistress.

Alice waved from where she now knelt on the chair. "And here I thought I was dinner."

Violet responded from the settee where she spoke with Delilah, "No, dear. You're dessert."

More laughter followed, and Anthony guided Lissa away from Leighhall as Pemberton motioned for Alice to join him to formally meet their host.

It was all rather civilized and yet not. Lissa found herself curious not only about Leighhall and his secrets, but also about what they would encounter for the rest of their stay. As Anthony introduced her to yet another couple, she knew in her heart that after this, she could never marry. Life was so much more than tea and dress fittings.

"Daguette, you look good enough to eat."

At Lord Rothbury's comment, she smiled. "And so do you, my lord. I have no doubt that Delilah will tell me exactly what you taste like."

The man's eyes widened before he pulled Delilah closer and whispered loudly for them all to hear, "Do not be telling *all* our secrets, my dear."

The woman rolled her eyes before patting him on his chest. "Do not worry. I would never say anything you wouldn't."

The lord stared at her a moment then grinned. "You are far too smart for me."

"Yes, but I do not stay with you because of your mind." As the woman's gaze roamed downward, Lord Rothbury stood straighter, obviously assuming his manhood was the woman's reason for staying.

But Lissa already knew it was for the man's wallet that Delilah remained with him.

It was an unfortunate place for a woman to be in. She herself wished to be the captain of her own fate. Too long had she allowed her grandmother to dictate her actions.

Just then, a footmen came into the room and rang a bell.

Anthony offered his arm, and she laid her hand atop it. He allowed the others to leave before moving forward. "Not exactly what I expected."

She leaned in as they strolled down the corridor. "What did you expect?"

"Honestly?"

She nodded, very curious what he had envisioned.

"I believe I expected an orgy of some type."

She chuckled softly. "Do not rule it out quite yet. For all we know, there may be a naked woman on the dining room table that we all must pull our food from."

"No." His eyes rounded at her comment.

"You did see our dressing room, did you not?"

As color rose up his neck and his Adam's apple bobbed, she grinned. She didn't know what half the items in there were, but she had some guesses. And her guess was that Anthony knew exactly how to use them.

CHAPTER ELEVEN

ANTHONY SAT WITH his back to the china cupboard, not wishing to look at it, and sipped his whisky. Pemberton was already in his cups and Buswick was well on his way there. Leighhall, he noticed, drank very little.

The dinner had been a far more normal affair than he'd expected, differing from a typical evening in London only by the ladies' dress and the few ribald comments and innuendos that peppered the conversation. What was very different was the jovial mood and relaxed camaraderie. That did give him pause. Was that due to the status of the ladies? Yet they still left the gentlemen to their drinks while they gathered in the parlor as usual.

"I say, young Bellamore, wherever did you find that pretty little morsel, Daguette? She's a special one, that one." Rothbury turned to the others. "I do believe she invited me to bed in French."

Pemberton guffawed. "Are you sure she didn't invite you to the kitchen?"

Not to be outdone, Buswick winked at Rothbury. "Your French is as bad as your breath, my man. She clearly invited you to a horse race, which, based upon your skills, I have no doubt you'd lose."

Seeing as no one actually expected an answer of him, Anthony took another sip of his drink, content to let the jovial mood continue.

"My question, Pemberton, is where did you find Alice? On the docks?" Leighhall's interest seemed more than just casual.

"Not at all. I found her in a decent brothel near Mayfair." Pemberton laughed. "She was so good and so willing to try anything, I just had to keep her." He lowered his brows, trying to put on a serious face, but failed miserably. "She was a lady's companion but found it far too boring."

"That doesn't surprise me." Buswick lifted his almost empty glass. "Here's to Alice—may she always be willing and wet."

The men cheered, and Pemberton basked in the glow of their admiration.

Leighhall set his glass down without taking a sip. "You always find the best whores. I really must meet up with you in Town next Season."

"The more the merrier, Leighhall." Pemberton grinned crookedly. "We old men need all the experiments we can get before we leave this earth. How's that Selene you have now?"

"She has the required physical attributes, but no imagination. I have Alberta for tomorrow. She's far more inventive with her body and willing to do anything. If any of you want a go at her tomorrow afternoon, you're welcome to her."

Anthony gritted his teeth at Leighhall's attitude. Yes, he understood the women were only mistresses, but the viscount made it sound as if they were dogs. No, less than dogs. The other men didn't speak so.

Maybe he was just used to having Lissa about. She had so much intelligence and skill. He hadn't even known how beautiful she was, or how alluring, until the day in Melton Village when she'd set about seducing him.

He found himself hard pressed to behave as he should. His only control was his respect for her, and also how much he cared for her wellbeing. On one hand, he wished to protect her from learning more than she already knew, and on the other, he wanted to teach her so much.

"I say, Bellamore, who will you have do the hunting tomorrow?" Buswick raised his brows.

"Do not the men hunt and the women stay here?"

Pemberton laughed loudly. "Really, Leighhall, did you not tell the man anything about this weekend?"

Leighhall shrugged. "Does it matter?"

Buswick lifted his glass to be refilled. "The hunt tomorrow is on foot. You can choose to be the hunter or the prey. Your Daguette will be the other."

"But there is no cheating." Leighhall said the words forcefully, making it clear they must play by his rules or not at all.

Anthony thought it best to learn more. "How does one cheat at hunting one's partner?"

Rothbury was happy to explain. "If the two determine a hiding place ahead of time or if the prey leaves obvious signs they are in the vicinity, like a ribbon on a branch or a piece of lace on the ground." He turned to Buswick. "Remember when Lord Archer thought himself clever by leaving lemon drops along his path so his mistress could find him, only to be bitten by ants?"

Buswick laughed. "I do. As I remember, she was far off his trail and didn't know where he was until he started yelling. I've never seen a man so happy to pay the forfeit."

Anthony didn't think it sounded very laughable. "What's the forfeit?"

Leighhall scowled, clearly angered by anyone who would cheat at his games. "Any cheater must walk back to the house naked."

Anthony sucked in a breath, not liking that forfeit at all. "And is there a great prize for the hunter who finds his prey first that such cheating is done?"

Pemberton, Buswick, and Rothbury looked at each other blankly before they all laughed.

Confused, Anthony looked to Leighhall, who smirked at the men. "There is no prize, unless you wish to brag that you can smell your whore's readiness faster than others. Of course, that's if you are the hunter. If you're the prey and your whore finds you first, I suppose you could brag that she is that anxious to be jocked."

"I see." Anthony pretended to ponder the issue. "So in essence, it is merely pride that drives the spectacle."

"Very good, Bellamore. Very good," Leighhall replied. "But do not underestimate a man's pride."

Anthony took another sip of whisky to hide his concern. This weekend gave Leighhall much that he could twist to get other men to do as he wished, while he himself seemed above it all, except whatever he did behind closed doors. Maybe a visit to the man's room while he was otherwise occupied could lead to his own secrets in addition to the room they'd found.

"I hear Prinny is getting impatient." Rothbury frowned before gesturing with his glass, spilling port on his black trousers. "It seems he's tired of waiting to be king."

Pemberton snorted before throwing back the rest of his scotch. "I don't see why. He has all the privilege and, might I add, women to enjoy without all the responsibility. Why the rush?"

Leighhall waved his hand to dismiss the notion. "That is just rumor. I heard from him just the other day, and he is in no hurry to take the country upon his shoulders just yet."

Surprised, Anthony turned toward Leighhall, who still sat at the head of the table as if presiding over a court himself. "You have the ear of the regent?"

"The ear? Our host is in regular correspondence with Prinny." Buswick, now definitely having a bit of a time walking, lost his balance and landed hard on a chair. "You, young Bellamore, are in the presence of one with more power than he admits to."

Leighhall, instead of lifting his chin as he usually did when pleased with accolades, seemed disturbed. "Do not exaggerate a casual friendship, Buswick." He turned to Anthony. "Prinny and I simply have a common hobby."

"Women!" Pemberton yelled as if he'd been asked what the

hobby was.

Leighhall took a deep breath then gave a single nod, obviously beginning to lose patience with his corned guests. The lords getting drunk must not have been planned. "Yes, that is how we became acquainted. We both enjoy a good rutting with a pliable and obedient trollop."

Anthony gave the man a smile then took another sip of his whisky, not revealing that he now felt his attendance at Woburn Manor was a waste of time. If Leighhall was friends with the regent, it was doubtful he'd be able to find anything with which to keep the man in check. Frustrated, he wished himself anywhere but with the viscount. Unfortunately, wishing and current circumstances did not meld well.

A footman came and stood next to Leighhall, but didn't say a word. Immediately, the viscount put down his drink. "Gentlemen, it is time to rejoin our various whores and wantons."

"Hope I remember which is mine." Pemberton laughed loudly before holding out his glass to have it refilled before he left the room.

Buswick rose. "I, for one, am happy to move to yet another enjoyable activity. What do you have planned for us this evening, Leighhall?"

The viscount rose and gestured toward the door. "The usual parlor games, nothing more."

Anthony stood as well, and Buswick clapped him on the shoulder. "Don't believe him, my young Bellamore. Our host always has a creative twist that we all appreciate in one way or another."

He forced himself not to stiffen as he strolled out with Buswick by his side. As soon as they entered the parlor, he stepped to the right and glanced over the room, quickly spotting Lissa, who sat next to Delilah in facing wingback chairs. Alice was sprawled upon the settee with Violet standing at one end. The other women present were looking out the window for some reason.

Leighhall immediately joined Selene at the window. "What is

it, my dear? I can't believe the moon would be nearly as interesting as you are."

Not wishing to hear any more of Leighhall's acting, Anthony moved to where Lissa sat. He couldn't resist laying his hand on her almost bare shoulder, the warmth of her skin seeping into his palm, making him feel more himself again. "Are you enjoying the evening so far?"

She looked up at him as she laid her hand over his. "I am indeed. There are so many interesting people here." Her eyes danced with humor.

"I agree. But I must say the most interesting is you." His gaze slipped from her face to her breasts pressed together by her stays and in danger of falling out. As he continued to look, he was quite sure he could see a bit of pink areola.

"My dear baron, if you keep staring at Daguette so, everyone will think you in love."

He blinked at being caught and met the warm gaze of Delilah. "Well, I hope so, because I am. Daguette has my heart."

Delilah placed her hand over her rather large bosom. "That's so wonderful to hear. But it saddens me that you cannot marry."

"It doesn't sadden me. I'd much rather spend my life with Daguette. Marrying someone would only pull me away from my love."

Delilah moved her gaze to Lissa. "Is he jesting?"

"No. Though I've told him numerous times that he cannot avoid his family obligations, he remains adamant."

He squeezed Lissa's shoulder slightly, proud of how well she acquitted herself in such an unusual situation. "I am that. I have an older brother who is married with a son. As far as I'm concerned, I am free to live my life as I choose." He sobered as if unhappy with his circumstance. "But I admit to hoping for advice from Lord Leighhall on how to accomplish that."

"My advice?"

Having seen Leighhall moving in their direction, Anthony wasn't surprised by the man joining the conversation. "Yes. It was one reason I'd hoped so much to attend your fete."

The viscount's brows rose. "And here I thought it was for the freedom to be social with your mistress."

"I admit that intrigued me greatly. But I also hoped you could advise me on how to manage my family's need to see me married, with my enjoyment of being with Daguette always. You have managed to stay unmarried, and you are older than I. I'm hoping you have strategies you could share."

"Strategies?" Leighhall appeared to ponder. "I'm not sure I have any. I simply told my family that I would marry when I wished."

"But what about your parents?"

Leighhall chuckled. "My father has passed and my mother is dependent on me for her comfort. She agrees with me that if I'm happy then she will be as well."

Anthony frowned, though he'd already known about the man's father. "I beg your forgiveness. I was unaware of your father's passing."

Leighhall waved off the apology. "It's of no matter. The bugger was worse than a wild boar. We are all better without him, especially my dear mother."

It was obvious the man had said the last to impress the women around him.

"Leighhall, what is our next adventure?" At Pemberton's shout from across the room, Leighhall moved on.

"I'd best save Rothbury from that Selene." Delilah rose before lowering her voice so only Anthony and Lissa could hear. "She made it clear to me that she is only with Leighhall for this weekend and is looking for a new protector. I will not let her take him from me." With that, she moved off.

He moved from behind Lissa's chair and sat on the arm next to her. "Do you wish to forgo the games?"

Lissa looked up at him. "Absolutely not." She leaned in and whispered, "I don't remember the last time I felt so comfortable. I know the Belinda School for Curious Ladies aspires to teach us new ideas, but I must say I have learned far more in the short time we've been here than I have in the last two months at school." She moved back. "I can't wait to see what the games are all about."

Her observation made him uneasy. How could she marry well, even among the middle class, if she had so much knowledge about this other side of life? Would her husband be pleased or horrified that she was so interested in sex? Even among the peerage, it depended on the man.

He froze as his mind connected the pieces of the puzzle that were Lissa. She wanted to marry middle class because she *couldn't* marry a peer. She wasn't a virgin. How could she hide that after the marriage was consummated? A peer would be furious. Why had he not figured it out before?

Immediately his mind raced to the wealthy men he'd pointed out to her in Talley on the Green. He tried to imagine her with each of them, but none of the matches felt right. He would have to give her future husband much more thought. And now he'd have to be sure that whomever he introduced her to, had no dealings with any of the men at Leighhall's party. He'd definitely made his promise to Lissa that much more difficult to fulfill.

"I wonder if we'll play charades." She set her hand on his thigh. "I do so enjoy them."

Though dinner was close to typical, he did worry about the games. If "hunting" took on a new meaning, what might "games" portend? He took her hand in his, feeling far more protective of her than he'd ever felt. He was responsible for her being in such a situation, and he would make sure she didn't do anything she didn't wish to do.

As Leighhall called for their attention, he stood, ready to make an excuse if Lissa wished to leave. As the game of Puss, Puss in the Corner was announced, he was relieved that there was no particular forfeit, though he needn't have worried, as Lissa was much faster than most of them. Leighhall didn't play, instead directing and judging.

Next was Hunt the Slipper. Each woman took off her shoe in an appropriate manner, except Alice, who made sure she lifted her skirts above the tops of her stockings before removing her slipper. Anthony did notice that Lissa untied her left boot, so as to keep her dagger in her right boot hidden. It was a reminder that she was neither the lady nor the mistress she appeared to be in her dresses. Only he knew the true Lissa, and a feeling of happy nostalgia filled him at that thought.

As the laughter died down from a joke Alice made after the game ended, Lissa yawned. Anthony glanced at the clock on the mantel to see it was only midnight but immediately rose from the floor where they all sat. "I fear I've grown tired after so much activity today. I hope you don't mind if Daguette and I retire early."

"Too much activity, you say?" Pemberton looked to everyone else. "It certainly wasn't with us."

As everyone laughed, Anthony helped Lissa to stand then wrapped his arm around her. "No, it wasn't with you, and I'm hoping for a bit more activity before sleeping, too." He winked, causing more laughter and a few ribald comments.

"Don't forget the dressing room." At Buswick's reminder, Anthony held back a grimace.

Lissa waved her hand. "Oh, I don't think so tonight. I prefer those manacles on the bedpost."

More laughter ensued, and they made their way out of the parlor. They had barely reached the stairs when they heard a woman's distinctive voice. "I'd be happy to help you hold 'em down, love." Which was followed by a squeal as Pemberton, no doubt, took Alice to task.

They climbed the stairs in silence, next to each other but not touching. Anthony didn't look forward to sleeping on the settee, but he would not make Lissa uncomfortable. After opening the door, he stepped aside so she could enter. No sooner had he turned and closed the door then her hands came around his waist, her cheek against his back.

"Thank you for bringing me with you." She squeezed him, the happiness in her voice making him want to turn around and see her face.

She quickly let go, and he turned just in time to see her dark eyes alight with joy, her lips parted in a wide smile, much like in France. "This"—she spread her arms wide—"is what life is, learning and experiencing new things. No wonder you won't give up your investigations." She flopped down on the settee and spread out as Alice had been. "I never knew about the life of a courtesan. I do believe I prefer their company over the *ton*." She paused. "Excepting my fellow curious ladies, who have wonderful hearts. But so do these women, or rather some of them."

She sat up straight. "That Selene is odd. How can a prude be a courtesan? And Alice..." She grinned. "She doesn't hide anything. I do believe I could be great friends with both Delilah and Violet. I wonder what this Alberta is like. Most likely another lady swooning over Leighhall's charming manner." Her nose wrinkled. "Delilah and Violet know it isn't sincere."

Since there was no other chair, he moved to the bed's foot post and leaned against it. "Did they have anything else to say about Leighhall or his activities?"

"Indeed they did." She sobered. "Delilah has been here the most, since she's been with Rothbury three years now. She said at least once each time Leighhall loses his temper about something and it is scary to behold. She also said she'd overheard his talking about some of his women, and it was quite unpleasant."

That was a mild way to phrase it, but he understood. "I'm sorry she had to hear that."

"Oh, but it wasn't all she heard. You're right. He is vengeful. She said he took revenge upon a woman just this year for something she did three years ago."

"What did she do?"

"She refused to lie with him when he chose her at a brothel. At a brothel, no less! It took him three years, but he finally managed his revenge by paying two men to tup her, which she loved, but they used no French letters. She became pregnant and had to leave the brothel, as that was their rule."

"And I imagine she had no way to support herself and the child."

Lissa shook her head. "No one knows what became of her. I wonder how two men tup one woman. Do they take turns?"

His anger at Leighhall turned faster than a water spout. The thought of another man with Lissa, never mind two, had him curling his fingers into fists. "You would not like it."

"Probably not, especially two men I didn't know."

He didn't care if she did know them. Two men were out of the question. Actually, any man was out of the question.

When the hell had he become possessive? No, not possessive, just protective. Risking his own life in his investigations was one matter, but even if there were no threat to them, he'd already risked her innocence, or rather her ignorance. No, that wasn't right either. He couldn't quite name it, but he wanted to protect her from more sexual knowledge than she needed. Something told him he wasn't making sense, but he ignored it. He simply needed to protect Lissa.

"Neither Violet nor Delilah care for Selene. I think it's because she acts as if there is some hierarchy among mistresses, which I've been assured there is not, at least among the ones housed by peers. She believes she is of better status, I think."

"Better status? How?" He'd never had a mistress, though he'd enjoyed many women's company from most levels of society. So his knowledge in the societal norms of fallen women was woefully lacking, not that he thought he'd ever need it.

Lissa sat straighter and lifted her chin like the finest debutante at a ball. "Why? Because she was the courtesan of Lord Morely, the very good friend of King George, until just a fortnight ago, when he was told some absolute lies about her and he threw her over." Lissa dropped her chin and grinned. "As she tells it, Leighhall was such a dear as to offer to take her on for a few weeks until she settled on a new protector."

Something clicked in his mind. "Selene was the mistress of Morely?"

"Yes. Why, is that important?"

"I don't know." He pushed away from the bedpost and strolled to the fireplace, which, now lit, gave plenty of warmth to the room on the cool autumn night. "This is the third connection to the royal family I've stumbled upon."

Lissa rose, turning to face him, her gaze intense with excitement. "What are the connections? Maybe if you talk through the information, we can find the common thread."

That did make sense, and if he admitted it only to himself, he did value her keen insight. "Very well. The first was Mrs. Boscawen, the laundress and seamstress to Queen Charlotte. Leighhall spent two nights at an inn with her en route to visiting her family. The second was this evening, when I discovered that Leighhall and the regent write letters to each other after some past escapade of a sexual nature, or so it was intimated."

She cocked her head. "And now his mistress for a few weeks is the discarded mistress of a man who everyone knows is great friend of the king." She dropped her hand as her brow furrowed. "Those are connections to the top three royals. It appears the viscount is well situated."

"Yes, it does." But Anthony's instinct was telling him there was more, and he began to pace. "The connection to the regent is direct, but precipitated by a common enjoyment of women. My guess is they shared one or participated in some, um, sexual event."

Lissa didn't say anything, but she did roll her eyes.

"The other two are connections to Prinny's parents, one a direct servant and the other a less-direct mistress of a close friend. Could it be coincidence?"

"Are you not the one who told me there are no coincidences and that someone just needs to look deeper to find the reason?" She folded her arms over her chest, which made it easier for him to think.

"That's true."

"Then you must look deeper. Think back on the women Leighhall has tupped." She smirked, obviously enjoying using the word. "Did any of them have *indirect* connections to any royals?"

He stifled a groan. "There have been so many."

"Then look back to the most recent ones. Whom did he tup before Mrs. Boscawen?"

"Lady Amherst was just before Mrs. Boscawen, and Mrs. Coster, a baker in Bedford."

Lissa's eyes rounded and she dropped her arms to her sides. "Lady Amherst? But she's married to an earl."

He turned away to keep his concentration and walked toward the bed. "Yes, Lord Amherst. He's..." He stopped mid-stride. "He's a godson of the king."

Lissa plopped on the bed next to him. "And what of Mrs. Coster, the baker?"

He started to shake his head but stopped and looked at Lissa. "Her son is one of the king's footmen."

She grabbed his arm. "That's it. That's the connection. Leighhall is tupping women who are close to people near the royal family, but why?"

He looked down at her and then wished he hadn't. Her neckline crinkled with her position and he could clearly see one of her breasts, the whole perfectly shaped breast, with a large dusty-rose areola and tiny nub. Spinning away and pulling his arm from her hands, he strode to the window to look out upon the black night, trying to focus on the discussion.

"Anthony?" Her confusion was clear in her tone.

"I must think upon it." But as he stared at the darkness, all he could see was the soft, pretty breast that he'd tasted for the briefest of moments earlier. Now all he wanted was to taste it again...and more.

"Could it be he was obtaining information? I can see where his flattery might turn the head of an unsuspecting woman."

He forced himself to focus on her words. Information. From

women. "By Jove, that's it! He's using these women to gather information about the king. But why?" He faced the room again, but didn't look at her. He felt he was close to something important some revelation. He just didn't know if whatever it was could aid him in his mission. "Why would Leighhall need information about the king?"

"Maybe he wants to ask him for something. Your king has many daughters, no? Maybe he wishes to improve his situation by marrying one of them."

It was a possibility, but there were easier ways of accomplishing that. "I believe the answer is located either in that secret room or the man's bedroom. I suggest we investigate both on the morrow. From what I've gathered, he will give us free rein of the house for *tupping* our mistresses again tomorrow before dinner, so that might be an excellent opportunity to further our search for answers."

"I agree." She jumped off the bed and moved to her trunk.

As she pulled the crepe shift out, he moved to the settee and sat to remove his boots. "I will sleep here. I do not wish to make you uncomfortable." He would be uncomfortable, but in a much better position than attempting to sleep on the bed without touching her.

"That's all well and good, but you will need to unbutton me first." Her booted feet came into view.

He looked up. "Yes, of course." Quickly, he rose, anxious for her to crawl into the bed, so he wouldn't have to worry about craving her. After unbuttoning the deep-blue dress, he untied the silken ties of the stays. "I believe that will accomplish what you need."

She held the dress to her chest and looked over her shoulder at him. "I have a feeling that you know that as well as I." Then, with a toss of her head, she strolled toward the armoire.

He ignored her comment, unwilling to discuss his skills with women, and dropped back down on the settee and removed his boots, greatcoat, and waistcoat. Then he lay back and closed his eyes. He didn't plan to open them again until morning, even though the room already cooled.

As he lay there, he heard the armoire open and imagined her hanging her dress, and with each small sound, he pictured her until he was confident she had brushed her hair and crawled into bed. When the cloth first touched him, his eyes popped open to the sight of her long black hair hanging over his chest as she covered him with a blanket.

He snapped his eyes shut once again. "Thank you."

She patted him on his shoulder. "We take care of each other, *mom ami.*"

The brush of her lips upon his forehead both startled and settled him. "Yes, we do. Always."

Even as he heard her pad over to the bed and climb upon it, his last word seemed to echo in the room, or was it in his head? Just as he started to drift off, he thought he heard it settle into his heart.

CHAPTER TWELVE

A SOFT CLICK sounded as the lock gave way to her hairpin. Quickly, Lissa looked to each entrance to the dining room. With no one about so early in the morning, she opened the secret door and pulled the china cupboard closed.

After securing the inside door, she stood absolutely still as the darkness enveloped her, except for the very small flame in her oil lamp she'd taken from their room while Anthony still dressed. The blackness didn't bother her, as she used to hide under the floorboards of the farmhouse in France after the war broke out, her family determined to keep her safe. Perhaps that was why she'd always enjoyed her forays at night to find food and treasures. She'd only robbed the living, staying far away from the battlefields where her grandmother stole from the pockets of the dead. The sight of blood was her greatest weakness.

Lengthening the wick to make the space brighter, she turned to face the room. The dark-red wallpaper didn't reflect the light well. Hugging the wall, she searched for another lantern as she walked by weapon after weapon, each hung masterfully on the wall to create a medley of armament that could have been a piece of art. It held a wide variety from ancient claymore swords to what looked to be a bearded axe of the Vikings to a Celtic crossbow. As much as she wanted to inspect each piece, her goal was more illumination, and hopefully more information. Coming upon a desk, she found what she needed and lit the large oil lamp that sat upon it.

The added light made half the large room visible. As she'd expected, there were no windows, the room being created in the center of the house. Looking back at the door she came through, it was clear it wasn't always a secret room, as it was framed in foot-wide walnut. It was probably a pass-through room, like the one at Dory's new home, where one room led into another, but someone must have walled it up, unless there was another entrance. Actually, finding another exit should be her first priority.

Glad that she'd worn her soft dance slippers so as to make as little noise as possible, she quietly walked across the hardwood floor, using her smaller lantern to shed additional light. As the opposite wall from the desk was revealed, she slowed. Looking back, she judged the distance to be at least thirty feet. Moving closer, she examined the scarred wall. Holes and marks covered it, as if someone had used it to practice with the weapons in the room. Once more she turned back to view the various weaponry now revealed. If Leighhall did indeed know how to use each one displayed, he was a much more dangerous man than they had thought.

Unease crept up her back, and she turned her attention to finding another way out. As expected, there was another door opposite the one she'd come in, but where it led to was the question. She hadn't explored nearly as much of the house as Anthony had, so she would confer with him. Still, if needed, she had an escape plan.

As the room itself held little besides old weapons, the practice wall, and the desk, she strode back to the desk, anxious to learn what she could and leave before too many people woke. There were three drawers on each side, but the top was littered with papers. Ads from the *London Gazette* and the *Morning Post* cluttered one side, while drawings of weapons sketched on paper were on the other. In the center was the inkwell and plume, as well as what looked like opened letters.

Careful not to move anything, she read what she could see. There were many pleasantries and a few references to weapons and gratefulness, but she couldn't read who they were from. One described a sexual exploit that included a basket from Asia, which she couldn't figure out, nor did she wish to. Finally, she carefully lifted a letter to see who the one beneath was from. Lady Amherst's name caught her attention. Skimming it, she found it simply an invitation, though rather explicit, to her home while her husband was in Town.

She was far more interested in the weapons than Leighhall's sexual adventures. Finding a letter mentioning the sword break, she gently lifted the one above it. It was instructions for receiving the weapon. Looking at the signature, her breath caught. It was signed with a very flamboyant letter P. Surely it couldn't be for Prinny, the regent. He would sign it with his name, or His Highness, or some such moniker, wouldn't he?

Anxious to learn more, she searched for more correspondence about weapons. Her gaze alighted on the word "musket," and she'd reached out to lift the paper above it when a sound at the door she'd entered stopped her. She snapped her head toward the other door, marking where it was before dousing the lantern on the desk.

As the door began to open, she dropped to the floor, extinguishing the flame of her own lantern as she crouched in the darkness. Was there a lantern at the door she'd missed that would soon flood the room with light? Even at the thought, her heart raced and she searched for a story to tell Leighhall if he found her.

The man walked slowly across the floor as if searching the shadows, a small amount of light from his lantern reflecting off the ceiling above her. As the footsteps grew louder, she pulled herself into a small ball beneath the desk. Her breathing escalated, making it hard to stay silent. She needed to remain calm.

It was no different than the night she'd hidden from soldiers who searched an abandoned home for valuables, not knowing she'd already taken what little there was. That night she escaped through a window by dousing their candles. She could do the same here if she had to.

With a plan in mind, her panic subsided, and she waited for her moment.

The footsteps drew closer, and she prepared herself. They stopped behind the desk, the light shifting over the top of it as if Leighhall searched for one letter in particular. Maybe he would find it and leave.

She watched the man's trousers where they touched his shoes, moving to the right as he shifted his weight. As long as he didn't decide to sit and pull the chair in, or push the chair in when he left, she might make it through with no detection.

A soft whistle left the man's lips above her.

Why would he do that?

His shadow grew larger as he bent to open the lowest drawer. The light scent of clove reached her. Had Leighhall been talking to Anthony? If so, Anthony would be worried about where she was.

As the lowest drawer shut, she heard a sniff. "Lissa?" Even as recognition dawned for her, he crouched low and stared at her. "What are you doing in here?" Though his voice was low, his surprise was clear.

Relief flooded her, and she smirked. "The same thing you are."

"Come out from there." He rose and lowered his hand to help her to stand.

She didn't need it, but was happy to accept. He had a strong grip that she appreciated. As soon as she stood next to him, she nodded to the top of the desk. "Some of these letters are about the weapons."

"I noticed. At least from what I could see without moving them." He let go of her hand to point below. "I believe the top drawers have the most important information, as they are locked."

"That's not a problem." She pulled her hairpin from her pocket and held it up.

He grasped her wrist. "Not now. When I came inside here, the servants were stoking the fires. We need to leave and come back this afternoon when Leighhall invites us to use the various rooms."

"That's a good plan." When he released her arm, she dropped the hairpin back into her pocket. "Maybe then we can discover where the other door goes to."

"Other door?"

"Yes. It's directly across from the one you came in."

He looked in the appropriate direction, but his lantern was far too low to see it. "We shall do that as well. But now we must leave."

Since her lantern was doused, she followed him as he led them back to the door. She couldn't help asking before he opened it, "You're not angry that I came in here without you?"

He looked back at her and smiled. "As soon as I sent the valet on his way, it's where I expected you to be, but when I entered and all was dark, I thought you may be with Delilah or Violet somewhere."

Pleased that he did not expect her to meekly wait for him, she rose on her toes and kissed him on the cheek. "I'm so glad I came."

His brow lowered, but he smiled, clearly uncomfortable. "I admit, it may not have been a good decision, but you are of great help."

She grinned. "And that's exactly why you should be happy I'm here."

He still didn't look certain, but he turned back to the door and doused his lantern before opening it. Light shone through the slit between the back piece of the china cabinet.

When he didn't immediately move forward, she assumed someone was in the room.

They seemed to stand there for almost twenty minutes, but

for all she knew it was only three. Finally, he moved the cabinet doors to the side and stepped out. She closed the door to the room behind them before following, then clicked the secret opening back into place. She had just closed the glass doors of the china cabinet when Anthony spoke.

"Lord Leighhall, just the person we'd hoped to see. Daguette was admiring that tea service you have on the top shelf. The one with the pansies on it. Where did you find that?"

She spun about to look inquiringly at Leighhall. "I really must purchase one. My dear mother had one quite similar, but instead of two flowers, it only had one."

Leighhall strode over and examined the set. "Hmm, I believe my own mother purchased that from Fortnum & Mason. But that was years before I was born. I doubt that you'll find it."

Anthony pulled her against him. "Would you consider selling this one?"

The viscount shook his head. "I'm sorry, Bellamore. It's my mother's, and she would not forgive me."

As the man looked to Lissa, she let her lower lip stick out, and he laughed, chucking her under the chin like a child. "Now don't be sad, mademoiselle. I'm sure young Bellamore here will purchase something even nicer for you."

She glanced at Anthony then looked to Leighhall. "My lord, you are indeed a good son."

For some reason, that made the man laugh. "You found yourself a gem, Bellamore." At that moment, the servants began loading the side table with food. "I just hope she hides as well as she pouts."

A shiver raced up her spine. "Hide? Why would I hide?"

The man's grin did not reach his eyes. "Because today we hunt. Did Bellamore not tell you? You are the prey."

Startled, she looked to Anthony, who quickly shook his head. "Actually, I had planned to let Daguette do the hunting. As you can see in her purple dress, she would be far too easy to find, and I wouldn't want her accused of cheating."

"Ah, I see you wish to follow the rules. That's wise of you." The man nodded, clearly impressed. "Now come and eat, for there's a frost on the fields and you'll need a full stomach. Sometimes the hunt can take hours, and—" Leighhall's head snapped to the doorway. "Alberta." Without another word, he left them to escort his other mistress, who was as dark and voluptuous as Selene was light and whisper thin.

Lissa leaned in. "What am I hunting?"

"Me."

She raised her brows, surprised and not a little concerned. "Surely I'm not expected to kill you."

"No." Anthony led her toward the sideboard. "You're expected to find me in the wood, and there is no cheating or you'll have to return to the house naked."

She lifted her chin. "I don't need to cheat. I'm an excellent tracker."

"Exactly why I chose to be the prey."

Flattered that he remembered her skill, she felt a strange gratefulness for his thoughtful decision. "And for that, I promise not to kill you."

He chuckled before handing her a plate with which to choose her food.

Despite what Leighhall said, she did not choose much, as she didn't wish a full stomach if she were to track. Once they had what they wanted, they settled at the table and were soon joined by Delilah and Rothbury as others trickled in.

There was much laughter and sense of anticipation as everyone enjoyed their tea and cocoa, making the hour rather enjoyable. It reminded Lissa of eating with the curious ladies, and she hoped Eleanor was enjoying her time at Dory's.

Eventually, Leighhall rose. "This morning we shall have a hunt of a special nature. You shall choose one of you to be the hunter and the other to be the prey. For example, Alberta here could be my prey. Her challenge would be to hide in the east wood without being found by me. Once I find her, I would bring her back to the tent at the entry point."

"What if you find Violet?" Lord Buswick asked the question, but clearly knew the answer, as he looked at Anthony as if to make the point clear.

"If you find another hunter's prey, you must not say anything to that hunter but continue on until you find your own. Telling someone the location of their prey is considered cheating."

Rothbury squeezed Delilah's shoulders. "And you don't want to cheat."

Leighhall's face took on a menacing look. "No one is allowed to cheat. No leaving a ribbon on a tree or making loud noises or deciding beforehand where you will be as prey."

Pemberton pointed to Lissa. "If you do, you must walk naked back to the house, and it's damn cold out there, so I won't be cheating...this time."

"Oh, I'm so relieved." At Violet's comment, laughter filled the room.

"This is very creative, my lord." Alberta gazed hungrily at Leighhall. "Will I be the prey or you?"

He lifted her chin with his finger. "You, of course, my dear. Best that I don't find you too quickly, or you may very well find yourself in the sling."

Alberta's large chest rose, threatening to spill out of her scooped neckline. As the sexual frisson between the two was palpable, the room fell silent. "Hmm, and if you find me last?"

If she hadn't been watching closely, Lissa would have missed the pure fury that filled the man's eyes, but she did catch it, and it chilled her.

"Then, my sweet, I will have no choice but to punish you."

Instead of heeding the warning, Alberta stoked the fire. "I guess we will just have to see how good a hunter you truly are."

As if he'd forgotten they all watched, Leighhall moved his finger down the woman's neck to wrap his hand around it. "I'm a very, very good hunter."

The woman's eyes widened with understanding. "I never

doubted that, my lord."

Appeased by her sudden capitulation, Leighhall turned back to them all. "Let us all don our coats and cloaks and remove to the tent before the east wood."

The mood of the guests remained jovial, which Lissa found odd. Had they not seen the look in Leighhall's eyes? That could well be, since he'd been looking at Alberta, and no one else was left on that side of the table besides Anthony and herself.

As they all walked briskly across the field, the sun broke through the many clouds, making the air warmer. Lissa slowed her step, forcing Anthony to also slow.

He looked at her in question.

When enough space was made between them and the two couples they'd been behind, she spoke quietly. "Did you see Leighhall's threat?"

Anthony nodded, but didn't say anything.

"The room is filled with weapons."

Again he nodded as if listening to her concerns about the hunt, but she understood that he too had seen the walls of the secret room.

"The far wall is a practice wall."

At that, his brows rose before he frowned. "I understand."

Relieved that he caught the connection she'd made between the weapons, the man, and the danger, she found her shoulders relaxing. Having Anthony by her side made her feel far safer. How odd that she hadn't realized that before. Even in France, she'd felt that way, as if she'd never get caught—or if she did, he'd be there. Then again, she was there for him too. They were friends, after all.

"Hey, Bellamore, I hope you aren't planning a meeting place."

At Buswick's call, Anthony laughed. "Hardly. I've never been in these woods, so I wouldn't begin to know what areas they contain."

Violet looked over her shoulder at them. "You will soon."

Her laughter caught the attention of Leighhall, who led the way. "You will all learn these woods, as they are different from the ones you last hunted in."

Did the man actually keep track of who came in what month and what woods? As if he'd read her mind, Buswick looked at them as they caught up and walked beside him. "Leighhall is nothing if not meticulously organized. His forethought is what makes coming here each time such fun."

Lissa tried to fit that in with the mess of correspondence she'd seen on his desk. The two behaviors didn't match. Then again, perhaps in his most private sanctuary he relaxed such strict tendencies. Maybe it was a need to control the situation when around others.

The white tent was large enough for all to sit and have a meal in, except no chairs or tables were present. It had obviously been set up simply to keep the elements at bay, specifically the morning frost. Her choice of boots for the day was much more appropriate than some of the footwear the other ladies sported, and her pelisse did provide some warmth. Though she wished she had her trousers instead of the deep purple dress with the scooped neck that she wore now. Unfortunately, she hadn't brought any, not wishing someone to recognize her in the future when she may have a need for wearing them out of necessity.

"My dear guests. For those chosen as prey, please step forward."

Anthony leaned in and gave her a kiss on the cheek before moving forward. The action was not lost on the few nearby, particularly Violet.

"Oh, he is a sweet one. I hope you get to keep him a long time."

Lissa clasped her hands to her chest. "He says he will never leave me."

"Yes, well, that is a lovely sentiment, but it's important to plan for those between times. We must always have the ability to be happy alone, so we are never too desperate."

There was a wealth of knowledge in the woman's eyes, and Lissa did not doubt she spoke from experience. "I will take that advice to heart."

"Good." Violet turned her attention back to those lined up before Leighhall.

Anthony, Buswick, and another gentleman stood with the women from the rest of the pairs. Even as she watched, she noted how much broader Anthony was. No wonder he passed for middle class so easily, yet he held himself as an aristocrat, which he was. Her anger at him over that had dissipated because he acted no different with her because of it, and he was becoming more comfortable with seeing her in a dress. She might just have to see tonight how comfortable he could be.

Even as the thought of undressing for him filled her head, Leighhall's voice caused it to vanish.

"Our prey will have twenty minutes to find a place to hide. I must now ask all my hunters to face the other way. I would not want you to have an idea of where the rabbit entered the wood."

As they turned around, Pemberton complained, "You too, Leighhall."

Leighhall strode around them and stood before all the hunters, his back to their prey. Lifting his watch, he waited a moment then called out, "You may leave, now!"

Lissa listened intently to the sounds behind her. The women's light tread was quick as they ran for the wood. The men seemed more purposeful, as if they knew where they would go. If she wasn't mistaken, two men headed straight, but one headed to the other end of the wood. That would be Anthony. How fun to use her tracking skills and her knowledge of her baron to find him.

Leighhall backed up into their line between Violet and Pemberton. As the others conversed to wile away the minutes, she thought about all she knew of Anthony's abilities in the woods. They were many, and if he wished to remain hidden a long time he could, but she was quite positive he would wish to be found relatively early. He'd always been protective of her, even while in

France, so he wouldn't want her to have to track for too long. Her concern was finding him *too* quickly. If Leighhall was not one of the first, if not *the* first, to find his prey, she was quite sure they would all know it.

"Really, Leighhall. Is it not time yet? My arse is cold and I need a willing woman to warm it."

"Control yourself, Pemberton. You still have three minutes."

She glanced past Violet to see Leighhall quite pleased that Pemberton was anxious. What was it that motivated such a man?

Finally, Leighhall held his arm up as he looked at his watch and brought it down. "Time to go hunting." The man spun and sprinted directly into the wood, as did many others.

She strolled forward, moving at a diagonal, following the matted footprints of one path crossing all others. As she entered the wood, it felt colder despite the fact very few leaves held to the trees to block any sunlight. Keeping her gaze on the ground, she followed the male footprints. She could be wrong and they might belong to Buswick, but she'd follow them anyway.

When the steps seemed to disappear, she grinned. Only Anthony would backtrack to throw her off his scent. Confident she had the right set, she returned the way she came until she could see where he continued. It was so much easier than tracking a hare or a fox.

When she came to a very small area covered in pine needles, she paused. It was impossible to see the tracks. With no help for it, she walked around the perimeter to see where he'd left the area.

A squeal rang out, and she halted. Then loud laughter followed. It sounded like Alice. If so, Pemberton either got lucky or the woman cheated.

She shivered. Hopefully, Leighhall had already found Alberta, or it would not be pleasant.

Resuming her trek about the needle circle, she found a broken twig just as raindrops started to sprinkle. Happy for her fur-lined bonnet, she continued into the wood. It took a few strides before she found his footsteps again, but then she heard a rustling behind her. Looking back, she watched as Delilah moved stealthily in the opposite direction.

Keeping silent, she watched until the woman was out of sight, then turned back to her track. The rain was beginning to affect the footprints, so she quickened her pursuit. Then, suddenly, the tracks stopped. She turned back to see if he'd backtracked again, but it didn't appear so. Coming back to where the footsteps ended, she reviewed the area. Nothing was disturbed, no twig broken.

Smiling, she looked up to see a rather low branch. If she had her trousers, she'd climb the tree, too. Instead, she stepped back, thankful for the slight cover of her bonnet as she looked up into the tree to find Anthony sitting on a branch a few above her. "Is it colder up there?"

He shook his head as he bent over to look at her. "I should have known you'd find me so quickly." He jumped down to another branch before sitting on the last one.

She stepped closer. "Has anyone beside Alice been found yet? Could you see from up there?"

He nodded as he jumped to the ground. "Indeed, I did. Alice, Alberta, Buswick, and at least six others have sought shelter under the tent."

Relieved they wouldn't be too early, she hooked her arm in his, and they started forward to join the others. "You didn't do much to cover your tracks."

"I didn't want you out here with Leighhall. I don't trust him."

Not knowing if others were near, since the rain was becoming steadier and the sound of it hitting the earth was growing louder, she put her finger to her lips. "We are all going to need to change once we get back. At least we can shelter in the tent a bit."

Just then, the rain doubled in intensity and Anthony slipped his arm from hers. "Run for the tent!"

She grabbed hold of her already wet skirts, lifted them high, and raced forward. Despite the sound of the rain, Anthony's thundering footsteps were clear behind her. As they raced out of the wood and the short distance to the tent, shouts from those undercover greeted them. No sooner had they stepped inside than others arrived as well.

Her pelisse was soaked, as was her bonnet. She untied the ruined hat and pulled it off, though it was too cold to shuck her pelisse. Glancing at others doing the same, she noticed someone was missing. "Where's Delilah?"

Anthony looked up from shaking his greatcoat free of water. "I don't see her, but Rothbury is here."

Lissa immediately strode up to Lord Rothbury. "Where's Delilah?"

He shrugged. "Don't know. Couldn't find her. The woman is too clever by half."

Placing her hands on her hips, she stared at the man. "So you ran for cover and left her out there?"

Anthony's hands on her shoulders just made her angrier, and she shrugged him off. "If you will excuse me."

"Where are you going?"

She turned on Rothbury. "To get Delilah."

"You can't." The man shook his head. "If she refuses to come in on her own, that's her decision. You're a hunter. You're not allowed to hunt my prey. That's cheating."

"No, it's not. It's caring enough that someone doesn't die of exposure." She stalked to the opening, but halted as Anthony stepped in front of her. "I'll find her."

She was about to refuse, but if she saw Delilah then he must have seen her too from his perch. "Fine. But if you're not back in ten minutes, I'm coming for you."

He gave her a nod and ran back out into the downpour.

"It's a good thing you didn't go, mademoiselle. As the hunter, that would have been cheating."

She turned at the sound of Leighhall's voice, even as fury filled her. "Yes, it would have been cheating death, but really, he's not such a great bedmate now, is he, my lord?"

The man took a step back then studied her.

Merde, she couldn't antagonize him or it could ruin Anthony's investigation. "But that is just what my mother taught me." She smiled. "I'm sure you were going to send servants out to look for her anyway." She waved her hand. "It is the way of us French, so filled with concern over our sisters."

At the mention of servants, she could see Leighhall hadn't even thought of that. He covered up his thoughtlessness easily. "I understand your concern. As young Bellamore will save the day, I will keep my servants dry." He turned from her and addressed them all. "And Alice, who cheated, can do her naked walk once inside the warm environs of the house."

Alice grinned. "That will be even more fun!"

The others went back to talking, but she turned to look out the opening of the tent. What if Anthony were the one to become sick? It had never occurred to her before, but now that he was out there, she couldn't stop watching.

CHAPTER THIRTEEN

ANTHONY CONTEMPLATED LISSA'S behavior from the warmth of the tub, which she'd had moved before the fire. She'd been out of sorts since he came back to the tent, both he and Delilah soaked to the skin.

Lissa's actions reminded him of the first time he'd come to the farmhouse in the devastated countryside of France. She'd held a pistol on him as he attempted to find out if the captain was there. If her grandmother had not come to the door to see who had arrived, he probably would have never discovered Lord Blackmore still lived. Only now, Lissa acted as if he were the one inside the house and anyone else was the enemy.

She'd ordered the hot bath and had the servants move the tub. Then she'd told the valet to return in an hour and had personally stripped Anthony of all his clothes. That she hadn't made a single inappropriate comment, or touched him except to peel his wet clothes from his body, concerned him, almost as much as her cutting her own wet clothes from her body before donning the dressing gown she now wore.

After dunking his head he lifted the soap to wash his hair, but she grabbed it from his hand.

"I'll do that. Lean your head back."

At her commanding tone, he did as she wished, the soapy water covering his nakedness for the most part. "Liss, what's wrong?"

Her hand moved the soap through his wet hair then began to massage his scalp. "Nothing's wrong."

Now that was a lie. "I thought we didn't lie to each other."

She pushed his head forward. "Dunk."

He waited, and when she didn't say anything else, he did as she asked. When he lifted his head again, he found her pouring a kettle of boiling water into a half-filled bucket of cold. "You don't have to serve me. The valet can do that."

Instead of answering, she strode toward him.

He barely had time to close his eyes before she dumped the bucket of warm water over his head. He wiped his eyes then turned to speak to her, but she was across the room at the armoire. It was not like her to avoid him. It wasn't like her to avoid *anything*. "Lissa, come here."

She turned quickly. "Has the bath grown cold? Let me get the towel."

He shook his head, not that she saw, since she'd already moved to lift the towel from the bed.

When she approached, he sensed that she would retreat once again, so instead of talking, he rose from the water.

Her gaze flowed over his body like the water as if she touched him, which sent his body into a sexual alert. As she stepped closer, she lifted the towel. He stepped from the tub and, instead of grabbing the towel, grabbed her to him.

Surprisingly, she didn't fight him, but wrapped the towel around him.

"Lissa, you've never been afraid to tell me what's on your mind. Why are you afraid now?"

She stopped rubbing his back, but didn't look at him. "I'm not afraid. I'm just angry."

Yes, she was angry, but there was more to it. "What are you angry about?"

She squirmed to be released, and he let her go, but the towel went with her and she didn't move far. Her gaze once again moved over him, but this time it was as if she were making sure all his limbs were still present.

He needed to try another tack. Holding his arms out, he cocked his head. "Am I acceptable?"

Her gaze flew to his and color came into her cheeks.

That shocked him, as he'd never seen her embarrassed. Something was definitely wrong.

She threw the towel at him and turned around. "How am I to know if you're acceptable? First, you're a soldier, and now you're a peer. I certainly don't know. What would I know about what is acceptable?"

He scooped up the towel and wrapped it around his hips before striding to stand in front of her. "I'm your friend, or I thought I was."

She searched his face as if looking for something. "*Oui. Mon ami* from France. The only one who knows my past." Her forehead puckered. "I did not like that you were so cold. I do not want you to die."

By the way she said it, he could tell she'd never thought of his dying before. He found that remarkable, as their escapades in France had put them in danger more times than not. Why was it an issue now?

She crossed her arms over her chest. "You were as cold as my grandfather's corpse. I don't know how you can still be alive."

A clue. "Your grandfather? I didn't know you knew your grandfather."

Her shoulders relaxed and a soft smile played upon her lips as she looked toward the window. "Grand-pére let me go everywhere with him. He defended me from my parents and taught me so much." Her smile disappeared. "One day, when I was but seven, he made me stay home, saying he had an important errand and I could not come. I was heartbroken. I wailed after he left and would not listen to anyone. I watched for him at the road, but as night fell and he didn't return, my father made me go inside."

His stomach tensed at what he was sure would come.

"The next day, my family grew worried and we started to search. We took the road and searched through the woods." Her gaze met his. "I found him. He was lying on the ground, his back to me, and I thought him asleep. I ran to him and hugged him." Even as she spoke, she shivered. "I hugged him, but he was so cold. I didn't understand. I shook him and he rolled over."

As if she were living the horror over again, her eyes widened and her mouth opened, but no sound emerged.

Anthony couldn't stay back any longer, and he pulled her stiff form to him. "You don't need to tell me."

"The blood. It was everywhere. They killed him."

Despite his hold, she remained stiff, no tears, no softening. He wanted to protect her from her memories, but he couldn't. It was frustrating. He could only protect her now.

She finally looked up at him. "He'd gone to buy me a new dress, but they killed him for the money. All that time I watched for him. But he was already dead from a dagger wound to his heart."

His own heart rolled over as emotion swept through him. She'd gone through so much, more than even he had known, and still remained strong, defiant, and so courageous. He didn't want her to ever have to be strong again. What he wanted was to be strong for her, protect her from any future threats or heartaches. Even as he cupped her head in his hands, he understood the feeling inside his chest. It was love, pure and simple. "Lissa."

Lowering his lips to hers, he kissed her tenderly, unable to say the words he felt, knowing she wouldn't understand, but willing to show her.

At first, she remained unmoving, but as if his touch were a flame to candle wax, her body melted, softening against his own, her lips moving beneath his. When she reached up and wrapped her arms around his neck, he dropped his hands to hold her and nudged her mouth open to enjoy her taste.

She deepened the kiss, tangling her tongue with his and pressing her soft curves to his hardness.

He couldn't deny the need in his heart nor the desire coursing through him. Unable to resist, he lifted her up and took two strides to gently deposit her on the bed.

At the break in their kiss, she frowned. "Come back."

He lay down next to her and leaned over her to cup her head with his hand. "I want you, Lissa."

She smiled slyly and lifted her arms above her head, revealing the bare skin between her breasts. "Finally."

He chuckled. He couldn't help it. The happiness inside him was fairly bursting. As she bent her knee to touch his hardening erection through the towel, his focus changed. Lowering his head, he took her mouth with his once again. He wanted to know every inch of her, love every hill and valley. Even as his tongue touched hers, he moved his hand between them to untie the belt at her waist. As it loosened, he pulled back and spread the dressing gown to reveal her pert breasts, taut nipples, and slender waist.

To have her bare before him with no danger of interruption caused his excitement to grow. Lowering his head, he took one hard peak into his mouth and savored.

Her hand at the back of his head held him to her, not simply giving him permission, but demanding his attention. He sucked lightly before gently rolling her nipple between his teeth.

Her back arched and her hand left his neck and ran over his back, while the other grasped his arse. Sensation shot through his balls and made him harder. He didn't want to love her quickly. He wished to enjoy every moment, so he moved lower, beyond her grasp, and paid heavy attention to her other breast.

Her soft moans encouraged him as he tasted his fill, nipping and sucking to his heart's content, and hers. Yet he wanted even more. Much more. He shifted his weight to the leg between hers and moved his other there as well. As he lifted, she grabbed at the towel, pulling it from beneath him and leaving him to feel her soft skin touch his.

"*Je te veux.*"

He looked up to see her watching him. "And you shall have me. I promise."

Seeming to accept that, she closed her eyes and smiled. "*Oui. A bon* promise."

He lowered his head to kiss the ribs beneath her breasts. Slowly, he made his way down her stomach to the dark curls at the juncture of her thighs, dropping kisses as he breathed in her apple scent and the muskiness of her readiness. The combination reflected who she was, complicated yet simple, beautiful yet strong.

He wanted to see her in ecstasy before making her his. He wanted to bring such a remarkable woman to the apex of life. Softly, he ran two fingers through her curls, barely touching what lay hidden beneath.

She moaned, bending her knees and raising her pelvis. "*S'il vous plait.*"

There was no possibility of his resisting such a plea, nor did he want to. He laid one hand on her thigh and lowered his head to grant her wish. He found her hard nub and licked upward then sideways and around it, listening to her loud breaths with each pass. He repeated the movements again and again, then pressed closer to suck on the tiny pinnacle, wanting to give her this ultimate experience.

She grabbed his shoulders as her hips rose, her pants harsh now as she reached for her release.

He stroked upward on her thigh before sliding his fingers along her moist folds to her entrance. Slowly, he pushed one inside her even as he released her nub and licked it. She was warm and tight and so close to her fulfillment.

Lissa squeezed his shoulders harder, soft cries coming from deep in her throat.

Those soft, yearning sounds urged him on to give his woman more pleasure.

His woman. Even as the words settled into his soul, he understood he could never let her go.

Tamping down his own need to make her his, he withdrew his finger before pushing two slowly inside her.

"*Oui. Oui.*" Her words were barely discernible between her breaths.

Pressing his mouth to her once more, he sucked gently as he moved his fingers, deepening his suction with every thrust.

Her cries grew louder until she tightened around his fingers and a scream filled the room.

He looked up to see her come apart for him. Her lithe body arched and strained while he continued moving his fingers within her, watching her until she let go of his shoulders and forcefully lifted his head.

Happiness settled over him like a warm blanket. He grinned, knowing well that her body was over sensitized from his skills. Waiting, he remained still, content where he was until her breathing slowed and her body grew limp. Then, without warning, he licked at her release.

"Oh." Her head came off the pillow as she looked at him wide-eyed.

He crawled up her body until he covered her. His hard erection pressed against one of her thighs as he kept himself leveraged on his elbows. "Did you enjoy?"

She nodded, gazing at him as if she didn't know him. "I didn't know you were such a lover. If I had, I would have not let you stay clothed for so long."

He chuckled, happy to have pleased her. "Does that mean you will keep me in this room naked for the remainder of our stay?"

Her gaze left his face as if she were thinking seriously about his question. Then a mischievous light came into her eyes as she looked askance at him. "Maybe not just in this room?"

"You would have me parade about below for all those women to see?"

Her brows lowered fast. "*Non.* They may not see or touch. *Tu es a moi!*"

He was hers? His heart gave a jolt of elation, but he tamped it down. The words meant far more to him than he was sure she meant them to be. He had no illusions about her feelings for him. He was a good friend and nothing more. But she was more to *him* now, and he planned to show her. "Then I will make you mine as well."

LISSA SUCKED IN her breath at the look in Anthony's eyes as he said those words. Pure possession filled his gaze, something she hadn't seen in him before, and it sent a thrill into her core as strong as if he'd touched her. As he moved back to kneel between her legs, that same gaze swept across her body, causing tingles to race over her skin. For the first time, the thought of being his mistress in truth filled her head, and with it came a feeling of excitement.

"You are truly beautiful."

She frowned, well aware that her breasts were small, even if slightly bigger since leaving France, and her hips were narrow, not voluptuous like those of the other ladies present. She didn't care that she looked as she did, but she was hardly beautiful. "*Mon ami*, we swore to never lie to each other."

"I do not lie. I know what I see."

His tone, so hard and forceful, surprised her. Maybe he needed spectacles. She was well aware he couldn't hit a bull's-eye with a dagger, though he came close. If he saw her as beautiful, she wouldn't argue. "Then I accept your assessment."

"As you should."

Usually, she would take umbrage with anyone who spoke so to her, but his gaze reflected his true appreciation of her form, and for the first time, she *felt* beautiful. Raising her arms, she smiled softly. "Come. Take me. Make me yours as you promised."

His face changed—a look came into his blue eyes that she

hadn't seen before—but as he lowered himself over her, her attention moved to his body. It was warm and hard, everywhere, making her feel truly delicate. Yet his hand as he brushed her hair away from her forehead was gentle and almost reverent. It reminded her of something, but before she could make the connection, his lips found hers in the gentlest of kisses.

She sighed, unable to help herself. There was something special that such a strong man could be so gentle. She did not *need* gentle, but she did like it on occasion, and this was definitely the occasion. Wrapping her arms around him, she kissed him back, enjoying the softness of his firm lips and the expansion of his chest as he breathed deeply.

He lifted his head and looked directly into her eyes. "I'm going to love you now."

Her heart hitched at his words, though she was quite sure he meant he would love her body. She had no time to question him as he lifted his hips and probed her entrance. Without thought, she widened her legs, bringing her knees up to welcome him. Her feelings were jumbled, but her body knew what it wanted. It wanted Anthony.

His entrance into her took all coherent thought away as he spread her, moving slowly inside until he could go no farther. If his goal was to make her his, he definitely did. There was so much of him that she felt as if she couldn't move. It was an unusual feeling, but it sensitized every inch of her body, even to the point that the hair from his chest against her nipples sent ripples of exhilaration to her very center.

She'd never been so sensitized after experiencing *la petite mort*. Yet here she was, on the verge of release, and he'd only just entered her.

He lifted his head, moving his chest from hers just a bit. "Am I too much?"

Her heart melted, and she lifted her hand to his cheek. "*Non. Just right.*"

As if he'd been prepared for a different answer, his hips relaxed into her, moving him just a bit deeper and causing a thrill that shocked her.

"I'm relieved. You feel so good that I don't want to move, but I also want to."

She understood exactly what he meant. So she lifted her head, which caused her sheath to contract about him. She whispered softly, "Move."

His body stiffened all around her, and she lowered her gaze to see his face taut with need. Then he moved, and what a glorious move it was. He pulled out to his tip then slowly came back into her.

Her body lit like the sky in a lightning storm. His controlled movements heightened her pleasure just a bit at a time until she wasn't sure she could take any more. She grabbed on to him, silently reaching for her peak, wanting him there with her. On his next stroke, he pulled back only to rush forward, rocking her body and sending her into the heavens.

She screamed as light seemed to burst through her like a sun. Another thrust and he found his own release inside her, which made the sun bigger, hotter, expanding her pleasure until it was beyond her, in her, around her, heating her until she burst into a million shards of ecstasy.

And there it was again, but so much bigger, so much stronger, *la petite mort*. She floated, not sure which way was up or down, but not caring as Anthony's arms wrapped around her, holding her tight to him, keeping her safe as he always did.

She held him against her heart, feeling tears at the edges of her eyes with no idea why except that she was happy, blissful. Never had she felt so satisfied and content. The thought had her searching her memories, but as much as she sought another time, there was none like this.

"Lissa?"

"Hmm." She couldn't seem to get her mouth to form any words yet. Her whole body felt as if she'd melted like ice in the spring.

His chuckle reverberated through her, sending off tiny sparks of delight.

"*Non.* Don't move," she managed.

"Well, we will have to eventually."

She meant to shake her head, but had no strength to do so. "Not yet."

He didn't respond for a long time, and she found herself drifting into sleep.

"You're mine now." His whispered words echoed in her head, forcing her to pay attention.

"*Oui.* And you're mine." And he was, at least for their stay. And then? Her contentment vanished. He'd promised to find her a husband, but she no longer wanted one. Could she possibly convince him to keep her as his mistress?

Even as the possibility presented itself, she knew it couldn't be. What would the duchess think, not to mention the men for whom Anthony worked? He may not need the money, as she had thought, but he needed the adventure.

That meant they only had the weekend before she would lose him. At that thought, she turned her head and licked at his ear.

"So you are awake." His voice was filled with good humor.

"I am. I'm simply enjoying—"

A knock at the door interrupted her.

Anthony lifted himself onto his elbows. "It must be the valet."

She'd forgotten they'd told him to come back. "Just send him away again."

"I would very much like to." He sighed. "I would like nothing more than to stay in here with you for the afternoon."

She winked. "That's sounds interesting. After all, we have yet to use these manacles." She reached above her head and to the left, where one was tucked beneath the pillow, and pulled it out.

Anthony's nostrils flared at the sight, and she was quite sure she would receive her wish.

But the man was far stronger than she, and he shook his head. "Not now. Maybe tonight. We must make use of this time when

Leighhall allows us to explore his house for places to enjoy each other. If you like, we could do that once we find the second entry to the weapons room."

Another knock sounded. "My lord."

Anthony looked at her with longing then pulled out of her. "One moment."

She felt lost at his exit, completely uncomfortable with such a feeling. As he rose from the bed, she covered herself. Irrationally, she felt irritated that he would leave her even knowing their investigation was critical to her dear friend's future.

As he walked across the room to the door, she found herself watching him, or rather his taut arse. She remained in bed as the valet entered and dressed Anthony, slowly reasoning herself out of her pique. Or maybe it was watching Anthony getting dressed that had her mood improving.

Once he was dressed, the valet headed for the door.

"Wait." Anthony moved across the room to her pile of wet clothing.

Tired of waiting for the valet, she'd cut her dress to get out of it, not wanting to waste a minute so she could get Anthony divested of his own clothes and into the hot tub and warmed up.

Anthony handed the valet the clothes. "You may dispose of these."

The valet looked aghast that he must touch her clothes, but did as told and left.

She chuckled, enjoying the fact the valet was scandalized. "I do believe he will be sick."

Anthony turned around and faced her. "I hope that's the case."

That his motivation had been for her had her laughing. "Well done, Lord Baron."

He bowed. "Thank you, mademoiselle." His brows drew together. "I do hope you have something else to wear for our afternoon stroll."

"Indeed, I do." Without warning, she threw back the covers

and languidly rose from the bed completely naked.

Anthony's eyes darkened, but he did not move.

Though she shouldn't, she still enjoyed walking to the armoire and taking her time deciding on a dress, though she only had enough for the weekend. She chose her green dinner dress that she had planned for the following evening because by then there would be no need to worry about what the guests thought of her for wearing it twice, as it would be their final night.

Turning to her trunk, she pulled out dry stockings then walked over to the settee where she'd left her stays. Lifting them from the back, she found them still damp. She refused to dampen another dress. She looked to Anthony, who she'd expected would have turned his back, but he hadn't. Instead, his gaze seemed to devour her from where he stood.

She sucked in her breath before finally shaking her head. "I will have to forgo the stays this afternoon. They are still damp."

He didn't say a word, but his nostrils flared.

Now knowing that he watched her, she found every movement she made, from pulling up her stockings and tying them to slipping into her kid shoes, aroused her. Even twisting her hair into a loose knot once more had her nipples hardening. Lastly, she added a dagger on her thigh. The dress had short sleeves, so she'd wear gloves to hide another weapon. Finally, she lifted her dress and brought it to him.

He took it, and as she lifted her arms, he settled the dress over her, smoothing it down the front over her breasts and then walking around her to pull it tight. Once it was secure in the back, she made to step away to add her other daggers, but he stopped her, instead taking her hand to bring her in front of the mirror.

Curious, she looked at him as he stood behind her. "Do you wish me to see something?"

"Yes. Look at you."

She did as he requested. Her gown hugged her waist and covered her breasts nicely without the stays to push them up to the scooped neckline.

He wrapped his arms around her. "You are beautiful."

Her chest tightened at his persistence, and she gave him a soft smile. Then she turned in his arms and kissed him, letting him know how happy he made her. She broke the kiss before they forgot what they were about and stepped back. "I just need my last daggers and I'll be ready."

Without the stays, she could only slip one in her hidden pocket and one in her glove. She held up a silk choker and gave it to him. "Please."

He tied it loosely, just as she liked it, then held out his arm. "Shall we explore, mademoiselle?"

"To find the perfect place for an assignation? Yes."

He chuckled as he led her from the room, little knowing that she meant exactly what she'd said.

Chapter Fourteen

ANTHONY LED LISSA out of the dining room, where they found a couple having sex on the table, but not before he had a good look at where the china cupboard was located on the wall. If he were correct, there had to be a room beyond the billiard room, which he must not have found on their arrival day.

She squeezed his arm as they started down the corridor. "That was an interesting place for a rendezvous, considering there are no doors."

He glanced down at her to see her grinning. He grinned as well. "Any place makes for a unique experience."

"Even in the dressing room?"

His body immediately heated. "You were in there."

Though he hadn't asked a question, she still nodded. "I believe there is much more I need to learn to truly be a mistress. You will teach me, of course."

He swallowed hard at the thoughts she instigated in his head. "I think we should focus on our place of discovery for this interlude first."

"I was just thinking of in the future, as in tonight."

The shock of desire that hit his groin had him coughing. "Yes, well, it's best not to plan but allow the atmosphere to dictate the terms." Though the atmosphere felt as if it would combust any minute. Even now, walking sedately past the library's closed doors, he wanted to press her to the wall and have her again. He should have never seen her in a dress or undressed or—

He forced his mind back on their task and nodded to the billiard room, where male voices could be heard.

Lissa sighed. "I guess those gentlemen must wait until this evening."

Since her comment started his mind in the wrong direction, he determined he needed her to focus as well. "I did enter the next set of doors, which are the ballroom, as are the set after them. I was hoping there was a room I missed, but we are almost to the end."

"Is there no other corridor? If not, the weapon room may well be off the ballroom."

That was a possibility, but if so, that would be very public when there was a ball. As they approached the end of the corridor, they could go no farther. "It appears we will need to search the ballroom, as you suggested."

They turned around and walked to the set of double doors. Opening one, he hoped the room would be unoccupied.

Lissa preceded him. "It's not particularly large, though it could take us a while."

He stepped to the right and viewed the entire room. She was correct—it was small for a ballroom, but checking every inch of wall would take quite some time. "I don't see another china cabinet or even bookcase in here that might be an entrance."

Lissa wandered into the middle of the room, the light from four sets of French doors illuminating the space. She slowly turned. "I imagine dancers escape to that terrace in the middle of events."

He strode across the empty room and looked out. The angle was wrong for a secret room to be connected. "I don't think we'll find what we're looking for in here. It's the wrong layout."

She looked at him over her shoulder. "But not if it's off that room." She pointed to her right, and he strode past the column in his line of sight.

She was already heading for the single door with a walnut doorframe much like in the rest of the house. Before he could reach her, she opened the door. "Oh."

When she didn't move inside, he quickened his pace. "What is it?"

"I believe this is where all the married men hide during a ball."

"Hide?" He stepped inside and to the right to examine the room. Though there were no windows, the sunlight from the ballroom was enough to see the interior. It was covered in pale green wallpaper with no design. On the walls hung a number of stuffed animal heads, a coat of arms, and two paintings of hunting dogs. Though smaller than the parlor, it boasted a large fireplace, at least a dozen wingback chairs, end tables, card tables, and a sideboard with a variety of liquors. "Yes, I imagine this would be the place to hide."

She stepped across the wooden floor toward a cabinet of rifles. "And look. I wonder if some of these were used on them." She waved her hand toward the animal heads on the walls.

He was less interested in what they were used for than in what they might be hiding. If he weren't mistaken, the wall with the gun cabinet could be the one for the secret room. Walking over, he began to run his hand along the side of the cabinet.

Lissa didn't say a word. Instead, she moved to the other side and began to feel along the wall as well.

He froze when his fingers encountered metal.

As if she sensed his excitement, she stopped. "You found it?"

He nodded then pushed down on what felt like a lever behind the cabinet. Immediately, there was a click.

Lissa walked over to stand next to him. "Now what?"

Studying the area, he saw there was only one way it could move, so he pushed. The whole gun case slid to the right, revealing a door.

"We found it." Lissa's whisper was filled with excitement as she grabbed on to his arm.

"I believe we did. Shall we check?"

Nodding excitedly, she let go of his arm and nudged him forward.

He turned the nob, expecting it to be locked, but it moved and the door opened inward to inky blackness. "We'll need a lantern."

"There must be one in here. Let's—"

The sound of the ballroom door opening interrupted her, and he quietly shut the secret door.

Without a word, Lissa tiptoed back to him, and they moved the silent gun case back into position. Just as he steeled himself for the click, Lissa let out a moan.

"Oh, Anthony, *mi amour.*"

He pulled her into his arms as a shadow blocked the light into the room. "I must have you." He lowered his head to her neck, undoing the tie at the back of her dress, waiting for the person to interrupt. When they didn't, he kept going, lowering her dress a bit and kissing her chest. *Ballocks.* He forgot she wore no stays. What was the person waiting for?

"Wait." Lissa's voice sounded breathless as she grabbed his shoulders.

He stopped. "But I can't." He hoped he sounded desperate, though anger was riding him hard.

"Please, Anthony. Someone is here."

He looked over his shoulder as if he hadn't known they had company. "Lord Leighhall." Quickly, he lifted Lissa's dress to cover her bare chest. "I didn't know you were there."

The man took a couple steps into the room. "I'm not surprised. I can see you were otherwise occupied." Though Leighhall spoke to Anthony, he continued to look at Lissa.

Quickly, Anthony tied the back of Lissa's dress before stepping around her. "I apologize if you didn't wish us in here."

Leighhall finally moved his gaze. "Not at all. Any room is open to you except other bedrooms." The man waved his finger. "I allow no orgies unless I'm invited."

"We don't participate in orgies." Lissa's voice was firm. "I do not allow another woman to touch my Anthony."

Leighhall's eyes fixed on her gloves. "No, I don't suppose you do. Why are you wearing gloves? It is not required at my house parties."

Lissa used her left hand to pull up her right glove. "As it happens, my Anthony likes the feel of silk on his—"

"Since you need this room, we shall continue our exploration of your beautiful home. You are indeed a most gracious host." Anthony glanced at Lissa, who appeared completely innocent in what she'd been about to say.

"I just came in to retrieve a couple of guns. Pemberton and I were having a bit of a debate."

Lissa visibly shivered. "Guns? I do not like them. They killed my family."

Leighhall's eyebrows rose. "My dear, if you had your eyes open, you would see there is an entire case of them." He pointed behind her.

Lissa turned to look. "Oh." Quickly, she turned back and pressed her forehead against his arm. "Take me away from here. I cannot bear it."

Anthony held her close and gave Leighhall an apologetic shrug. "I think it best we find another room in which to play." Leading Lissa past the man, he continued out the door before crooning to her, "I'm here. We shall find someplace else. I promise we won't go in there again." He continued until they had left the ballroom and headed for the stairs.

When he felt her shaking, he grew alarmed and stopped. "Lissa, what is it?"

She lifted her face, chuckling. "I don't suppose we should tell our host that I'm a crack shot."

Relieved, he shook his head. "There are many things we won't be telling our host."

"And there's much he's not telling us. We need to get back in that room."

He continued to lead them to the stairs. "Yes, we do. Maybe tonight, after all are asleep."

"That's a good plan. And that gives us time to enjoy the afternoon in another room, like maybe the dressing room?"

His body reacted at her suggestion, but he refused to be distracted. "No, it's a good time to rest so you are awake when everyone is asleep."

She gave him her perfected pout. "I'll never be able to sleep."

"Then I suggest you read. I will be rejoining the men after a little more exploration."

When they reached the top of the stairs, she dropped her hand from his arm and strode purposefully toward their room. "Exploration? Surely, I can help with that."

Despite enjoying her company, he didn't wish to risk her again. She meant too much to him. "Nothing exciting. Just the rooms I haven't explored yet."

"Oh. Very well." She remained silent until she reached the door. She opened it, stepped inside, and halted, immediately turning to face him. "You said you were concerned that Leighhall is a great friend of the regent and therefore untouchable."

He quickly closed the door behind him, moving to his travel trunk and opening it. "Yes. My fear is that if he is such a good friend, no matter what we discover about him, it won't make a difference. I've never failed at providing my client with what they need, but if Leighhall is so well favored, there will be nothing to stop him from ruining Lady Harewood's reputation."

"Then why hide the weapons? If he truly is so protected, why not display them? He had the gun case in that small room. What's different about the ones in his weapon room that he won't show anyone, nor even let any servant in to clean it?"

Even as she made her point, hope rose in his chest. "That's true. But we don't know that he doesn't allow a servant in. You only heard that through rumor." He rummaged through his shaving case to pull out three keys, pocketing them before closing the trunk.

She wrinkled her nose before turning and walking further into the room, pulling off one of her gloves. "That's true. It was terribly clean, from what I noticed. I could see that burly butler being allowed in. He looks as if he'd die protecting Leighhall."

"Still, your point is sound. Why not display such a unique collection?"

She pulled off her other glove, palming her dagger. "Are they illegal here in England?"

He'd asked that very question of Mr. Stochbury at Talley on the Green, and at the time, none of the ones he knew of were outlawed, just out of use.

At the thought of Stochbury and his promise to introduce Lissa to the man, he stiffened. How could he possibly keep that promise now?

"Anthony?"

"Yes?" He found her standing by the bookcase. He'd completely lost track of their conversation.

"I asked if any of those weapons were illegal here in your country."

"No. So again, why hide them? They are of no particular value."

She pulled a book from the shelf and turned back to face him. "Then maybe they are stolen?"

Her explanation made the most sense, but even then, the regent would protect the viscount unless he'd stolen them from the king himself, which was unlikely, since the king had little interest in weapons. Now, the regent *did* enjoy collecting weapons, which only made the connection between the two men that much stronger. "That may be the case, but even then, it would not be enough to keep Leighhall at bay." He turned back toward the door. "I'm going to search his rooms. Maybe I'll find something there that will aid us in our quest."

"Are you sure you don't wish me to accompany you? I may notice something you don't."

Even as she said the words, he had to tamp down a harsh

refusal. He'd seen the way Leighhall's gaze had latched on to Lissa. The last place he wanted her was in the man's bedroom. "No, it's better that I go. If we are both caught there, we will have broken one of Leighhall's rules about exploring other bedrooms. It would not go well for us, I'm sure."

She cocked her head as if trying to find another excuse to leave with him, but finally she sighed. "Very well. You go." She waved him toward the door. "I shall see what folly Lady Fancy falls into."

"I'll look forward to hearing all about it." He opened the door before the actual acts that might be described in such a book had him halting. "Or maybe not." He quickly stepped out to the sound of her laughter.

What was he going to do about Lissa? Even as he walked toward the stairs, he tried to answer that question, but as he crossed the landing and moved up the steps to the other corridor of bedrooms, he didn't have an answer.

A doorway opening behind him had him plastering himself against the wall. As Maria and her benefactor strolled toward the staircase, he let out his breath. Now was not the time to be musing over Lissa. He needed to be alert in case Leighhall or the man's valet decided to go to his room.

After the couple descended the stairs, Anthony moved quickly to the last door on the right. He tried turning the knob, but it was locked. Taking a ring of three skeleton keys from his waistcoat pocket, he inserted one into the lock. It took a few minutes and the second key, but finally there was a soft click and he turned the knob, slipping into the room.

Turning around, he found the bedroom appointed like any other viscount's. Its wallpaper was gold with trees and bushes. The four-poster bed curtains were a dark-golden velvet, and the window curtains, which were partially open, illuminated two chairs at a small table on one side and a wingback chair before the fireplace. There were two armoires and a chest of drawers as well as a table for shaving.

Moving toward the bed, he found no manacles or devices, but that wasn't what he searched for. On the bedside table there was a note, and he quickly unfolded it. It was nothing more than Leighhall's mother informing him of her next visit. Studying the room, he saw nothing untoward about it, and everything was in its place except for the note.

He walked around the bed past a full-length mirror to a door, which most likely led to a dressing room and then another bedroom for the future lady of the manor.

Opening the door, he froze in shock. He swallowed hard at the apparatus inside.

Manacles hung from two poles that would have all but the tallest of women on their toes. Two more were anchored to the floor. On a table nearby lay a whip, a quirk, and screws. None of which would have been so alarming if not for the dried blood on all of them, including the manacles. This was no pleasure room. It was a torture chamber.

Hearing movement behind the door to the connecting room, he quickly backed out and softly closed the door. Unsettled by what he'd seen, he strode to the exit. Just as he reached for the door, a giggle could be heard in the corridor outside. Leaning his ear against the wood panel, he listened. Soft conversation ensued, making him itch to leave, but he couldn't be seen leaving Leighhall's room. He glanced toward the closed door of what should have been the dressing room, expecting it to open at any moment.

Finally, in the corridor a door opened, but it did not shut, and giggles turned to moaning. If the couple were having sex in their doorway, Anthony would have to risk it, because he refused to stay in Leighhall's room for one more minute. Carefully, he cracked open the bedroom door. As he'd guessed, a couple had opened the door to their room, but never shut it. Slipping into the corridor, he relocked the viscount's bedroom then strode forward.

As he reached the doorway, he found Violet bent over the

foot of the bed as Buswick pumped into her. Softly, he walked past and to the stairs.

Anthony hadn't expected Leighhall to be as dangerous as he now knew him to be. All he wanted was to take Lissa and leave. Every instinct inside him was telling him they weren't safe.

As he headed back toward his room, he contemplated his options. If he left, Lady Harewood's reputation may well be forfeit. If he didn't, then Lissa could be hurt.

His protective instincts rose hard. They would leave. He just needed an excuse.

He opened the door, and Lissa looked up from her book. She'd taken her hair down, and it fell half behind her and half over her left shoulder. How could he have not realized how beautiful she was in addition to her cleverness and courage?

"Were you not able to enter any other rooms?"

He closed the door and leaned back against it, not sure how to explain his need to keep her safe.

She set the book down and stood. "What is it? Did you hear something?"

"No." He wouldn't lie, nor would he tell her what he saw. "But I now know that Leighhall is indeed a dangerous man."

She walked toward him, her brow furrowed in concern, before setting her hand upon his arm. "We had guessed that, especially with the practice wall in his weapons room."

He hadn't thought twice about the practice wall for weapons, but then again, he didn't actually see it, as his lantern had not revealed it. That it existed had his stomach tightening. "I believe we should leave."

"Leave? But we haven't found what we need. We can't leave. Dory needs us to find something. I'm sure once we get into the weapons room tonight, we will have all that we need. Did you find anything in Leighhall's bedroom that will help?"

"No. But it may be too dangerous to enter Leighhall's secret room again. I will just have to tell Lord Harewood that I couldn't find anything."

Her dark-brown eyes studied him. "Anthony, I haven't seen you this tense since the time those three men caught us in the stables of Comte de Lancey."

Unwittingly, she'd given him a way to explain. "This is much like that. There is great danger to you here. Like then, I need you to be safe."

She frowned. "But at that time you needed me safe so I could fetch the coachman while you provided a distraction. Do you feel I will need to run to the stables for your coachman?"

He curled his hands into fists and walked away from her touch. He wanted to tell her how he felt about her, but he couldn't. She wouldn't understand, perhaps perceive him differently, possibly as a threat to her future plans. She definitely did not want a peer as a husband.

Even as the thought surfaced, he understood exactly how much she meant to him. He'd broach that quandary if and when the time made it possible. First, he needed her to agree to leave. "I'm quite sure we will need my coachman, but only to drive us away from here."

She wrinkled her nose and set a hand on her hip. "I do not think it wise to leave now. We need to try one more time to see what we can discover in the weapon room. Then, if you like, we can leave tomorrow. But we will need a good excuse."

He didn't want to leave tomorrow, but his instinct told him that telling her he loved her and needed to protect her would do the opposite of what he hoped. "Very well. We will try once more, but then we leave. No information is worth dying for."

Her eyes widened before she nodded in understanding. "You must have found something for such a change in plans. What did you find?"

"Blood."

Her face drained of color, and he cursed himself for revealing the truth. He knew how much she feared blood. He strode across the room and held her to him. "I should not have told you."

She lifted her head from his shoulder. "No. I asked and you

did not lie. That is very important to me." She cocked her head. "It is best I know, so I am better prepared."

One moment he forgot how delicate she was, and the next he was reminded how strong she could be. He cupped her head and kissed her with all the possessiveness he felt.

She matched his passion, pulling herself closer as she opened to him.

The need to claim her again ran up his spine, and he quickly untied the back of her dress to splay one hand over her bare back and down to the curve of her small buttocks.

She arched toward his hand, offering him her arse.

The need to possess her heart, soul, and body grew stronger until her hand found his hard erection and squeezed him through his pantaloons. He growled before bending her back and slipping his fingers between her legs, moisture greeting him. "I want you again."

She let out a raspy chuckle. "And I want the sling, so I say we agree."

He froze, his body practically pulsing, demanding he take her. He took a deep breath, refusing to rip her clothes from her body. He wasn't sure if she meant to be a temptress or if she wasn't aware of what she did, but he had to stay in control.

Removing his fingers, he withdrew his hand from her dress.

Her moan of disappointment echoed through his groin, but he forced himself to set her back enough to look her in the eyes. "Have you ever experienced a sling?"

She shook her head. "You'll have to teach me how it works, probably with a number of other items in that dressing room."

He swallowed hard as the images of the items he had seen in the room flew through his head, making his body reverberate with need.

She sauntered by him, her dress slipping past her shoulders, catching on her hard nipples. "But I was most curious about that sling."

He couldn't hold back any longer and rushed her, throwing

her over his shoulder like Pemberton had done to Alice on the stairs. He strode to the dressing room door and had opened it when a knock sounded on the bedroom door. "Go away." His words were barely discernible with the predatory growl in his voice.

"A package from Lord Leighhall, sir."

He halted, the heat in his loins disappearing faster that a thin sheet of ice on a pond on a sunny spring day. Lissa didn't move either. Slowly, he put her down, and she pulled her dress up to cover herself. They stared at each other for a moment.

She gestured toward the door to the corridor. "We should probably see what it is."

He agreed, but couldn't quite get his voice to work, yet his body cooled so quickly as to almost make him shiver. Without saying anything, he turned and walked to the door as if he'd find a live snake curled up outside. Opening it, he looked about to see no one was there, but a bundle wrapped in brown paper sat on the floor.

He glanced down the corridor to see other packages. If every guest received one, then it must not be anything dangerous. Picking it up, he brought it inside and set it on the settee.

Lissa peered over his shoulder. "What is it?"

"I don't know, but every guest received one."

She breathed out heavily before plopping down on the settee next to the package. "In that case, let's see what it is. Maybe it's something for tonight's activities."

She was right, of course, and he admonished himself for his abundance of concern. Untying the wrapping, he lifted the note. *For the bacchanalian celebration on our last evening. Please enjoy your costume and come prepared for a carnal experience fit for the gods. Of course, we will need a maiden to be sacrificed to those fickle deities. L*

The image of Leighhall's dressing room immediately came to mind.

"I'm sure he doesn't mean a real sacrifice." Lissa peeled back layers of the brown paper. "He did say *carnal*, so I imagine we will have some final sexual show."

Even as she lifted the white toga from the folded pile, he couldn't agree with her. His only hope was that Pemberton, Buswick, and Rothbury would never come back if such sacrifices were the norm.

"I do believe this is rather short." She handed him the toga. "Do you think that's mine?"

He held the white garment against him. "I hope so. It barely covers me."

"I don't know. I think it quite fetching." She reached into the paper. "Especially with this gold leaf circlet." She held it out to him. "See if it fits."

He took the gold-painted wreath and set it on his head.

She laughed. "I do believe that's your costume."

He did not find it humorous at all. "What else is in there?"

She lifted a sheer crepe toga with a golden rope belt from the package. "I hope there is more to this." She pulled out two gold metal circles and frowned. "Do you think these are for the shoulder?" She clipped one to the material.

He swallowed at what she was expected to wear, the tension in his lower abdomen already affecting him. Leighhall obviously knew exactly what would make his guests excited. The gold medallions were meant to clip to her nipples, the sheer material showing every other part of her body. Almost afraid to know, he still asked, "Is there anything else?"

"I don't think so." She shook out the paper, and a gold chain fell to the floor. She lifted it, showing it had a small white piece of silk attached to part of it. "Is this for my head?"

Gritting his teeth, he took the chain from her and held it out with two hands. "This material is to cover the front of your pelvis."

She frowned. "But for that to be, the chain in the middle would have to go between—Oh." Her skin flushed. "That seems uncomfortable. And why cover so little there when everything else is visible? It doesn't make sense."

Sometimes he wished she wasn't so analytical. "The gold pieces go on your breasts, not the material."

She picked up one and held it in front of her. "If it's not clipped to the toga, then it would be clipped to my nipple?" Her chest rose suddenly, as if the thought stimulated her.

He simply nodded.

She laid out the sheer toga on the settee and added the metal undergarments beneath it. "I might wear this in here, but I refuse to wear it before anyone else."

"I wouldn't allow you to."

Her gaze snapped to his. "Wouldn't *allow* me? That is not your place."

It wasn't difficult to see her dander was up. Instead of arguing the fact that he was responsible for her, he held up his own toga against himself. It would barely cover his private parts, and that only if he didn't get an erection. It also draped from one shoulder down to his hip, leaving half his torso exposed. "Would you allow me to go below before everyone like this?"

She opened her mouth to answer then snapped it shut. Instead, she shook her head, folded up her costume, and laid it on the settee. "I can't believe he thinks we would wear these."

He handed her his toga, quite sure that Leighhall expected all his rules to be obeyed, which meant he had to get Lissa off the property before tomorrow evening. "I suggest we get some rest before dinner. We will have a long night."

CHAPTER FIFTEEN

LISSA FOLLOWED ANTHONY as he led the way down the dark corridor toward the ballroom. They'd had to wait until after five in the morning before Pemberton and Alice had said goodnight to Leighhall. The sun would be up in less than an hour, so they needed to find something quickly.

She almost wished they could stay for the bacchanal now that she'd discovered all the women were spending the morning hours in the parlor making changes to their costumes. Delilah said that Leighhall always sent revealing costumes for the last night, and they always modified them. Maybe if Anthony found something, she could convince him to stay.

At the first set of doors to the ballroom, he stopped and slowly opened one so they could slip inside with no noise at all. Thankful she'd worn her maroon evening dress for its lack of decoration and dark color, she stood in the dark, cavernous room as he closed the door behind them. How could he see in the almost-complete darkness? Luckily, there was a muted light coming in from the terrace doors, no doubt from the moon through the clouds, a sign a storm was rolling in.

Anthony took her hand and led the way to the gentlemen's room then suddenly stopped.

She froze. Had he heard something?

He reached out to what looked like a column, but she'd

didn't remember one being there.

He swore under his breath, which made her look closer. The column was opposite another, which was across from another and another. It was clearly set up for the event later that evening. Each column had rope nailed into it halfway up, with the rest lying on the ground. In the middle of the four columns was what looked like a sideboard that had been covered in a tablecloth. As the purpose for the setup became clear, she shivered.

The carnal sacrifice. Did Leighhall really believe one of them would allow themselves to be tied onto that sideboard?

The answer came swiftly. He did.

Anthony tugged her forward, and soon they were before the gun case. She could only tell because her hand touched the glass. Anthony handed her the lamp he carried and went about finding the hidden latch. The click was the only sound as the case moved across the floor.

She felt his hand reach for hers, and she grasped it as he pulled her forward into absolute darkness.

He closed the door before using flint and tinder to light the lantern she held. Once there was light, they moved toward the desk.

He lit the larger lantern. "I want to see the rest of the room before reviewing these papers. Can you get into the locked drawers?"

She grinned and pulled a hairpin from her hair. "I can."

He leaned forward and kissed her briefly, then turned and moved along the wall, studying the weapons.

Immediately, she set the small lantern on the desk and bent over the top drawer. After inserting her hairpin, it took but seconds before she heard the tiny click. Opening the drawer, she found more letters, but left them to work on the next locked drawer.

When she opened that one, she sucked in her breath. It was filled with old gold coins and pieces of jewelry. Did Leighhall collect stolen treasure as well? She and her grandmother could live the rest of their lives with but half of what was there. Glancing up to see where Anthony was, she found him studying the marks in the practice wall.

Quickly, she dropped a few pieces of jewelry into her hidden pockets then filled her hand with gold coins and slipped them into her boots. She grabbed more and stuffed them beneath her breasts and into her stays, thankful once again that her chest was on the smaller size.

"Did you find anything?" Anthony strode toward the desk.

"Indeed I did. Look." She pointed to the open drawer of wealth.

He didn't appear impressed. "Unless that's stolen, that won't help us."

That he could be so unimpressed with such a hoard reminded her that he was from a far different class than her, something that was easy to forget with him. "That drawer over there has more letters."

"This may help." He pulled the drawer completely out and set it on the chair behind the desk to study the letters. The only furniture in the entire room was a few small tables for lanterns.

Now that Anthony had lit a few more lanterns, most of the room could be seen, though a few dark spots still remained. The walls were covered with old weaponry, no two pieces alike. Everything from blades, to guns, to whips, and a few she didn't recognize. They were hung from just above the floor to about twelve feet high.

It would have passed for a room in a museum if it weren't for the blank wall planked in wood. Now that the wall was lit in full, faded figures could be made out on it. Two were sketched, one an outline and one a complete painting. Scratches and holes were all over each figure as well as in the large spaces between them. The open space in the middle would make practicing with the various weapons easy. She shivered. If Leighhall were moderately skillful with even half the weapons, it made him extremely dangerous. Truly understanding Anthony's concern, she moved her attention to the letters on the desk.

Maybe she needed to review the ones about women as well as the ones on weapons. She skimmed the contents of the top letters nearest her. Three were about women and one on a weapon, but then she noticed a pattern in the ones about women. "Anthony, whoever is writing to Leighhall about the ladies he's tupping starts the letters out by being grateful for the information."

Anthony looked over. "What information?"

"It doesn't say. But the signature on them changes. Sometimes it's an elaborate *P* and sometimes it's a plain capital *R*. Another has a small *g*. The handwriting, though, looks the same. Why would someone not sign their name?"

He stepped next to her. "Because he's worried that if the letter falls into the wrong hands, he'll be discovered?"

She met his gaze, anticipation filling her at the prospect of figuring out what Leighhall hid, besides the ancient weapons.

Anthony pointed to another letter. "This one discusses how the claymore will be delivered and hopes it is equal to Leighhall's trouble." He carefully lifted the letter that was on top of the signature. "This one was signed with the plain capital *R*. It sounds like Leighhall is receiving the weapons as gifts for providing information."

Even as Anthony said the words, the content she'd read clicked into place. "That has to be it, but to what purpose?"

"We need to keep reading." He turned back to the letters in the drawer.

With a better idea of what she needed to find, she walked around the desk searching for what kind of information was being provided.

"Ballocks."

At Anthony's vulgar swear, she looked up. "What is it?"

"This one references poison that could be slipped into food."

She widened her eyes. Murder? Suddenly, the villager's comments drifted through her head. *But they do say there is a locked room at Woburn Manor that the lord doesn't allow anyone into, not even to clean it. Some say he does terrible things to his staff in there.*

She looked around her. If people were tortured in the room, they wouldn't be heard. But she'd seen no dried blood. In fact, the room was very clean, with no dust on the weapons and the floor polished to a shine except where scratches from the weapons had marred it. Someone other than Leighhall was allowed inside. But none of that related to poison, or rather, not directly. "Poison is another weapon that causes death."

"True. Keep searching."

She returned her attention to the papers scattered across the desk. She'd just read a phrase commending Leighhall's loyalty when a noise came from the china cupboard door. She snapped her gaze from it to Anthony, apprehension skittering up her spine. It could be the staff beginning the day, or it could be Leighhall! She pointed to the lantern and mouthed, *Light.*

Anthony immediately reached for it as she raced to the other side of the room to douse the other three. She had two of the three out when the door started to open. Quickly, she extinguished the last before crouching down to the floor, having seen Anthony do the same behind the desk.

Unfortunately, light flooded the room as Leighhall stepped inside followed by his butler.

"Who dares come in here?" The viscount's fury was clear in his tone. "Show yourself. Now!"

Hoping Anthony wouldn't listen, she clasped the dagger in her pocket and slowly rose.

"You!" Leighhall strode forward, and the rage in his eyes had her taking a step back.

His expression changed from anger to calculation in an instant. "You doxy. How did you get in here?"

Knowing his opinion of women, she cowered, hoping to lessen his anger. "I was just getting a closer look at the china. I wanted to see who made it. When I set it back, I must have hit something, because the cupboard opened." She took another step back and hunched her shoulders, making herself as small a threat as possible.

Leighhall stopped in front of her, his gaze moving over her as if he were deciding what sexual position he'd like first, or what part of her body he would torture. She couldn't be sure which.

Grasping the dagger in her hand harder, she lowered her gaze in submission, but as she did, she caught a glimpse of Anthony crawling behind the butler.

Leighhall's finger raised her chin, but she kept her eyes lowered so he wouldn't see the disgust at his touch. "The door to this room is locked, my dear liar."

She snapped her gaze up to his and widened her eyes, shaking her head and dislodging his hand. "No, I swear. It was unlocked. I locked it once I came in." She looked away toward the butler as Anthony rose behind the man. Quickly she brought her gaze to Leighhall's again. "When I saw the weapons, I grew fearful. I don't like guns." She shivered.

A loud *thwap*, followed by a thump, had Leighhall turning to find the butler on the floor and Anthony standing there with a battle axe in his hand.

For a moment, he looked like a vengeful Viking to her, which she fully appreciated. But then she moved to get away from Leighhall.

How the man could turn and react to Anthony's presence yet still reach out and grab her arm, she wasn't sure, but his deadly quickness told her much about her opponent. "Now it makes sense."

"Let her go."

Leighhall laughed. "No. I want to know who sent you."

Anthony's brow furrowed as if he didn't know what the man spoke of. "No one sent me. I came here because I admired you, but in the span of two days I have discovered you are hardly one to be admired."

"You can drop the lie. You're here to stop me, but you can't. Everything is in motion, and you, and she"—Leighhall tugged

Lissa toward him, holding her against his chest—"will quietly disappear." The man chuckled. "Of course, I will have some fun with her first, but alas, you will not be alive long enough to watch."

She'd thought Anthony looked like a Viking before, but now his gaze grew intense, almost glowing like an avenging angel's. She felt Leighhall shift his weight as if expecting Anthony to attack. The slight movement gave her the space to pull her dagger from her pocket. Thrusting backward, she felt it sink deep between the man's ribs as his hold loosened.

Pulling out of his grasp, she spun, making the mistake of looking at the damage she'd done. Blood seeped through Leighhall's white shirt, and she froze.

"You bitch!"

She jumped at the rage in his voice, which allowed her to step further away, though she couldn't take her eyes from the blood. She heard Anthony's footsteps advancing across the floor.

Spinning around, Leighhall unhooked a crossbow from the wall before turning and aiming it at Anthony.

Her heart shuddered, breaking her trance. She reached for a weapon on the wall next to her, lifting a chakram from its hook, and sent it hurtling through the air just before Leighhall released the arrow. Her weapon hit his arm as he loosed the arrow, which buried itself into the wall far from Anthony.

She had but a moment of relief. "Anthony, behind you!"

The butler swung a claymore at Anthony, who turned in time to block it with his battle axe.

Leighhall threw down the crossbow and turned on her. Without a word, he pulled a broadsword from its mount, the metal screeching as it slid from its hooks.

She ran to the other side of the room and lifted from the wall a curved saber, a weapon she knew well.

Leighhall halted, no doubt surprised by her action. Then an evil grin twisted his lips and he pulled the sword breaker from the wall, advancing on her while the sound of Anthony's weapon clashing with the butler's filled the room.

She swallowed hard. The chance the saber would break was slim, but if her blade was caught, he'd have her. Keeping her gaze away from the blood soaking the man's shirt, she focused on his sword.

His first hit ran up her arms with its strength. She may know how to wield a saber, but having a trained man attacking her with a broadsword would wear her strength down in minutes. The sounds of weapons clashing told her Anthony was occupied, so she'd have to fend for herself, just as she had in France before meeting him. She moved deeper into the shadows, the two lanterns Leighhall and his butler had set on tables near the door giving limited light.

"You can't hide from me, trollop."

She cringed at his words, not because they were crude but because of the sheer hate within them. Saving her strength, she didn't respond, keeping her gaze fixed on his sword. As it descended toward her, she brought her own blade up, deflecting his and using the momentum to spin about and into an even darker area. Her maroon dress would make her a difficult target.

Leighhall paused, clearly perplexed. "Who are you? Are you a spy for the queen?"

She just shrugged, not willing to divulge anything.

He advanced again. She backed up farther, but her retreat was halted by the door she'd entered through.

Leighhall grinned. "It's a pity I won't be able to enjoy you first, but you are far too dangerous to keep."

He brought the sword up with two hands and swung down.

She braced for the impact, but it didn't come as Anthony tackled Leighhall from the side, dislodging the sword from his grasp.

Relief flooded her and tears of thankfulness itched the back of her eyes, but as the two men rolled back the other way, the flash of the sword breaker caught the light.

Anthony held no weapon and fought to keep the sword

breaker from his body.

Ignoring the prone butler, she searched the wall for something she could use to help. She didn't dare let loose a dagger when they changed positions so quickly. She also wasn't sure she could stomach more blood.

Her gaze lit on a shield. Raising herself on her toes, she struggled to get the heavy shield loose. Finally, she jumped and hit it, knocking it from the wall. The noise was ignored by the two men bent on killing each other.

Grabbing up the heavy shield, she waited. As the two rolled closer, she could see the sweat on Anthony's forehead. Watching the sword breaker come so close to his throat had her hands sweating, making it that much harder to hold the shield.

She couldn't let her emotions cloud her actions. That was weakness. Fortifying her resolve, she waited for the right moment.

And then it came.

Leighhall was atop Anthony, using his leverage to push the sword breaker down.

She lifted the shield and slammed it against the man's head.

Instantly, Leighhall went limp and Anthony rolled him off. Jumping to his feet, he grasped her to him. "Lissa. My Lissa."

She melted into his embrace, relief causing her to shiver. Never had she been so scared of losing someone, not even in France. She didn't understand it, but she wanted to cry when she should be laughing.

Anthony moved his hands to her shoulders and pushed her back, inspecting her. "You are not hurt?"

She shook her head, even as she noticed a nasty red bump starting to swell on the right side of his forehead.

"Lissa." He cupped her face in his hands and kissed her gently. "We must leave. Now."

She looked at the two prone bodies. "Are they dead?"

He grimaced. "No. And we will not kill them."

She kept silent about Leighhall's stab wound. He might well

die. "Let us go."

He took her hand and headed for the door to the gun case.

"Wait." Breaking his hold, she ran to the drawer on the chair and grabbed a bunch of letters, stuffing them into her hidden pockets. She looked longingly at the drawer of coins and jewels, but time was of the essence.

Running back to Anthony, she took his hand and let him lead her out. Even as the gun case moved back into place with a click, they were silently traversing the ballroom, the light outside proving the sun had risen but was firmly packed behind thick clouds.

Anthony opened one of the French doors to the terrace, and they were hit with cold winter wind.

Without a word, she followed him out and across the gardens to the stable. When they arrived, they found his coachman had started to prepare the coach, but the horses had yet to be harnessed.

Anthony handed her into the coach, which at least kept the wind away. Anxious about the delay, she watched as Anthony helped the coachman connect the horses. Though Anthony had had her pack before going to sleep, they hadn't planned to leave until after breakfast, so their clothes remained in their room. Maybe Leighhall would burn their belongings out of spite.

Finally, Anthony opened the door and joined her, the cold air filling the space. He carried in a wool blanket. "This should help us stay warm until we reach the first inn." He sat next to her, pulling her close to his side, then covered them in the blanket as the coach headed down the drive.

Despite the warmth of both Anthony and the blanket, she shivered, unable to keep from watching out the window, expecting a gunshot at any moment.

"I promise we will obtain feet warmers and more blankets as soon as we get to an inn."

She grasped his hand, still reeling with a mix of emotions like the dancers of the scotch reel. "I'm not cold. Not now. I'm worried."

He squeezed her hand. "Yes, we left a mess behind. Leighhall will hunt us down once he wakes."

"If he wakes." Her words came out in a whisper, but Anthony heard her.

"You're worried about the stab wound."

She nodded, relieved that he was so observant.

"If that butler wakes soon, I'm sure he'll get Leighhall the attention he needs. Which means we must figure out what Leighhall was up to, or we will have no defense against him."

Happy to have her mind on something other than the possibility they were being followed, she ran over the information they had accumulated so far. "We know he was being gifted with weapons, which he appears to be obsessed with."

"I would agree. And we know that he was gathering information from the women he tupped." His mouth quirked up as he said the word.

She grinned, surprised she could after what had just happened. "*Oui*, and you said they were all connected in some way to the king and his family and friends."

"Clearly, Leighhall was spying on the king, but to what purpose? The war with France is over, so I can't see any Frenchman finding the information of any consequence."

She pondered the puzzle of who would benefit from knowing the king's actions. "I understand your king is mad. So who would care what he did or whom he spoke to?"

Anthony stiffened next to her, alerting her that he may have an idea. "What was the signature you noticed on the letters on the desk?"

"There were three. There was an ornate *P*, a capital *R*, and a small *g*."

She waited as Anthony thought. Then his brows rose before lowering once more before he shook his head. "It can't be."

She shifted on the seat so she could face him. "What can't it be?"

"Not what, who. Those initials could stand for Prinny, regent, and George. All the same person."

"That doesn't make sense. Wouldn't the regent already have people reporting to him on his father's activities?"

"Yes, he would, which is why I don't understand. Hopefully, there will be something in those letters you pocketed that will help us put the pieces together. In the meantime, we have to assume Leighhall is acting under the command of the regent, which makes him even more dangerous."

She sat back, trying to imagine a ruler being grateful to the likes of Leighhall. "One letter did praise Leighhall's loyalty."

Anthony leaned back against the seat as well and linked his fingers with hers. "Then there is only one thing we can do to protect you."

She turned her head to look at him. "Protect me?"

"Yes. My dear Daguette, you not only stole those letters, but you stabbed a peer."

A strong foreboding filled her. "I also stole some coins and jewels."

He sat straight again and stared at her in surprise. "Lissa, why?"

She didn't want to tell him. He would object, tell her she would be an outlaw if she followed through on her plan to live independently by committing crimes. But they had promised each other long ago that they would not lie to each other. Seeing no help for it, she answered, "I decided to collect valuables so I could sustain Grand-maman and myself without having to marry. You saw Leighhall's drawer. He had plenty."

As his eyes rounded, she rushed on. "I know what you would say. *Oui*, it is wrong. But *mon ami*, I cannot live under the rule of a man. I need to live, not exist. Even your middle-class tradesmen and lawyers would stifle me." She folded her arms, knowing he'd try to convince her otherwise.

"I know."

"I would rather be a mistress than a w—What?" She unfolded

her arms and stared at him.

"I said, I know. You would be miserable as a wife." His gaze was soft, caring, making her belly feel as if little minnows swam inside her.

"Then you can see why I had to steal."

"I can." He nodded then took a deep breath. "Unfortunately, because you stabbed a peer and stole from him, there is only one way we can save you from going to prison."

"*Oui*, I know. I must hide. I can give you half of what I took and you will take care of Grand-maman. *Non?*"

"No, hiding won't be an option. They will find you. Leighhall is nothing if not thorough."

Her heart skipped a beat and her hands grew clammy. What he said was true. Leighhall would never give up. "*Mon ami*, you must hide me."

"I cannot. There is only one avenue for us to take to keep you out of prison." His gaze was no longer soft, but determined.

When Anthony was determined, he succeeded. She already felt safe. "Tell me."

"We must go to Gretna Green."

CHAPTER SIXTEEN

ANTHONY WAITED FOR Lissa's temper to erupt, but instead she looked blankly at him. "Where is Gretna Green?"

Ballocks. He'd forgotten she wouldn't know. She wasn't raised in England. She hadn't even known that at twenty-one she didn't need her guardian's permission to marry. "It's in Scotland, just over the border. It is not far from my parents' estate and mine."

"I don't understand why going to Scotland will save me. Please explain."

As he studied her, it was clear to him that even if he hadn't fallen in love with her, he would still make the sacrifice for her. He just hoped she wouldn't hate him for long. "Gretna Green is the place couples go to get married to go against their parents' wishes or to avoid the reading of the banns."

Her mouth opened and closed before opening again to speak. "Married? I can't. I just told you I can't. You *agreed* I can't."

Though he knew the odds were not in his favor, he had had the hope that she might at least consider him. "And so I did, because I know you well. I admit that marriage to me would only protect you somewhat, as I am but a baron. However, my father is the Duke of Roxburgh and has much sway."

She wrinkled her nose. "Would he not help me simply because you are his son and I am a friend?"

His gut reacted to her argument, but he tried to keep his hurt at bay. "No. My father, unlike myself, is a traditionalist. He believes in the hierarchy of society. Since you are French and a woman of the gentry, he would feel no responsibility. That you have traveled alone with me and not only caused a peer to bleed, but stole, would have my father calling the magistrate himself."

She looked away, obviously not happy with him. He had no doubt she searched for other solutions to her dilemma. "Would he help you if I were your mistress in truth?"

Again his stomach tightened as if punched. "No. He is faithful to my mother and does not believe a man needs a mistress if he chooses his wife wisely."

Her shoulders slumped. "Is there not another country I could go to? I cannot return to France. As you know, my activities in the past there would have me hanged."

He could listen to no more excuses. He turned her face toward him. "Lissa, would it really be such a terrible life being married to me?"

She blinked as if she'd not thought about the fact it would be him, which did ease him a bit. "No, I suppose it would not be terrible, but I would still be married. You would look at me differently, expect me to conform to what a baroness would do. Truly, can you see me hosting a dinner party at your estate?"

He chuckled, an image appearing in his head of her in male clothing sitting at the other end of the table opposite him with a dozen fancy-dressed guests between them. "No, I can't, but I wouldn't expect you to act the baroness any more than I act the baron."

She cocked her head, finally looking into his eyes thoughtfully. "Would you really do this for me? You told me you would never marry."

In that moment, he almost couldn't keep his feelings at bay, but he swallowed them down hard. "I would do this for you." He couldn't bring himself to say it was because they were friends.

She rolled her lips in, her resistance still in place.

Cupping her chin, he stared into her eyes. "I cannot bear the thought of you in Newgate, buried deep in a squalid chamber with fifteen or so other women, starving or sick with disease. Or worse, trading your charms with a dirty turnkey just to eat. You deserve more."

She looked down, clearly hiding something. Finally, she met his gaze again. "Could I continue to aid you in your investigations?"

Hope surged through him. "If that is what you'd like to do."

"And would you take care of Grand-maman?"

That she was possibly capitulating had his heart racing. "Of course."

She leaned closer, her mouth almost touching his. "And can we get a sling?" Her breath across his lips held his attention before her words registered.

The spike of desire that shot through him would not be denied, and he crushed her to him, taking her lips, demanding she submit.

But Lissa never submitted. Instead, her tongue dove into his mouth, fighting for dominance, even as he felt her hand on his growing erection.

With the need of a dying man for his last breath, he threw off the blanket and pulled her over to sit on his lap facing him, happy to allow her to have her way with him.

She didn't release his mouth, but did release him from his pantaloons beneath her. She finally broke their kiss and rose on her knees to position herself above him.

He expected her to take him inside her, but she remained there looking at him, even as the coach jostled them.

His patience having evaporated with her kiss, he pulled her neckline down to free a hard nipple.

She yanked his head up, surprising him.

"You did not answer my question, *mon amour*."

He tried to remember what she asked, but he couldn't think with her bare, taut peak just inches away.

"Do you promise to get me a sling?"

"By Jove, yes!"

As soon as he agreed, she came down upon him in one hard thrust, almost sending him into his release. He grabbed her waist to keep her from moving as he struggled to stay in control, but the coach rocked them as it bounced along, his driver understanding his need to be away.

She rubbed herself against him even though she didn't lift, and he groaned with his need to let go. Desperate, he sucked on her nipple, teasing it with his teeth, wanting her as ready as he was. If he could just hold on…

His decision was taken from him as the coach hit a particularly deep hole, jolting them both, breaking his tenuous control.

Shouting his release, he heard it echoed by Lissa as she arched hard against him, riding him like a wild horse, matching his fever with her own.

When he was spent, she fell forward onto him, and he wrapped his arms around her even as they hit yet another large hole.

"Oh." Her exclamation was followed by her lifting from him, and he loosened his arms.

He didn't mind, as he completely understood how sensitive it was for her.

She pivoted her body and flopped onto the seat next to him.

He let his head fall back on the seat and turned to look at her. "So your answer is yes?"

Her eyes remained closed as she relaxed into the cushions. She didn't say anything, but her nod had joy filling him. Now, he just had one last monumental task to complete before he could be truly happy—help her see that she loved him.

Doubt crept into his head, but he refused to listen. Surely, over time, she would care for him like he did her.

Yet even as he rebuttoned his pantaloons, the harsh reality of what they were about to do and all the ramifications set in. Lifting the blanket from the coach floor, he spread it over them, already growing cold. His first order of business was to marry her and keep her safe. He would worry about the rest after he'd accomplished that much.

The coach slowed, and he looked out at the gray day to see them pulling into an inn. He had no doubt that either Leighhall followed them himself or his butler, if not others under his employ. A plan took shape even as his coachman opened the door.

Turning to Lissa, he found her asleep and reluctantly woke her. "We're at an inn."

She blinked a few times before gathering the blanket about her. He helped her down then gave instructions to his coachman to continue on to Bellamore without them once he and the horses had rested.

After entering the inn, he ordered hot soup in a private dining room.

Lissa clutched the blanket tight about her, despite the warmth of the room. But once the food arrived, she threw it back and repositioned her dress to hide her assets. "I wouldn't want anyone to have a bad impression of your betrothed." She grimaced as if being betrothed was the worst possible fate, besides prison. "I'd rather be in a warm pair of trousers and greatcoat."

Of course! He should have thought of that. He leaned in and kissed her. "And you will."

"I will?" She frowned at him, clearly puzzled by his exuberance.

"My coach will continue on to my estate, while we take horses to Gretna Green. Stay here and eat your fill." He stood, kissing her one more time, lingering probably longer than was prudent. He pulled himself away and headed out to talk to the innkeeper.

It didn't take long to get the required clothes Lissa needed, along with two good horses. He just wished it wasn't so cold, but the greatcoat would keep her warm and they would stop at another inn for the night. Striding back into the private dining room, he found all the food gone and Lissa pacing.

"What is it?"

She stopped, relief obvious in her face. "I wasn't sure if something had happened to you. You were gone a long time, and this dress makes it unacceptable to go out alone looking for you. Did you find me some clothes?"

"I did." He handed over the pile.

"It will feel good to move freely again." She turned her back. "I will need your assistance once more, my handsome lady's maid."

He forced himself to simply undo the buttons and step away. Knowing they needed to make good time, he turned his back as she dressed. If he watched, he had no doubt he would take her again.

"I'm ready."

He turned to find the youth he'd always known. Yet he knew well the woman beneath the clothing, and he would do anything to keep her safe.

She moved to her discarded clothing and expertly folded everything within the red dress, before tying it into a sack.

"The letters?" He hoped they weren't crushed in her clothing.

She patted the pocket of the waistcoat and the greatcoat. "All here, though folded."

"Do you need me to take some?"

She shook her head. "No. If we're caught, I don't want you to have any, so you can claim you don't know."

Her response eased his heart. That she cared enough about him to want to protect him had hope building. "I promise you, we will not be caught."

"You cannot promise that, Anthony. You can only promise to try to keep us free."

That had been a phrase he used with her many times in France, when she promised she knew the area or that they wouldn't be caught. "You are correct." He gestured and allowed her to precede him out.

Once they were on the road, he set a brisk pace, confident in Lissa's ability to keep it up. Even so, by time they stopped at an inn for the night, she looked tired. The room they shared was sparse and chilly, so they kept their clothes on except for their outerwear, and he fell asleep with her in his arms.

In the morning, he insisted she drink two cups of warm cocoa, despite her readiness to leave. It was as if now that they had a plan, she couldn't wait to execute it. He hoped she wouldn't regret it later.

Luckily, the clouds had dissipated after a cold, rainy night, and the sun made it feel a little warmer. After a couple of hours, they stopped on the side of the road to eat some of their provisions.

"Oh no!"

At Lissa's exclamation, he jumped up from the log he'd been sitting on while she tended to her needs in the woods. "Lissa!"

She tramped through the forest like a charging sheep. "I'm supposed to be back at school today."

He'd completely forgotten. Her limitations in England were far stricter than when they were in France. "You won't be, but at least you'll return married, which will help a bit."

She scowled at him as she waved her hand. "It's not me I'm concerned about. It's Eleanor. She will have to face the duchess alone. She is not good at lying, so she will tell Lady Northwick that I went to visit my grandmother and haven't returned. Then they will send someone to my grandmother."

"If that occurs, it will delay their searching for you anywhere else and give us time to go back and explain."

"Yes, I suppose. But I'm concerned about Eleanor. She will worry. She worries about everyone. She's like a mother hen with her chickens."

He swallowed the last bite of scone and walked his horse closer to hers. "I will have a letter sent to the duchess and Lady Eleanor. You can write whatever you wish to appease everyone's concerns."

She looked askance at him. "Thank you. Though I don't think I'll be able to appease anyone, but then again, that was never my intention." She winked at him before mounting up.

He settled onto his own horse, and they continued north.

Arriving in Gretna Green well after sunset, he found them a room at a decent inn and left Lissa to wash up.

Striding toward the blacksmith shop, the place he was told he could get married, he frowned. The building was dark—as well it should be, since the blacksmith had finished his work for the day hours ago. Still, Anthony knocked on the door. When no one answered, he started to head back toward the inn, nervous that they would need to wait yet another night.

"Looking to get married, lad?" An old man across the road stood outside a croft smoking his pipe.

Anthony changed his path and walked toward the man. "Yes, I was. Will the blacksmith marry us this evening?"

The old man studied him from beneath bushy eyebrows. "Aye, for a price."

"I'd be happy to pay the price. Can you tell me where I can find him?"

"I can do better. You go fetch your lass, and I'll have Mungan meet you over there." He gestured with his pipe toward the blacksmith's place.

"Thank you, sir. I am much obliged."

The old man chuckled. "Any sassenach that comes to our village at this time of night to get married is bound to be besotted. I'm just helping love along."

Anthony smiled. "That I am." Giving the man a short bow, he strode toward the inn.

As he stepped into their room, he found Lissa trying to button the back of her dress. "Here, let me." He stepped up behind her and buttoned the red, very wrinkled dress up to her neck.

She turned around, a self-deprecating smile on her lips. "It's not the height of fashion, nor in good condition, but I thought it better than the trousers."

He spoke without thinking. "I'm not marrying your clothes. I'm marrying you. I will buy you whatever clothing you wish once we're married."

Her smile faltered. "I believe you already bought me, as your mistress, much clothing, like this dress."

He did not want her as his mistress. He never had. She was his friend and now his betrothed. He loved her. He didn't wish her to think of herself in such terms. "True, but only for a part you played in an investigation, much like when you dress as a young man. It does not mean you are one." He held his arm out toward the door, anxious for her to be his. "The blacksmith is even now getting ready for us. Are you ready?"

She took a deep breath and nodded, but didn't say anything as she walked past him.

He opened the door for her, and they descended the stairs to the main floor. The quiet hum of conversation greeted them as they passed by the main dining area and walked outside into the moonlit road.

"It's so quiet." Lissa's words were barely above a whisper.

"Most of the villagers are home after their toils of the day. I'm sure come morning, there will be plenty of activity here."

They approached the blacksmith's, and Anthony could see the old man had been true to his word, as light shone from within. He stopped before the door under the single lantern and faced his soon-to-be wife, taking her hands in his. "Lissa, I know that you are unsure about this step. I promise you, I will do all in my power to care for you and protect you. I don't ever want you to regret marrying me."

Her dark gaze roamed his face. "Long ago, what seems like a lifetime, I thought to marry Etienne. It never happened. The war took him and life became survival. You arrived and became my friend. So much has changed. What that young woman dreamed for then is far different than what I look for from life now. I do know that I can trust you, and that's why I will take this step with you."

The tension in his chest lessened and he kissed her, the woman he loved, the woman he respected, the woman he'd never let go.

When they parted, she smiled at him.

Feeling as if they'd already said their vows, he opened the door and took her inside.

⇛⇚

THE NEXT MORNING, Anthony woke and stretched before reaching out for his wife. The ceremony had been brief, the blacksmith presiding with his wife and the old man from the street present to bear witness. Anthony and Lissa returned to the inn for dinner and consummated their marriage not once, not twice, but three times.

Even with his eyes closed, he smiled. He had a wife. And such a lovely, passionate, and clever one at that.

When his hand found nothing but cold linens, he opened his eyes.

Lissa, in only the shirt from her male clothing, sat at the small table in the warm room, poring over the letters she'd taken from Leighhall.

He sat up, the covers falling to his waist. "Do you not wish to give your new husband a kiss? I promise you can kiss me wherever you wish."

She shook her head and didn't look at him.

Not necessarily insulted but definitely deflated, he threw the covers off and strode naked to see what had her so engrossed. Standing next to her, he could see she had organized the letters into piles on the small table. "What have you discovered?"

She rolled her lips in, holding a letter in her hand as if deciding where it should go. Finally, she set it on her lap, released her lips, and looked up at him. "I think the regent wants to poison the king."

"*What?*" The accusation was regicide and beyond comprehension.

She pointed to one pile. "These are all questions being asked about when and what the king eats and who is with him." She moved her hand to another pile. "These ask about different poisons and how long they take to kill someone." She moved her hand again. "These are letters requesting the names of people who have the skills to enter buildings without detection, and these here are promising gratitude in the forms of weapons and favors."

His stomach felt as if it were filled with lead shot. Hoping she didn't understand the connection between the correspondence, since it was only one-sided, letters received by Leighhall, he pointed to the letter in her lap. "What is that one?"

She held it up for him to take without looking.

Dread filled him as he read a complete plan to poison the king with the help of an agent that Leighhall would hire on behalf of the regent. Not only was his wife in danger, but so was he, and possibly anyone they knew. Leighhall undoubtedly knew they had these letters and would stop at nothing to get them back.

The king!

Never mind their own danger, when was the poison to be fed to the king? This was far more serious than even Anthony had suspected. He'd unknowingly dragged Lissa into a plot against the king's life. "We must leave at once."

"I know." She sounded disappointed, and her shoulders slumped forward as she methodically began to gather the piles of letters together.

Despite the need to hurry, he knelt beside her and laid his hand on her arm. "Tell me what is wrong."

She cocked her head, and her gaze softened. "I had hoped, just for a day, that we could live as a simple couple enjoying each other and celebrating our marriage." Her gaze drifted. "But I think safety, security, and happiness is not my fate."

His heart rebelled at such ideas. With his hand, he gently coaxed her to look at him. "I do not agree with you on your fate. I promise you." He held his hand up as she opened her mouth to no doubt caution him against promising. "I promise you that when all is resolved, we shall return to this very inn and spend a day or two alone as simple folk."

Her attempt at a smile was sad at best and scratched at his heart. "I would enjoy that." She held his gaze for a long moment before returning her attention to the table and slipping her arm from beneath his hand.

He was quite sure she didn't believe he could keep that promise, but he would. Rising, he walked to the washstand, rearranging his plans based on the new information.

He dressed in silence, the weight of their circumstances and that of the country filling his head. He had no doubt Lissa pondered the situation as well, and he could only wonder about what her thoughts were. He hoped none of them included fleeing back to France.

When they gathered their few belongings, they left the room and exited the inn. To any passersby, they appeared to be two brothers, and in no time, they were headed out of the village, at which point he urged his mount into a gallop.

After a while, he eased up on the pace, not wanting to harm the horses, though in his mind, he had already arrived at his father's estate and was organizing what he would say.

Lissa rode beside him, watching the edges of the road as she usually did, always alert to danger.

He counted himself fortunate yet again that he had made her his wife. No other woman had her talents or uniqueness. He would never force her to change. "We should be there in another hour. Do you need to rest?"

She shook her head. "You never told me about your estate. Is it very large?"

Of course, she would expect them to go home. "Bellamore will have to wait. We go to Narborough Park, my father's estate."

She pulled up on the reins so fast that he was a full length ahead before he realized she'd stopped. Turning his horse around, he frowned at her. "What is it?"

"I can't meet your parents."

Befuddled, he brought his mount forward so they faced each other. "Of course you can. You're my wife."

She cocked her head, looking at him as if he should be in Bedlam. "Do I look like a baroness?" She gestured to her trousers.

"No. But won't that be the fun of it?"

Her eyes narrowed. "Anthony, do not tell me you want your parents' first impression of me to be this." Again she gestured to her clothing. "Your father is a duke."

Ballocks. He hadn't thought of the long-term results of their showing up dirty from the road and looking as they did. "It can't be helped. Now that we know what is afoot, we cannot wait."

Her nose twitched. "This is not good. They will never believe I am worthy of you."

"It's not for them to determine your worth. You determine it. In my eyes, you are worthy of a true baron, not a man who eschews his title to roam about the country investigating people."

She sighed, looking away. "You do not understand."

He was sure he did. She wished to look her best for his parents, but she needed to understand that was all it was. "Then help me understand."

Her gaze came back to his, and it sparkled with unshed tears. "They will know me for what I am." She shook her head at him. "I am not worthy of you. I am not from landed gentry. Grand-maman lied to you and Captain Blackmore. That farmhouse where we lived in France was not where we moved to after the mansion was burned. It was the house I grew up in, and my mother before me. I am no more than the child of a farmer and a lady's maid."

Stunned, he stared at her. He always knew Madame Fontaine was a wily woman, so it did not surprise him that she thought to make the most of having saved the captain's life, but for Lissa to believe that her birth made a difference stymied him. She thought of herself as "no more than"? But she was much more. He needed her to understand it didn't matter to him.

No, it wasn't him she truly worried about. It was his parents. Pure happiness filled him, and he grinned at her.

"Are you laughing at me?"

She was so incredulous that he let his mirth out, laughing, even as he shook his head. "I'm not laughing at you. I'm laughing at everyone's assumptions." He cupped her cheek and gazed into her dark brown eyes. "Lissa, my father, the Duke of Roxburgh, married my mother, a shopkeeper."

CHAPTER SEVENTEEN

L ISSA STARED AT the man who was now her husband in absolute disbelief. First, he was middle class. Then he was a peer. Now he was both? "A shopkeeper?"

"Yes. My mother kept a shop much like the one we visited in the village of Talley on the Green, only hers was in the village of Intervale. My father was traveling through and stopped to buy a gift for a woman he was hoping to court." He waved his hand. "It's a long story, and my mother tells it much better than I. Suffice it to say, despite turning him down twice, she finally accepted his proposal." He spread his arms out. "So you see? You do not have to worry. My parents will welcome you, and my father will especially because he'd given up on me ever marrying."

She could admit, if only to herself, that it did make the thought of meeting Anthony's parents a bit more bearable, but just a bit. "Is there other information I should be made aware of before we continue to your parents' home?"

He sobered instantly. "Yes. I told you about the factory accident, so you know what happened. My father gets around on a wooden piece, which is not quite as distracting as my mother's face. She has many scars, much like those from smallpox. When people first meet her, they tend to stare, so if you can avoid doing that, it would go a long way in her accepting you."

Immediately, the tension left her. She could imagine the stares the woman must get. "I can do that."

He looked at her a long moment before nodding. "Yes, you can. Now, we need to get there as soon as possible to confer with my father."

He was right, of course. Even now the king's life could be in danger. "Then lead the way." She held her hand out for him to proceed.

Turning his horse around, he set a fast pace once again.

She didn't mind the pace. Riding slow always made her uneasy, as if she were easy prey, which she would be. Back in France, it was those very people that she'd robbed.

It didn't take long before the forest gave way to rolling hills, far different from those closer to London. As they topped one hill, Anthony slowed to a stop.

She rode up next to him to see a large, sprawling mansion. She knew it was Narborough Park. At the thought of Anthony growing up in such a place, her hands began to sweat. She'd looted places like that, not lived in them.

As if he sensed her unease, he set his hand over hers on the reins. "We're almost there. Don't let the size bother you. They only use one wing now." He let go. "Come. I'll race you to the gate."

Before she could argue, he was off. Immediately, she set her horse to a gallop and gained on him. Just when she thought she was going to win, he pulled ahead before slowing the horse as they passed through the open main gate.

She pointed at him, not willing to look down the drive. "That wasn't fair. You had a head start."

He grinned. "Yes, I did. Now let's get to the house so we can solve this major dilemma."

Very much aware that he had called the race to distract her, she turned to face the massive stone building. Maybe they'd send her around back to the servants' entrance.

As soon as they arrived, two stablemen came to take their

horses, both assuring Anthony they would be well taken care of.

He took her hand and walked her up the five steps to the large wooden door, which opened before he could knock.

"Anthony!" A woman no taller than herself in a blue muslin dress ran out and embraced him, making him stumble back a few steps.

He held her close before setting her back. That was when Lissa saw the deep divot marks on her beautiful face and knew it was his mother. She appeared to have once been blonde, but there was much white in her hair. Her face had few wrinkles and her nose was turned up, making her look like a child. But she was not delicate. She appeared strong, and Lissa could imagine her having to be to keep four boys from misbehaving.

"And who is this you've brought us? Are you still collecting strays?"

Anthony turned rather red at his mother's question.

Lissa quite enjoyed that, so she kept silent, waiting to see what he would say.

"Mother, this is actually my wife in disguise. Your Grace, it is my pleasure to introduce you to my wife, Baroness Bellamore. Lissa, this is my mother."

Belatedly remembering her manners, Lissa curtsied, which felt a bit odd in trousers.

"Wife? Disguise? Oh, I must hear all about this." The woman moved in front of Lissa and took her hands. "My dear, I cannot begin to tell you how happy you have made me." Then she let go of one hand, tucked the other one around her arm, and proceeded to lead them into the house.

As soon as the butler closed the door, Anthony halted his mother. "Where might I find Father? I have urgent business with him."

Lady Roxburgh's brows rose high. "Does this have to do with the disguise?"

"Yes." Anthony seemed to suddenly not know what to do with his hands, as he pulled up his collar then tugged down on his greatcoat.

Lissa found that very interesting. Was he uncomfortable telling his mother about his current profession?

Her Grace waved him off. "He's in the study fiddling, as usual."

Without a word, Anthony headed past the stairs down a corridor, and Lissa found herself alone with his mother.

"Come, let us get you into more comfortable clothes, though truth be told, those look rather freeing."

Her only clothing was still tied to her horse, and if she donned it, she would hardly be presentable. "I'm afraid I have nothing to wear, Your Grace."

The woman waved off her comment and started up the grand staircase, making a show of having to lift the skirt of her dress. "That's of no matter. I have plenty of clothing here, including some from my daughters-in-law. I'm quite sure we can find something that will fit. And do call me Frances, or even Mother if you like. I really have little use for these grand titles."

Lissa found herself frozen on the third stair staring at the woman as tears filled her eyes.

Lady Roxburgh stopped and turned not four steps above her. "What is it, dear?"

Lissa shook her head, trying to understand why the thought of calling the woman Mother made her want to cry. "My mother died when I was twelve. I never thought to call anyone that again." Only by saying it did it make sense, though even so, she wasn't entirely sure it did.

Her Grace descended to where she stood and took both her hands once again. "I would be honored if you would call me Mother, but only if you wish to. And I must call you something other than baroness." Her Grace grimaced as if the title was her least favorite. "What is your given name?"

"My name is Lissette. I'm French." Lissa wasn't even sure why she blurted that out, but it was done now.

"Hmm, I don't know any French. It's a pretty name, but I'm

sure your mum called you that. Would it be acceptable to call you Lizzy?"

Her throat closed at the nickname, one her grandfather had given her. Instead of answering, she nodded.

"Wonderful. Now come, Lizzy." Her Grace took Lissa's hand and led her up the stairs. "I want to hear all about why you're dressed as a young man and how you managed to get my son to marry you."

Lissa would not lie about the reason they were married, so she would focus mostly on the investigation she and Anthony had been conducting—leaving out all the sordid details, of course.

Within minutes, she was in a room with a maid helping her into a fine muslin rose day dress. Her male shirt had been determined too rough, and she'd been given a shift, stays, and new stockings. Though they wanted to take her boots and daggers, she insisted on keeping them.

Lady Roxburgh sat on the wingback chair in the room supervising the transformation, even to the point of how Lissa's hair should be swept up. Finally, everything was as the duchess wished, and Her Grace shooed the maid away.

"Now come sit with me and explain everything." She patted the wingback chair next to the one she was in, smiling with anticipation.

Lissa moved to the chair and sat, quite pleased with such a broad opening. It allowed her to speak about what she wished to speak about. "Do you know your son has been investigating people for various lords?"

"Of course. He doesn't divulge much in his letters, but it does sound as if he's enjoying himself, as I told him to."

Lissa frowned, as that was not the impression she had from Anthony. "He has told me that his family is not pleased with his activities."

Her Grace sighed. "Yes, well, that would be his father and three brothers. They can be quite boring in their traditions, but I told him to enjoy his life however he wished. When he was young, he thought of himself as expendable—and yes, at the age of but seven, that is what he called himself. There was no way I could sway him otherwise, as his father and brothers had truly made him feel that way, though not intentionally. I do hope he has overcome that flaw. But yes, I told him because he was a fourth son, it gave him the freedom to do whatever he wished with his life."

Lissa's admiration for Lady Roxburgh grew at how clever she was, though she'd keep the fact that Anthony still considered himself expendable to herself. Even at the thought, her stomach clenched. He truly didn't realize how important he was.

"So your disguise has to do with his latest investigation?" Her Grace's blue eyes, the same color as Anthony's, shone with excitement.

Pleased that the woman was far from the typical duchess, Lissa continued. "I'm sure Anthony is telling His Grace about this even as I speak, so you should know as well. We stumbled upon a plot to kill the king."

"What? No one can get to the king, especially now, with his ailment."

She leaned forward, happy to have someone to talk with about it. "We knew there was something afoot with a certain lord, and so Anthony garnered an invitation into the man's home through your eldest, Lord Ferncroft. While there, we discovered a secret room. Unfortunately, the lord discovered us and a fight ensued."

Her Grace's eyes widened. "Is that how my son got that terrible bruise on his forehead?"

"Indeed it is. As we escaped, I stuffed my pockets with letters we had found, but hadn't had a chance to read, in the hopes they would help us. It was after we rode to Gretna Green and married that we were finally able to read them. You see, when I grabbed up the letters, I also inadvertently scooped up a few valuables. Anthony was afraid the lord in question would bring me before a magistrate, so he married me to protect me."

Anthony's mother studied her then began to shake her head. "No." She continued moving. "No, my son would not marry you simply to protect you."

Confused, Lissa pressed the point. "I promise you, he did. We have been friends for well on three years now, so he feels a certain obligation toward me. It's what I felt when protecting him in France. I know you wished your son a love match like you and the duke, but I promise you, we will rub along nicely." She smiled, hoping the woman wouldn't be too crushed.

But Lady Roxburgh kept shaking her head. "I understand you believe that, as I imagine he hasn't told you how he feels about you, but the truth is, he could've found a way to protect you without binding himself to you for the rest of his life. No, my son loves you."

Lissa shook her own head but stopped as she thought back on their time since reuniting. There had been a definite shift in how he treated her the day they discovered the gun case entrance to the secret room. Could he truly be in love with her? Her belly turned in on itself and she rolled in her lips, not sure how to feel about such a revelation…if it were true.

"Don't worry. All will be well. My son is a smart man. He would know the right woman for him, and if you have been friends for such a length of time, then that is a strong foundation."

Though the woman's words were meant to soothe Lissa, they didn't. In fact, they made her feel guilty.

She rose from the chair and walked to the dressing table. What she felt for Anthony was not the same as what she felt for Etienne. It was very different. It was fondness, respect, protectiveness, enjoyment, and pleasure.

She stared at herself in the mirror. But that *was* what she'd felt for Etienne, and yet it wasn't the same. Could it be her age now that made it feel different? Anthony understood her, and she him. They had the same spirit, as it were. They were a pair, alike, with a strong bond. She'd never been friends with Etienne. Could that be it?

Her Grace rose. "Well, I best set the staff to packing."

"Packing?" Lissa frowned, not sure why Lady Roxburgh would need to leave. She wasn't in danger.

"Yes. If I know my husband, and I do, we will all be leaving here by tomorrow morning. If the king is involved, then there is no time to waste. Yes, we are almost hermits up here, but my husband still has close friends, and he will want to take care of this. Besides, you cannot settle in at Bellamore until all is resolved."

"Why?" Lissa had hoped they could leave the issue with the duke and she could see her new home. One that was truly hers.

The woman stopped on her way to the door. "Because, my dear, Anthony's coachman has already been here to let us know that a Lord Leighhall has visited Bellamore and demanded to see my son. The coachman warned us not to let Anthony go home. Something to do with having burned his coach. As I understand it, the poor coachman barely had time to separate the horses and flee." The woman winked before walking out.

Lissa stared at the closed door, her mind racing. Leighhall had burned the coach they were supposed to be in? A shiver raced up her spine, and she crossed her arms over her chest. Suddenly, understanding dawned. Anthony's mother had already known something was wrong! Had she asked for details because her husband wouldn't tell her, or was she testing her new daughter-in-law?

Lissa moved closer to the fire, feeling cold. For the second time since being sent to the Belinda School for Curious Ladies, she felt her life was no longer under her control. Now she was married to a baron. A man of wit and humor, but also with great honor and responsibility, who may, possibly, love her.

She held her hands out to the warmth, thinking of how gentle or passionate he could be in bed, how often he grinned, or how much he enjoyed the puzzle of life. These were all similarities they had. She needed time to sort out her own feelings. She cared for him greatly, of that she knew. When Leighhall had lifted the crossbow, her fury had been all consuming, but that was because he was her friend. He would feel the same way.

And maybe he did. His mother was not in his life anymore. She might not realize the man he was, the steadfast and loyal friend he could be. That was the most likely explanation.

Feeling more comfortable with her thoughts, she moved back to the dressing table, curious about why Her Grace had been so particular about her—

The door flew open, banging against the wall as Anthony strode in. "We leave in an hour."

It appeared his mother had been correct. "Where are we going?"

He stopped at the opposite wall and turned. "We go to Silver Meadows to enlist the Duke of Northwick's aid in speaking with the regent."

A wave of cool air seemed to envelop her, and she wished herself back by the fireplace. "The regent? But he's—"

"I know. But my father makes an excellent point. We give the regent a chance to blame the whole affair on Leighhall. Prinny can claim it was the viscount's idea and he was just humoring Leighhall, or some such story. Then we'll have him." He punctuated his statement by grasping the air in front of him.

"And if he doesn't blame it all on Leighhall?" She hoped the men had come up with a second option.

"Then he'd have to throw two dukes and a baron into Newgate, and that would cause quite a fuss."

"A fuss?" Her heart began to race. "A fuss is not enough. You can't go to the regent with your plan unless you have a better alternative."

His smile faded. "What do you suggest? We can't very well take out an ad in the morning *Gazette*. The idea is for the regent to be assured that very few are a party to this information."

She crossed her arms and shook her head. "No. That may be good for the regent, but it's not good for you. Take the Captain. Take the Earl of Harewood. Take every peer you can so it's impossible for the regent to do anything else."

He stared at her, his eyes wide as if her idea was addle-brained. But a slow smile began to lift his lips as he strode across the room and kissed her.

It was a quick, hard, sensuous kiss. And then his lips left hers, his smile wide. "You are brilliant!"

Surprised by his sudden acceptance, she wrinkled her nose. "I am?"

"Yes. You are also beautiful in that dress. I'm afraid there won't be time to gather more clothes for the trip, as we leave so soon. Already a footman is riding fast to let the Duke of North-wick know to expect us."

Relieved that he would accept her plan and hopefully not be thrown in prison, she relaxed. "I don't need any other clothes except a pelisse or cloak. Oh, and I would like to keep the clothing I brought with me. After all, that is my wedding dress."

He cupped her cheek. "Yes, it is, and I've already ordered it to be packed. Lissa, everything is going to be fixed. I prom—"

She placed her finger over his lips. "No. Don't. I'm simply happy that we have a way forward."

He held her hand and sucked her finger into his mouth, sending shivers of desire coursing through her. Then he pulled her in and kissed her again, this time gently. When he let her go, he started for the door. "I'll let my father know the change in strategy and have more letters sent." He stopped halfway out of the room. "I did let the Duke of Northwick know of our marriage. I hope that will relieve Lady Eleanor."

Her heart melted that he'd thought of her friend. "I am grateful."

A quick smile lifted his lips, and he left.

Now was the time of reckoning. It was as if her whole life was culminating in the next few days. Either they would all be safe and Leighhall would no longer be a threat, or she and her husband would be thrown in prison.

Husband. The word echoed in her head, and she sat abruptly on the chair at the dressing table. She now had a husband, and she was worried about him far more than she was worried for her *friend*

CHAPTER EIGHTEEN

Silver Meadows, the Belinda School for Curious Ladies
A week later

LISSA PACED THROUGH the parlor, past the portrait of Belinda Mabry and her friends, and into the dining area before turning back. She itched to go out and practice throwing her daggers, but she'd been forbidden due to the cold. The duchess had kept a close watch on her since they'd arrived and Lissa admitted to a shortened version of the truth.

"Dague, you're going to give me a migraine." Ellie pulled out another stich in her embroidery loop. "Do sit down."

A shiver raced up Lissa's spine. "You can't call me Dague anymore. It could put my life in danger now."

"I apologize. I forgot. Lissette, please sit down."

Sophie tsked. "She's worried."

That got Ellie's attention. "Are you?"

Lissa stopped, finding the question a bit absurd. "Of course I am. Anthony is my husband now, even if it is just a marriage of convenience."

"I'd be thrilled with a marriage of convenience. I so dread having to experience another Season." Sophie patted Eleanor's arm in sympathy, but Eleanor wasn't distracted. "If it's just a marriage of convenience, then why worry?"

Lissa moved to stand behind a straight-back chair that faced the two ladies and the portrait, gripping the top of it. "Because he's been my friend for years. I care about him, not to mention if they all fail, I'll be sent to prison, too. It will be my fault. If I didn't go with him to Leighhall's, I would have never discovered the truth, and he'd be safe now."

Sophie studied her as she did everyone. "Are you not looking forward to your new life as a baroness?"

Lissa hadn't thought so far ahead, but now that Sophie mentioned it, she could easily imagine what it would be like. "No, I am not looking forward to life as a baroness, but I am looking forward to being Anthony's wife. I know we wouldn't remain at Bellamore long. He would still do his investigations, only I would help. We are good together in figuring out puzzles." She smiled as she thought of their recent adventure. "And that's not the only way in which we are good together."

"Lissette!" Ellie put down her embroidery. "You certainly don't mean…"

Lissa grinned, happy to enlighten her friends as she had Dory. "I do mean. He is an excellent lover, and I have learned so much more than what is in the duchess's secret book."

Eleanor blushed and Sophie appeared puzzled.

"Ellie, did you not share the *Education of the Feminine Species* with Sophie?"

The blush grew darker. "No. I haven't even gone beyond the title page myself."

Dumbfounded, Lissa stared at her friend. "But why?"

Ellie looked at her and then at Sophie and then back at Lissa. "If you insist. I didn't want to know about what I would never have the chance to experience."

"What?"

"No. Don't say that." Sophie wrapped her arms around Ellie.

The woman gave a curt nod. "It's true. I am not sought after by anyone, except for an occasional old man with poor intentions. I've resigned myself to being a spinster."

Lissa remembered wanting to be just that, but now, she couldn't imagine her future without Anthony in it. It was a sobering thought. Also a revealing one that required examination.

"Ellie." Sophie's soft voice in such a commanding tone was odd. "You are not going to be a spinster. You are a beautiful woman, with a large, caring heart, that any man should be pleased to have for a wife."

Ellie sniffed and nodded, but Lissa could sense her friend didn't believe any of it, even if it was true. "This is why I never wished to marry. Why is it that we must impress the men and *they* decide whom they want? Why can't they impress us and we choose whom *we* want?"

"Because that's not the way of the *ton*." Ellie said the words with finality, but her lips did quirk up at the idea of having the choice.

"Would you choose Anthony?"

Sophie's question caught Lissa by surprise. Would she? "I suppose if I absolutely had to choose a husband, I would choose him."

"Now, that's what I thought after he first visited here." Ellie slapped her leg with her statement, causing the embroidery loop to fall from her lap.

Yet at that time, if someone asked if she'd choose him, Lissa would have said… What would she have said? She would have said yes because, based on her knowledge then, he wasn't a peer and had wealth. And now?

"You love him."

She snapped her gaze back to Sophie. "What? Why would you say that?"

"Because it's true." Sophie's green gaze didn't waver.

Was it? Was that why she'd been pacing the confines of Silver Meadows for three hours worried she'd never see Anthony again? The answer was so obvious, she couldn't believe she'd missed it. Sophie was correct.

Somewhere between being friends and being married, she'd

fallen in love with Anthony. She loved him with all of her heart, her every breath, her very being.

The butler stepped into the parlor. "Lady Bellamore, you wished to know when a carriage entered the gate. I have been informed that—"

She didn't wait for Harrison to finish, but ran past the man and out the front door.

The Northwick coach was followed by the Roxburgh coach, which was the one in which she was most interested. More coaches came down the lane behind it. Were there people inside, or had they all been thrown in prison? Surely the other coaches would have returned to their homes if no one rode in them. Hope sparked in the depths of her soul.

Unable to wait, she hurried down the grand steps of the mansion, not for the first time wishing there weren't so many. By time she reached the bottom, the first coach was coming to a halt and her breath was making small clouds in the cold air.

She ran to the second coach.

Just as it came to a halt, the door opened and Anthony jumped out. "Lissa."

She ran into his arms, tears in her eyes that he was back, even not knowing the outcome. To hold him again meant more to her than breathing.

"Lissa, all is fine. Everything is fixed." He lifted her face and wiped at her tears. "Are these tears of happiness?"

She tried to speak but had to swallow hard to get her voice to work. "No. They are tears of relief…and love." Her heart skidded to a halt. She wasn't sure what he would think.

His smile widened. "Here I already thought I couldn't be happier, and yet you make me more so. *Je'taime aussi*. With all of my heart."

She shivered with happiness and kissed him, showing him how full her heart was now that she had him back.

A male clearing his throat had them separating, and she blushed to find the Duke of Roxburgh looking at them, his brows raised in question.

Anthony addressed his father. "We were just celebrating that Lissa loves me."

"I would think you would be celebrating that we weren't all thrown in prison and that Leighhall will be on his way to Australia soon, his estates forfeited to the Crown."

"Father, that's an excellent point."

Lissa had been so worried about Anthony, she'd forgotten all about the plot. "Is the king still alive?"

His Grace nodded. "He is. The regent was aware of Leighhall's fascination with weapons and his ideas for killing the king, but he simply replied to Leighhall as a pastime. He didn't expect anyone to learn of it and was quite furious."

"At least, that's what he stated." Anthony rolled his eyes, clearly not believing any of it. "And now he'll be able to take all his weapons back. That's why Leighhall hid them. They were gifts from the regent."

"So was the king actually in danger?" Had they really traveled so far, so fast, for no reason?

"No, according to the regent." Lord Roxburgh exchanged a look with his son before continuing. "However, it is unclear if the king would have remained so. We were delayed because the regent insisted on sending men to bring Leighhall to him. They found the viscount taking his anger out on a woman in his dressing room. Fortunately, they interrupted in time and she was still alive." He looked at his son thoughtfully, and his gaze softened. "I'm glad you escaped when you did."

A hard shiver raced through her at the thought of how easily she and Anthony could have become two of the viscount's victims.

"Hear, hear." Lord Harewood strode up with Dory on his arm.

Lissa stared at her friend, who not only appeared blissfully happy, but even more beautiful in her maroon pelisse that matched her hair perfectly. "You went with them?" Lissa gestured toward Lord Harewood.

"Of course not. My husband wouldn't allow me in the same town as that man. It makes me shiver thinking about how I was at a house party with him. Though it is odd that a thought can make me shiver when it's such a beautiful autumn day, even if a bit cold. It's fascinating that despite the warmth of the sun, it is still so cold, yet in the summer, the sun does add warmth. I'm sure Ellie could explain such an odd circumstance. Though I can't imagine—"

"Dory," Lord Harewood interrupted his wife, a smile on his face.

She laughed before grasping his arm. "I was rambling again, wasn't I?" She turned her gaze back on them. "I'm so thankful that all of us are out of harm's way and have nothing else to worry over."

"I agree." Lord Harewood held his hand out to Anthony. "Thank you for your assistance in this matter. If I had known how dangerous it would become, I assure you that I wouldn't have hired you."

Anthony shook the man's hand. "If that had been the circumstance, then we would all have to look over our shoulders for the rest of our lives. No, it was fortunate that you did."

"I suppose you're correct." Lord Harewood turned to Dory. "Shall we go in and celebrate?"

At Dory's nod, they walked toward the house.

"Hired?" His Grace frowned. "Tell me you did not accept payment for your investigation."

Anthony shrugged. "I had to. It makes these lords more comfortable, and the work is usually much less dangerous than when I was with the Bow Street Runners."

His father's eyes rounded before he shook his head. "I don't want to hear anymore." Turning about, albeit awkwardly, the man started for the house, his wooden leg making his walk more that of a sailor than a duke.

Anthony pulled Lissa close. "We should celebrate our success."

Just as she recognized his intentions, his mouth came down on hers in another kiss, but this one was far more passionate than the last, and she couldn't resist wrapping her arms around his neck and pressing herself into him despite the presence of others walking past.

When she was breathless, he broke away. "I'd best get you inside. You'll freeze out here." Anthony's arms loosened from around her.

"I don't feel cold. All I feel is warmth." She gazed into his eyes, seeing and feeling the love he professed. "Maybe we could make use of this coach and relieve ourselves of some of these clothes?"

Anthony's nostrils flared, sending heat flooding her body. Then he lifted her in his arms and deposited her inside the coach. "Coachman, bring us to Ravenridge. And when we get there, bring us back."

She laughed at his orders and scrambled onto the seat as he jumped in to join her.

"My wife's wishes always come first."

She eyed him slyly. "I *wish* that all my clothes would come off."

He laughed. "What an odd coincidence, as I was just wishing the same thing."

As he pulled her back up against him to undo her buttons, she sighed. "I do believe we are perfectly matched. If I'd known that disarming the baron would have led to such happiness, I would have done so years ago."

His lips found her neck, and he murmured against her skin, "But you didn't know I was a baron."

She cocked her head. "True, and you didn't see me as a woman."

He pulled away her dress to cup her breasts. "But I do now and am I ever pleased to do so. I have no defense against you."

At the feel of his fingers upon her, she arched into his hands, the shock of desire burning her up. "I'm the one defenseless."

He slipped his fingers deeper into her dress and pulled out a dagger. "Liar."

She laughed until his mouth came down on her bared breast and the dagger dropped to the coach floor. As the excitement of his touch filled her body and her heart, her last lucid thought flitted through her head: *Mon amour, ma vie.* My love, my life.

EPILOGUE

Hawthorne Park
December 1817

"DOES YOUR BROTHER always require payment for favors?"
Lissa's question interrupted Anthony's thoughts on what to tell his brother and what not to tell him as they awaited Darius's entrance into the library.

He was quite happy to return his attention to her. "Yes, he does. But to be fair, we have always bartered in this way. My father encouraged it as a way to sharpen our intelligence, though sometimes it cultivated rather devious thoughts."

"Oh, now that sounds like a promising story." She sat in one of the two wingback chairs before the desk, looking every bit the baroness, from her swept-up hair beneath her cap to the green travel dress and pelisse she wore—not that he could tell her that, as she wasn't comfortable with her new title yet.

He moved closer and sat on the arm of the other chair. "Stories, as in many. The four of us often tried to outdo each other. One time when Darius asked a favor of—"

"I do hope I'm not hearing my name taken in vain."

At his brother's voice, Anthony rose and turned toward the door. "Not at all. Just sharing childhood memories."

Darius grimaced. "I've tried very hard to forget most of those.

As I was the oldest, Father more often than not put the blame on me."

"Well, we all did look up to you so much."

Darius snorted as he strode by and clapped Anthony on the shoulder. "No use trying to speak to my ego to lessen your payment. I have a real need, and I believe you are the perfect person to accomplish the fulfillment of it."

He strode to where Lissa sat. "It is a pleasure to see you again, mademoiselle."

"It is baroness now." Though she didn't smile, Anthony was pleased that she at least acknowledged her title.

"Is this true?" Darius looked from her nodding to Anthony.

He grinned. "Indeed it is. Since she was also at the house party, I was able to further pursue my interest, and we were married shortly afterward."

"You married in Scotland?"

At the utter disbelief in Darius's voice, he laughed. "Yes. That is what one does when one cannot possibly wait."

His brother shook his head. "I should have guessed that you couldn't even follow the traditional route to marriage."

As Darius turned his back to walk around his desk, Anthony glanced at Lissa, who was trying hard not to laugh.

Darius took his seat, and Anthony returned to the arm of the chair, but at his brother's stern look, he quickly slipped down onto the cushion. "So how can we repay you? As you can see, we are very grateful to have been at that particular house party, and it wouldn't have happened if you hadn't obtained an invitation for me."

"So then your goals were met."

Anthony looked at Lissa before turning back to his brother. He *did* need to tell him about Leighhall. "They were, but we became involved in a rather unfortunate discovery. We stumbled upon evidence that Lord Leighhall was a traitor, and I had to enlist Father's help in bringing it to the regent's attention."

Darius's eyes widened before his brows lowered and he

shook his head. "Can you not even attend a house party without causing a fuss?"

Anthony coughed to hide a chuckle. He did so enjoy being the bane of his brother's neatly ordered existence. "I hope it will appease you to know that the lord in question was arrested and sent to Australia, but he died before ever embarking. Dysentery, I believe it was."

"I certainly hope my name is not associated with the man's. Do not tell anyone that I obtained that invitation on your behalf."

Anthony put his hand to his chest. "I promise to remain silent."

"Good. Very good." His brother relaxed back in his chair. "Now to my own goal, which you will help me with."

Anthony didn't care for Darius's tone, but for Lissa, he was willing to pay his brother's price. "Yes. We are anxious to show our appreciation." He stifled a smile. Darius was clearly not happy that he was so cheerful about it. Usually, they all complained when having to repay the debt, but he genuinely wished to.

"I need a wife."

The payment was so unexpected that he coughed to hide a chuckle. "Yes, well, you said so last time we were here."

Darius leaned back in his chair and clasped his hands together, a habit he used often when scolding someone or setting down rules. "So I did. However, I wish a wife by Christmastide."

"The Season starts in a fortnight. Unless you wish to make your own trip to Gretna Green, you'll need at least three weeks for the posting of the banns. Of course, that's if you reached a settlement by the end of the week."

"I didn't say by the Season. I'm not such a simpleton as that, nor desperate enough to marry a woman by whisking her off to Scotland."

Lissa ignored the insult and leaned forward in her chair. "My lord, do you mean to marry a woman you've never met in the next month?"

"I do."

"But why?"

It was exactly what Anthony wished to know, but if he asked, Darius wouldn't tell him. Would he reveal his motives to Lissa?

Darius looked down at his hands for a long while as if choosing his words carefully. Finally, he focused on Lissa. "My lady, I am a widower with two children. I knew my late wife well, having courted her for the full Season. However, she was a mistake." He held up his hand to avoid interruption. "It was not her fault. I simply chose unwisely. But now I need a mother for my children, and if she's somewhat comely, I will be able to do my duty and beget a second son to ensure my legacy."

Anthony couldn't keep himself from asking, "Why so quickly?"

Darius sighed, clearly not happy with his own situation. "I am being bombarded with invitations, which is no great feat to ignore. However, I spent the Season avoiding well-intended mothers and faint-hearted young women. I need a woman of strength who will let me be when I need to be alone."

For the first time, Anthony recognized true worry and even fear in his brother's gray gaze. He wanted a woman who could handle his being absent for days at a time until his black mood passed. "I understand. It will be difficult on such a short timeline. But is there a reason for urgency?"

Darius looked at Lissa before returning his gaze to Anthony. "There is. I wish my children to have at least one parent about. You and I both know that a nanny is not enough."

The memory of the long weeks Anthony and his brothers had gone without seeing either of their parents while they recovered from the factory accident came to mind unbidden and unwanted. Their mother had been their light and their father their strength, and with both being treated in Town, they'd been left with a nanny. They'd bonded together, learning to depend on one another, but after two months, when they'd finally been allowed to see their parents, one of them was always at their side.

Darius's wife had been gone a good year, which meant that every time he slipped away, his children had only each other.

Anthony found himself nodding. "I see."

Lissa looked at him, letting him know he'd have to take her into his confidence later.

"Good." Darius rose from his chair. "Then you know my requirements."

Anthony rose as well. "I believe I do. A strong woman, who will be a mother to your children, and who is pleasant to look upon. She must be a bit older than the typical debutante but still willing to have a child of her own. She must also be willing to marry within the month."

Darius raised his right brow. "You were listening."

Anthony ignored the surprise in his brother's statement. "My only question is, do you wish to meet her before the wedding?"

The silence that followed made it clear that Darius was undecided.

Lissa surprised Anthony by rising and laying her hand on the desk. "My lord, do you not wish to at least gaze upon the woman you plan to live the rest of your life with?"

Darius stared at her as if he hadn't considered the gravity of his plan. Finally, he shook his head. "No. My brother will know the right woman for me and my children. Her outward appearance is of not of great consequence. It is her character that is most important."

His words and his rush made it clear that Darius's black moods had become worse after his wife's passing. He wanted to give his children the best chance for a successful life, even if he couldn't be there to see it. The realization was sobering.

Anthony held out his hand to his wife. "Come. We have a new mission with a fast-approaching deadline."

Though he expected she might balk, she took his arm. He returned his gaze to his brother. "I will send you word as soon as I have identified someone. Do you wish me to negotiate the settlement or will you?"

"I will."

It relieved Anthony that his brother wanted to be involved in that, at least. "Then we best leave, as we have much to do."

"Safe travels, Anthony, Baroness. And congratulations on your nuptials."

Anthony led Lissa out to the coach. He was surprised when she didn't immediately ask questions, but instead sat across from him gazing out the window. They were at least a mile from Hawthorne Park when she finally turned to him. "Thank you for including me in fulfilling your payment."

That was the last statement he'd expected to hear. "How could I not? We're married. We are now a team in our investigations."

Her eyes glistened with unshed tears. "I had hoped, but I wasn't sure. I was afraid you would look at me differently now that I'm your wife."

Surprised, he grabbed on to the side of the coach and moved to sit next to her. "I married you because I love you, not because of who I think you should be, but because of who you are."

She leaned in and kissed his cheek. "And I am so grateful that you will not change."

He took her hand, intending to pull her close for a kiss, but then she clasped his hand in both of hers.

"Now tell me why your brother needs a wife so quickly. He fears something. Does he fly into rages and hurt his children?"

Not a little shocked by her deduction, he scowled. "No, of course not. Darius would rather drown than hurt his children. He loves them, which is why he needs a wife."

"That's a relief. He did seem to have their welfare as his primary motivation. So he doesn't truly want a wife, but more a mother for his children."

Relieved that she understood so quickly, he relaxed. "Yes. Darius suffers from what he calls his black moods. They are not violent moods, more a deep melancholy that can last a fortnight."

"A fortnight?" Lissa's eyes rounded.

He held up his hand. "They don't always last that long. It can be just an afternoon. He has no control over them, and when they happen, he hides away. He says he's not fit company for anyone. Our parents were very involved in raising us, as odd as that is for those in the peerage, and Darius wants his children to have the same life."

"I see. With his sequestering himself, his children would have no one now that his wife has passed. That relieves my mind greatly."

"I'm pleased."

She turned and faced him. "It relieves my mind because I know exactly who should be his wife."

"What?" Doubt fought with excitement, which he tamped down. "Whom do you know who would marry a man without seeing him just to be a mother, as in truly being with the children, and not a typical wife? Most ladies of the *ton* have little to do with their children until it is time to marry them off or send them to school."

Lissa didn't smile, obviously understanding the importance of the task. "Lady Eleanor Dulac. She said to me just last week that she would be happy with a marriage of convenience if she could avoid another Season. Not only is Ellie my age, she's a woman of strong character, and she mothers every Curious Lady at the school. I do believe she and your brother would fit well."

Thinking on what little he knew of Lady Eleanor, he did see the possibilities. "Then I suggest that once we reach Bellamore, we send a letter off immediately to see if she would be interested."

"You still wish to go to Bellamore?"

Lissa's question made sense, since time was of the essence, but it was important that she feel comfortable in her new life circumstance before they rushed into their next mission. "I do. You can meet the staff and explore your new home. We can send the chest we're carrying with a letter instead of stopping at Leighhall's mother's home now."

Lissa wrinkled her nose. "I suppose."

"Trust me. Your gift of the china and the coins to the woman is kindness itself. She doesn't need to meet you."

"I just didn't think it fair that her son's actions leave her destitute. I did want to meet her to see if she were the cause of his cruel behavior."

He studied his wife, not at all surprised by her comment. "I can tell you that when I asked Leighhall how he kept his family at bay when it came to marrying that he said he simply told them he would marry when he chose. Based on how he thought of women, I believe that his mother is not the one at fault here. However, if she were, would you decide not to turn over the chest?"

Lissa appeared nonplussed at the question, and she didn't rush to answer. "You do have enough wealth that those coins mean little to you?"

He nodded, very aware of what she was thinking. "And I have plenty with which to keep Madame Fontaine in the luxury she wishes in her final years."

Finally, Lissa shook her head. "Then I can forgo meeting Leighhall's mother. As you pointed out, it doesn't matter. I will write her a letter." A sly smile lifted her lips. "I'll sign it Daguette."

He rather liked that idea. There was no need to associate with the Leighhall name, especially as they were to start their new life together. "Then I suggest we relax, as we won't reach Bellamore until late tonight."

"Oh, I can think of other ways we can pass the time." Lissa pulled on the finger of her glove and then the next, making it quite clear what she wished to do.

His body reacted to her suggestion immediately, and he quickly unbuttoned his greatcoat.

"Will we each have our own bedroom at Bellamore?" She pulled her glove off and started on the next.

Though the question was casually spoken, he could sense

there was more behind it. "Yes, we will. This way we can enjoy alternating our sleeping spaces."

He felt her relax at his answer before the second glove came off and she reached up to unclasp her cloak. "That pleases me. I'm sure I will wish to tup you often."

He laughed out loud, her statement was so unexpected. "I will be happy to be of service to my Lady Baroness."

She sobered at his address, and he scolded himself for not holding his tongue.

"As a baroness, I suppose I will have to give up my plan to have manacles installed on your bed." Her statement was followed by such a heavy sigh that he was quite sure she was serious.

"Lissa?" He gently coaxed her chin up. "You do not have to give up anything. In fact, I was going to save this until we reached Bellamore, but I think it important to tell you now."

Her deep brown gaze didn't leave his face as her brow puckered. "What is it?"

"It's my wedding gift to you."

"My wedding gift?" She looked about the coach as if expecting it to be hidden somewhere. "I do hope it isn't silver." Her eyes lit. "Is it a new dagger?"

He bit down on his smile and shook his head.

She stared at his greatcoat lying on the opposite seat where he'd thrown it. "Will it fit in your pocket?"

"No. The only item small enough to fit in my pocket is the one on your hand."

She lifted her left hand. The gold band with a large ruby surrounded by small diamonds and a sapphire on each side sparkled in the sunlight that filtered into the coach. "It's a beautiful gift." She dropped her hand. "If my ring is not my wedding present, then what is?"

He let his smile grow wide. "I had a sling installed in your dressing room."

Her eyes rounded, and for a minute, he thought she was

horrified—before she threw her arms around him, sending him backward against the side of the coach. *"Mon Dieu! Tu es le meilleur mari de tous les temps!"*

He laughed as he held her close. So he was the greatest husband of all time, was he? "And you, my love are the most interesting, intelligent, and passionate wife in all of England."

She lifted her head from his shoulder and gave him a soft look he'd only seen a handful of times. "My soldier, my thief, my baron, my husband. You are *my* Anthony forever." Her lips found his in a gentle kiss that told him very clearly that he was not expendable after all.

The End

About the Author

Lexi Post is a New York Times and USA Today best-selling author of romance inspired by the classics. She spent years in higher education taking and teaching courses about the classical literature she loved. From Edgar Allan Poe's short story "The Masque of the Red Death" to Tolstoy's *War and Peace*, she's read, studied, and taught wonderful classics.

But Lexi's first love is romance novels so she married her two first loves, romance and the classics. Whether it's dashing dukes, hot immortals, sizzling cowboys, or hunks from out of this world, Lexi provides a sensuous experience with a "whole lotta story."

Lexi is living her own happily ever after with her husband and her two cats in Florida. She makes her own ice cream every weekend, loves bright colors, and you'll never see her without a hat.

Website: lexipostbooks.com
Lexi Post Updates: app.mailerlite.com/webforms/landing/c1w1g3
Facebook: facebook.com/lexipostbooks
Twitter: @LexiPost
Instagram: instagram.com/lexipostbooks
Amazon Author Page: http://amzn.to/1IEL2cc
BookBub: bookbub.com/authors/lexi-post
D2D: books2read.com/author/lexi-post/subscribe/1/16171
Goodreads: goodreads.com/goodreadscomLexiPost
Instagram: instagram.com/lexipostbooks
Blog: happilyeverafterthoughts.com
Pinterest: pinterest.com/lexipost77
Email: lexi@lexipostbooks.com